# SANTA FE RUN

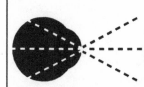

# SANTA FE RUN

## PRESTON LEWIS

**WHEELER PUBLISHING**
A part of Gale, a Cengage Company

Farmington Hills, Mich • San Francisco • New York • Waterville, Maine
Meriden, Conn • Mason, Ohio • Chicago

Copyright © 1993 by Preston Lewis.
Wheeler Publishing, a part of Gale, a Cengage Company.

**ALL RIGHTS RESERVED**
Wheeler Publishing Large Print Western.
The text of this Large Print edition is unabridged.
Other aspects of the book may vary from the original edition.
Set in 16 pt. Plantin.

LIBRARY OF CONGRESS CIP DATA ON FILE.
CATALOGUING IN PUBLICATION FOR THIS BOOK
IS AVAILABLE FROM THE LIBRARY OF CONGRESS

ISBN-13: 978-1-4328-6697-6 (softcover alk. paper)

Published in 2019 by arrangement with Preston Lewis

Printed in Mexico
1 2 3 4 5 6 7 23 22 21 20 19

*For Marc, my brother,*
*and*
*Lee Ann, a fellow writer*

# SANTA FE RUN

"Dismount!" cried the lieutenant, and the black troopers of Company C, 11th U.S. Cavalry, obeyed in unison.

Saddles creaked and horses whinnied as the sixty cavalrymen dropped to the hard-packed ground. Jonah winced as his swollen feet hit earth and tried to burst the seams on his ill-fitting boots. Drooping his arms over his saddle, Jonah looked about at his silent mates. For a moment he wondered if their joints had rusted or if their muscles had stiffened as much as his from the long ride. He rested his chin on his saddle's sticky leather and stared west across thirty miles of open prairie toward the mountains standing like tombstones on the horizon. Somewhere out there was Pachise, damn his Apache hide, and until he was returned to the reservation no trooper at Fort Bansom would have rest.

With the resignation of a man who has

failed to catch a ghost, the lieutenant softly gave the order to attend the horses and strode away to report to the colonel. Jonah envied him about as much as he would a man thrown in a pit of rattlesnakes, the colonel being half as congenial and twice as crooked as any rattler.

As the other soldiers led their mounts toward the stables, Jonah lingered, gazing through the shimmering summer heat which made the mountains dance in the distance. His eyelids fell. He no longer saw the mountains, just his bed, and he wished he were in it. It was a pleasant thought — the first he had had in days — until it was shattered. An excruciating pain shot from his left foot and rattled around his brain, then returned to his foot. He hopped on his right foot and grabbed for his left. Momentarily stunned, he at first thought Grant had stepped on him, but his horse remained motionless. Then Jonah's blurry eyes slowly came into focus on Skully, gaunt and grim.

"No cause, Skully, to stomp on a man's achin' feet," Jonah called, raising as much anger as his weary mind and body could muster.

"Just checkin' if you still among the livin', Jonah," Skully said, motioning toward the troopers moving to the stables.

8

"Stomping on my foot's a good way to get yourself kilt, Skully. Do it again and I might save Pachise a bullet."

Skully's disposition favored New Mexico weather — it changed, but mostly for the worse. He lapped his knee and bared his teeth without laughing. "Thought a scorpion was on your boot," Skully growled and motioned again to the retreating troopers. "They'll beat us to the chow if we don't hurry. Anyway, you wouldn't shoot your best friend."

Jonah grabbed Grant's reins and led the animal toward the stables, Skully walking by his side. "Why I put up with you, Skully, I never will understand. One of these days you'll gets me into more trouble that I can ever pull myself out of." They joined the other troopers and tied their horses to the picket line.

Gladdened by the prospect of having only to care for their mounts before tending their own needs — food, baths, and sleep — the black soldiers hurried with their horses. Each trooper performed the prescribed ritual by rote: unsaddle his horse, water him, comb him, feed the animal a healthy portion of corn, water him well again. The horses always came first, whether at the post or away on patrol. Only after the horses were tended could the men attend their own needs.

The soldiers, all muttering softly to their sweaty steeds, understood they would perish in Apache country without their US-branded mounts, but that dwindled in importance now that the troops had safely returned to Fort Bansom. In the New Mexico badlands outside the perimeter of Fort Bansom and beyond the boundaries of the Bosque Bonito Reservation, the soldiers seldom cussed out their horses as they did at the picket rope outside the stables. Away from the fort, the horses shared all the hazards with the men — poor food, insufficient water, pirating varmints, venomous insects, dangerous thunderstorms and, worst of all, the dreaded Apaches. But back at the fort, the horses received preferential treatment. Stable call came just after reveille. The horses, not the men, were fed first each day. Even daily sick call came only after the horses had been tended. The Army rationale piqued the men.

"Life shore would be easier if I just had four legs," said one of the black troopers.

"If you weren't no slave hoss," answered another.

"Ain't no such thing as a slave hoss," responded the first. "No sir, hosses get too good a treatment for 'em to be any slaves."

"Don't tell me that," piped in another. "All hosses be slaves. Yes sir, they either does that what we tell them or we whip 'em. So ya'll don't tell me that. I wouldn't blame every hoss in this fort for running away."

"Ya'll hush now," said Jonah, entering the conversation from down the line. "Ya'll be giving Grant here ideas and I don't want him running up north where all the horses are emancipated."

A few snickered, but Jonah's humor had a hard edge. Little more than four years ago, most of the men standing at the picket line had been slaves, the private chattel of owners ranging from the benevolent to the malicious. Some troopers bore scars, ugly reminders of their servitude.

Although it was against regulations and not befitting a man of his rank, Jonah took off his army blouse with its twill yellow corporal stripes and hung it on a picket line stake. Shirtless he had worked the cotton fields of Alabama, and he still preferred to feel the hot sun on his back and the dry breezes cooling the sweat off his chest. He unbuttoned his longjohns and pulled the top off so it hung over his light blue pants. As he unsaddled his horse, his muscles rippled under smooth black skin. His body was strong and hard, his hands big but gentle. He moved unhurried to tend Grant, while beside him Skully had already stripped his horse of its gear and was rubbing him down with fast, brusque strokes of the curry comb. Jonah eased his saddle to the ground in front of Grant, and the blowing horse nudged him. Then Jonah pulled the saddle blanket off and fanned the animal with it, just as Skully untied his mount to lead into the stable.

"You're forgettin' a cocklebur in his mane and a couple in his tail, Skully. You might oughts to water him a little more."

"Ain't it enough for you, Jonah, to take care of Grant? You don't have to be no mother hen for every boss in this army."

"Give your hoss a name. It'll help you think more highly of him."

Skully eased his animal back away from the picket line, but stopped to stare at Jonah. His deep set eyes, peeping out from under his drooping forehead, betrayed no emotion. "I remember how Grant got his name."

Jonah, dropping his head, did too.

"You was running your finger over the brand and you asked that white stable sergeant what it meant. 'That's a U and an S', he told you, and then asked you if you knows what U.S. stands for. You being so smart told him you did. 'Ulysses S. Grant', you told him and he jus' laugh and laugh and call you a dumb bastard and say it stands for United States. And you tell him that on this hoss the U.S. stands for Grant and that's what you is gonna call him. You gave him a name, but he's still a hoss."

"No reason to fun a man cause he can't read, Skully."

"Leaving a cocklebur or two in a hoss is no reason to stop a starving man from getting something to eat as soon as he can."

"But filling your belly's no cause to ignore your hoss's needs. Grant may belong to the Army, but he's the closest I ever had to my own animal. I'm gonna take care of him the bestest I can."

"I'm not a-waitin' on you to care for Grant," Skully said, bending over to pick up his saddle. "If they finish mess 'fore you get there, you want me to save you a plate?"

"Jus' remember to bring me a handful of sugar."

"For Grant?"

Jonah nodded.

Skully shrugged. "That hoss gonna outlive you and probably the rest of us, good as you treat him." Skully joined the other troopers leading their mounts into the

13

stables. Jonah tended his horse in solitude.

Picking up the curry comb Skully had discarded in the dirt, Jonah began to untangle the matted hair in Grant's mane. When the horse quit blowing so hard, he fetched a wooden bucket of water from the trough. When the horse finished drinking, Jonah brought him a bucket of corn. The hungry horse devoured the corn as Jonah ran his hand along the sorrel's ribs. The corporal shook his head. Dammit if Grant wasn't losing too much weight with all this chasing of Pachise.

Until five months ago, life at Fort Bansom had been routine, the troopers' major duty being to keep the Apaches on one end of the Bosque Bonito Reservation, the Navajos on the other. The only thing the Apaches and Navajos hated more than each other was learning the white man's way of farming. But one morning after the Apaches had been issued ten days of rations, the tribe was gone, having followed Pachise from the reservation in the night. Tranquil guard duty had given way to long marches fraught with frustration and an occasional casualty. Pachise and his tribe had been living on the run, terrorizing the settlers scrounging to make homes out of the unpromising lands of New Mexico Territory. There in the southeastern quadrant of New Mexico there was no rich soil, just a sandy mixture that sprouted gama grass and sparse plants good for nothing except the Apaches. It didn't even rain enough to bathe a lizard. Why any white person would ever stake out a claim in this forbidding country was a mystery to Jonah.

Jonah despised Pachise, the renegade Apache leader. Since that morning five months ago, Company C and the two other units of the 11th Cavalry at Fort Bansom, located on the reservation itself, had been searching for Pachise. Despite innumerable forays into the countryside, the soldiers had had no success in bringing Pachise back, unless the capture of six old squaws, two wrinkled men too feeble to fight and a dozen tired ponies could be considered victory. The Apaches were like the wolves that roamed the mountains; they traveled and attacked in groups until they were threatened. Then they would split up into smaller, more mobile bands and spread out like grains of sand tossed into the New Mexico winds, leaving not one trail, but dozens for the 11th Cavalry to follow. Unlike the sands, which were forever separated, the Apaches would reassemble some place else, like wolves, to renew their attacks. For the past five months it seemed as though the 11th Cavalry had been chasing the wind itself.

Since Pachise's disappearance, Jonah had watched with mounting concern the deleterious effects of the hard marches on Grant. The sorrel needed more rest. He was losing his strength and stamina. His diet in recent weeks had consisted of too much gama grass and too little corn. As Jonah pulled cockleburs from Grant's tail, he whispered apologies to his horse for all the trouble Pachise had caused. A soldier from Company B ambled by, Jonah noting his presence by the sweet odor wafting from his corncob pipe.

"Already taken Pachise to the stockade, have you?" he teased. "Colonel Stubby is gonna be mighty displeased when he hears you boys couldn't catch a few barefooted and naked Apaches."

"We didn't gets him, but he didn't gets us, either," Jonah responded, lifting Grant's legs to check his hooves for stone bruises. "Company B had lesser luck their last try. Brought back a wounded man, I remembers."

The soldier nodded and pulled the pipe from between his teeth. "Shot hisself in the leg cleaning his pistol."

"Us boys in Company C didn't shoot none of ourselves. We know how to clean our guns."

"Colonel Stubby weren't none too well pleased with that casualty." The trooper laughed and continued his stroll across the grounds.

Jonah fetched another bucket of water. While Grant drank, Jonah carried his saddle and equipment into the stable. When he came out, Skully was sitting on the bucket.

"You take his water away, Skully?"

"He's through, Jonah. Don't matter none for you. They're through with the grub. Be breakfast 'fore you get anything on your empty stomach."

"I got hardtack I can eat. Did you bring the sugar?" Jonah asked.

Skully extended his closed hand and dropped a ball of brown sugar into Jonah's palm. "You keep on eatin' that hardtack you teeth gonna fall out or it'll clog up your innards for damn sure."

"Now don't you worry none 'bout that, Skully. I's just gotta do what Grant needs doing for him," Jonah said, sticking the sugar under the horse's nose. "See how lean he's getting? Needs more fat. I'm gonna see he gets more corn later."

"Just like you, Jonah. You always got that

17

animal on your mind. I shore hope nothing ever happens to that dumb hoss, 'cause you'd never get over it."

"Nothin's gonna happen to this hoss, Skully. That's why I's takin' good care of him. Something this slave learned while caring for animals on the farm, you takes care of them like you supposed to and they'll live as old as you."

"You're something, Jonah. That hoss ain't even yours and you're treatin' him like a son," Skully said. He glanced away and watched a solitary rider coming toward them.

Skully spat in the direction of the horseman, a lean man with an unnatural riding form. His left arm bounced oddly with the horse's gait. When the rider came within thirty feet of Skully and Jonah, he reined in his horse, stared at Skully for an instant, then prodded his horse on past. Strapped over the back of the horseman's saddle, a gray longcoat drooped over either flank. It looked to Skully like a confederate officer's coat.

Jonah hummed as he untied Grant from the picket line.

"Did you see that, Jonah?"

"See what?"

"That feller's coat. He must've been some

'federate soldier or somethin',"  Skully
sneered.

# CHAPTER 2

Morgan Garrett reined up his horse and stared. Black soldiers. One, tending his horse, was obscured, but the other black trooper, sitting on an overturned water bucket, stared back. The war lingered too fresh in his memory to care for the sight of blue uniforms, much less colored soldiers wearing them.

Garrett nudged his mount forward. At least he'd made it to Fort Bansom. He'd buried one man who hadn't. Had Garrett been a couple hours earlier on the trail, it might have been himself bristling with arrows, spread-eagled on the ground while the buzzards picked at his flesh. He shuddered. Garrett's right arm still ached from scratching out a shallow grave with his tin plate. Burying a man was hard work without a shovel and with but one good arm.

Garrett's stomach knotted in hunger as he rode onto the large parade ground centered among the squat adobe buildings. He wished for a good meal, but he'd settle for a bad one.

To his left four long barracks stood in a precise row and behind them an uneven rank of cottonwood trees grew along the hanks of the Loco River. To his right, for officers no doubt, eight smaller dwellings with covered porches offering shade stood behind freshly planted saplings that gave more promise than shade. Far behind the officers' quarters was the post hospital. Ahead of Garrett the headquarters, the quartermaster's building and another building he picked for the sutler's store anchored the north end of the parade ground. He twisted in his saddle to look around, confirming that twin stables with giant corrals in back were all that he had passed. Garrett pointed his horse toward the faded sign over the door of what he hoped was the sutler's store, but at this distance the sign was unreadable.

Behind the headquarters building he spied men working in gardens, among vibrant stalks of corn, squat squash bushes and spindly bean plants, the first real green he'd seen for days. Beyond the vegetables and the irrigation ditch which watered them a cluster of four more adobe buildings formed the Indian agency for the Bosque Bonito Reservation. Those buildings, like all in the fort, were sired of mud and straw, sun-baked adobe with flat roofs and small windows. What Fort Bansom lacked in shade it made up for in ugliness.

Garrett pulled his horse up near the building and gazed at the sign that had seen too little paint to begin with and too much New Mexico sun since. Squinting at the sun-bleached wood, Garrett could just make out traces of letters that spelled "Sutler." He dismounted. After tying the chestnut's reins to a post, Garrett sidled up to an unwashed window and looked inside, but the filth on the glass screened out what was beyond. Garrett moved for the door, pulled off his hat, wiped the sweat from his brow, eased the door open and stepped quietly inside. A spindly clerk, his back to the door, continued to stack canned tomatoes on a far corner of the counter.

"Ahem," Garrett cleared his throat.

The clerk spun around, dropping a can of tomatoes, which rolled across the plank floor toward Garrett. As the clerk scrambled for it, he dropped two more cans from his arms. A jumpy fellow, Garrett thought. He wore wire-rimmed glasses, the thick lenses making his eyes appear bigger than his narrow face could handle. He was a slight man with thin lips, a slender but defiant nose and thinning black hair as unruly as New Mexico Territory. He squatted, as edgy as a penned horse in front of a prairie fire, and fumbled around for the tins of tomatoes. Behind those thick glasses, his brown eyes seemed to cower. Garrett grinned and immediately the clerk's thin lips bloomed into a full smile.

"Welcome to Fort Bansom, mister," he said, picking up two of the tomato tins. He added them to the stack on the counter as Garrett shoved a third can with his boot. The clerk grabbed it, added it to the pile and stepped behind the counter. "Benjamin Franklin Tilman's the name, and I'm at your service with the best selection of goods between Santa Fe and El Paso. Yes, sir, I'm at your service."

"Looking for a place to stay. And first, a meal."

"This is a store, not a hotel," the clerk intoned. "But you leave it to Benjamin Franklin Tilman here and I'll take care of you as if this were the grandest city in all the West."

"Something to eat. That possible?"

"Anything's possible with Benjamin Franklin Tilman, sir. You just take a seat at a table there and tell me what you have in mind. I'll endeavor to satisfy all your needs, unless of course, you have a hankering for female companionship. Not much of that in these parts unless you've a notion for Indian flesh." Tilman motioned to a worn chair beside a dilapidated table, a dog-eared deck of cards spread across it. Garrett sat down, then the clerk joined him. Gathering the deck of cards, Tilman nodded Garrett's way and began shuffling them without looking, all the time focusing his eyes on Garrett.

"Now you may be saying that this Benjamin Franklin Tilman is as crazy as a drunk Indian or that New Mexico Territory drives a man out of his mind. Well, you may be right, but you'll find I'm as sane as they come, at least in New Mexico. Of course, when William Fitzgerald's in here I keep a hold of my tongue. Fitzgerald, he's got the contract to operate this and the issue house over at the Indian agency. Now when he's not here, like now, I'm the boss. I rule the store."

Garrett looked about the room, the shelf-lined walls sparsely settled with merchandise, the plank floor sprouting an occasional table of goods. Near the counter, which doubled as a bar, four tables and companion chairs were worn from use. Garrett glanced back at Tilman.

"How's all this affect you?" asked Tilman, who dropped the cards long enough to brush back from over his spectacles a sweat-matted clump of stringy black hair. "I'm prepared to give you the best prices we've got on anything you need in this store. Of course, I don't tell William Fitzgerald this, and if he should come in the store, all deals are off and I shall be forced to charge you our highest price — our trooper price.

"You see, sir, in this store we have three prices. The trooper price is marked up considerably, at least three or four times cost. Few of these black boys can read and not many can cipher so William Fitzgerald has seen fit to set up special prices for them. Of course, Colonel Stubby, he knows about the trooper prices. He profits from them. Now our next rates are for the officers and they're well above, no less than double, the price an honest man would charge. The officers think it's just the troopers getting robbed. Ha! They're getting taken, too. Now Colonel Stubby doesn't realize that. William Fitzgerald tells him freight costs make it impossible to sell things for any less and make a profit. I've seen the books because I keep them, so believe me, I'm right.

"Then we come to Benjamin Franklin Tilman's prices which are enough for any store owner to make a decent, but honest living. You take whatever you need and be assured I will not overcharge you as long as no one else is in the store." Tilman stopped shuffling the cards.

Before answering, Garrett waited a moment to see if Tilman was really giving him a chance to respond or just catching a breath before continuing his spiel. "I have little money and can spare no more than two bits for food, if I'm to have money for a place to sleep."

"A man in dire need, are you?" said Tilman, resuming his card shuffling. "Probably pretty tough for a one-armed man to earn much money. No insult intended, mind you, but I can't help but notice your left arm is useless. Man in your shape can't farm, can he? Can't chop wood, if there were any to be found around here, can he? Can't handle many a job too easily. Most jobs out here in this part of the country a man needs two good arms. Of course, not everything requires all your arms and hands. Can you read and write?"

Garrett stared at Tilman, uncertain of his motives.

"Can you?" the clerk repeated.

"Well enough to get by and maybe better

26

than most," answered Garrett, tapping his fingers on the table. His stomach ached for food and he feared he was no closer to easing his hunger than when he walked in.

"What about arithmetic? You any good at it? I mean can you add, subtract, multiply and maybe do a little long division? Lot of folks can't, you understand, so don't be ashamed to admit it," said Tilman, suspending his shuffling and pulling a dirty rag from his pocket to blow his nose.

"I'm fair at it."

"Now we're getting somewhere." The clerk arose from his chair and walked behind the wooden counter along the side wall. From the worn roll top desk behind the counter, Tilman fetched a sheet of paper, a writing pen and an ink well.

Returning to the table, he placed them in front of Garrett. That done, Tilman slumped back into his chair.

"Sign your name on the paper, please," said Tilman with unflinching eyes.

Garrett dipped the pen in the ink well and with a flourish of his good right hand, signed his name, then pushed the paper over to Tilman.

"Not bad, not bad at all, Mr. Morgan Garrett. Do one more thing for me. Add the year of your birth to this year and let me see if you can figure."

Garrett scratched his head, dipped the pen in the ink well and added the two years. He shook his head and shoved the paper across the table at Tilman. "You're about the strangest man I ever did meet, Mr. Tilman."

"I told you I was crazy," Tilman said, examining the paper. "Good, you can add. Well, that's a relief to know because I have a proposition for you. You need some money, right? I need some help. Yes, sir, you would think no more business than I've had since you've been here I wouldn't need any assistance, but you're wrong. Between this store and the issue house at the Indian agency, I stay busy, particularly around payday, which is a month overdue for these troopers. You ever worked in a store before?"

"Had a little experience in Texas in a place quite a bit more honest than this."

"Mister, I don't set the prices. I just charge whatever I have to. As long as William Fitzgerald gets a sizeable profit, he doesn't pay much attention to the operation, except looking over the books nightly. He leaves me in charge. You see, I can hire for him and keep most of his books — several sets in fact. I could use a honest man to help out. You'll be asked to do nothing dishonest by me."

Garrett paused, scratched his head while mulling over the offer. "I need a meal more than a job."

"I'll give you twenty dollars a month. That's more than the troopers make and I'll throw in the keeping of your horse and give you a room. I got a shelf of books for amusement and you can share meals with me. I'm no great cook, but it's better than army grub. A one-armed man is not going to find many better meals or deals."

"Why you doing me a favor?"

"No favor. Nobody does anybody a favor in this world, no sir. Everybody uses everybody else and I'll use you. I never saw a lame man I didn't feel sorry for and you look like an honest man. I need some honorable company here for a change. Somebody to help out. Yeah, I can use the help, but I need somebody to talk to other than crooked Fitzgerald, ignorant troopers and pompous cavalry officers.

"You know the War of the Rebellion was the worst thing that ever happened to the West," said Tilman. "Yes, sir, it sure was. Every officer out here today is a cocky son of a bitch. They've tasted the intoxicating wine of war and they miss it. They sure as heck do. And all of them are brevet officers with rank way above their abilities. You take

Colonel Stubby here. He was a brevet general of some type during the war and he thinks he's as good a soldier as General Grant or Sheridan or Sherman. Imagine that, would you?"

Garrett leaned across the table and extended his hand. "I'll accept your offer, work being hard to come by in these parts."

"Sure you'll accept. You have no choice, do you?" Tilman said, shaking Garrett's hand, then continuing his tirade. "Hell, if I'd known there were generals like Colonel Stubby in charge of the U.S. Army, I would've joined up with the Apaches. Did you fight in the war?"

"For the Confederacy."

"Glad to hear it. I'm a Pennsylvanian but I'd enlisted in the Confederate Army myself if I'd known there was a Colonel Stubby in the ranks of the Union. He's too pompous about his contributions to the war, freeing these slaves and all that. Hell, all he did was just change places with you southerners. Now he's running a plantation in New Mexico with two hundred and fifty uniformed slaves. Thinks he's the Napoleon of New Mexico, mind you. Why that's what's so funny about this Pachise fellow, an Apache savage that's taken his tribe into hiding. The Napoleon of New Mexico can't even catch the darned women and children in his tribe, much less Pachise himself. Indians don't fight like you Confederates did. But will the Napoleon of the West change his tactics? No sir, not at all. He keeps expecting the Apaches to fight full-scale battles over strategic sites that mean nothing to the Indian. This whole damn desolate country is home for the Apaches. Taken together, the land has strategic value to the savage, but a mere portion has none. The Apache has no supply line that can be cut because he manages off the land where he is. He has no capital city. No railroads or crucial bridges. He's just a nomad, but Colonel Stubby can't accept that and fight with the same hit-and-run style Pachise uses."

Garrett's patience was growing much shorter than Tilman's breath. "Now am I going to work for you or not? If so, where do I need to start?"

"No rush, is there? Tomorrow will be fine. Start off after a good night's rest."

"I'd get better sleep on a full stomach. When do I eat?"

"Later, after Colonel Stubby comes for his little liquid refreshment. He always ventures over when a patrol returns, and one came in today. Empty handed, of course. I want you to see Colonel Stubby. He always gets a bottle of whiskey — on the house, of course. We play a game of entering it on his account, just so the other officers won't get too wise, although they should have an idea since they get a free drink now and then. Colonel Stubby will take his bottle and sit down at this table, in your chair, and his junior officers will join him. He'll shake his head over the failure of another patrol, then pour each officer a drink. After asking for their suggestions, which he will ignore, they'll down their shot of whiskey. Then Colonel Stubby will drink his and keep refilling his own glass, not theirs. Looks to me he could at least share his whiskey a little more freely since it doesn't cost him a thing. Now you just watch."

"I'll take your word for it," said Garrett, tiring of the droning monotony of Tilman's voice. "If I could eat your words I'd be a full man right now, Mr. Tilman."

"Don't call me mister. I prefer Benjamin Franklin Tilman, but that's too long. Just call me Ben. What about you?"

"Call me Mister Garrett!" He grinned. "Otherwise, Morgan will do."

"You got some funny streak in you, Morgan. If you'd just learn to talk a little more you'd be all right."

"Don't have a chance when you've got the floor," Morgan shot back.

"Funny again," said Tilman, rising from his chair at the sound of men muttering outside. He strode behind his counter. "Sounds like the esteemed colonel is coming, so you just wait there. See what happens."

Garrett watched Tilman pick up a feather duster and attack the stack of tomato tins on the counter. When the door opened, Garrett glanced toward the parade of entering officers, led by a short, squat colonel, chewing on a cigar butt. By appearance alone, Garrett thought, the colonel deserved Tilman's poor estimation. His shirt tail hung out in back, his trousers tucked in one boot and out the other, his uniform blouse unbuttoned halfway down the front, exposing sweat-stained underclothes. By comparison, the junior officers came neatly dressed, including the dust-covered lieutenant who looked like he had just returned from patrol.

The colonel swaggered up to the counter. "Benjamin Franklin Tilman, give me the regular and put it on my account," the colonel commanded.

"Yes sir," said Tilman. "Any luck with Pachise this time?"

The colonel scowled at the dust-covered lieutenant. "We'll get him soon. I've got a plan."

Tilman nodded as though he'd heard the colonel's plans before. As the colonel turned toward the tables with bottle in hand, Tilman winked at Garrett. The junior officers each grabbed a glass provided by Tilman, the last man taking two since the colonel had forgotten one for himself, and followed their commanding officer to Garrett's table.

"You're in my chair there, mister," said the colonel, approaching Garrett. "Find yourself another place to roost. I have important Army business to discuss with my officers."

Morgan Garrett didn't blink an eye. "Garrett's my name, sir, and I'm not accustomed to being ordered around by soldiers in blue uniforms."

"Mr. Garrett, then, is that your nag out front with CSA on the saddle. Now, if it is and you are a former Confederate, I would suggest you move your butt or I'll check for your amnesty papers. If you don't have them, I'll put you in the stockade."

"You are most persuasive, Colonel Stubby."

The lieutenant in the dusty uniform snickered, then stifled it when the colonel shot an icy gaze his way.

"What did you call me, Garrett?"

"Colonel Stubby," the gray-eyed Garrett responded, then glanced at Tilman, whose eyes showed fear, but whose hand was stifling a nervous chuckle.

"Who called me that?" the colonel bellowed, banging the bottle on the table, spreading his legs apart and shoving his fists into his abundant waist.

"One of the troopers, sir. I asked when I came in for the man in charge and that's what the soldier told me," Garrett lied. "That not right?"

"The name is Orville C. Fulton, *Colonel* Orville C. Fulton, brevet brigadier general, U.S. Army, and I suggest you not forget it. Now get out of my way."

Garrett knew he had spurred a high-strung horse. He pushed himself back from the table, but before he could stand Tilman was beside him.

"Sorry about this, Colonel. This man's new here. I hired him today to help out in the store. He didn't realize he was making a mistake. Why I'm sure he would be delighted to buy you another bottle of liquor just to show there's no hard feelings by it all."

"Okay, Benjamin Franklin Tilman, but

you'd better teach this fellow something about Army ways, things he should have learned in the Confederate Army, even if he did indeed fight for the South against his own country."

Garrett moved from the chair, holding his limp arm so it would not dangle as noticeably.

"Too bad that U.S. rifleman wasn't a better shot," huffed the colonel.

Ignoring that final remark, Garrett followed Tilman behind the counter where the clerk picked out another bottle of liquor and delivered it to the colonel. Tilman's face broke into a silent, mocking smile only Garrett could see. Tilman winked, then resumed his feather dusting.

Just as Tilman had predicted, the colonel poured a round of drinks and then asked for suggestions, all the while chewing furiously on his cigar which was down to a nub. Garrett watched Colonel Fulton intently, taking in the officer's overbearing demeanor and disliking him more each moment. Between lecturing his Army inferiors and taking swigs of liquor, Fulton spit bullets of tobacco onto the floor from his disintegrating cigar.

"I guess I'll be forced to lead a patrol myself out to catch Pachise. None of you can bring him and his band back in," Fulton kept repeating, his officers nodding but staring blankly at the walls. "If I had command of real troopers instead of these niggers, we'd soon catch that renegade."

"But sir," interrupted one officer, "these men are better than most white men I've commanded."

"Dammit, Lieutenant," Fulton shot back, "I don't want to hear you making excuses for them. They disgust me and you do too when you take up for them. Gentlemen, this is enough for today. I am retiring to my quarters and will expect each of you to do a better job catching that red bastard than you have to date." Fulton scowled, looked around the room and stood up from the table. He grabbed both liquor bottles and stormed out the door, slamming it behind him.

The other officers waited in silence, giving Fulton time enough to reach his quarters before they started for theirs. Then they marched out in the order of their rank.

"You pretty near got me in trouble, Benjamin Franklin Tilman," said Garrett, getting the jump on the spindly clerk just opening his mouth.

"It wasn't me that called him Colonel Stubby — your mouth's the one that created that mess. Hell, he'll not remember a thing tomorrow, not after he's had a chance to kiss not one, but two bottles, all night. Anyway, you should've known Stubby wasn't his real name."

"I did."

"Then why'd you call him Colonel Stubby?"

"I never got any amnesty papers. Thought that was a good way to change the subject. I didn't care to spend a night in his stockade, even if it is free. Anyway, where's the name Stubby come from?"

"Oh, it's these troopers. Everybody at Fort Bansom has a nickname and Fulton's is Stubby. Fact is, that's what everybody calls him to his back, but as I recollect, you're the first to call him that to his face."

"I'm honored," Garrett said with a grin and a mock bow.

"Now just why the troopers call him that, I'm not sure," continued Tilman. "Some said it was because he's always chewing on a cigar, others said it was because he's short. But yes sir, you're the first man to call him that to his face. Hell, this may make you a hero here on the Bosque Bonito Reservation because the only person that likes him is himself. He hates me."

38

"You did pester him a bit much," Garrett replied.

"That's not it. He thinks I'll reveal his corruption. I am the only one other than William Fitzgerald that knows the kind of rake-off he gets here at Fort Bansom."

"All this talking has made me hungry, Ben, and I'm not kidding. Are we ever going to eat?"

"Yes sir, you'll get to eat, don't you fret. We have at our selection the finest choice of canned goods between El Paso and Santa Fe. I'll have something going as soon as I lock up and you get your horse cared for. Grab your belongings off your mount and take the animal to the corral. Tell the stable sergeant you've been hired at the store and he'll handle things from there. Come around to the back door when you're finished and I'll let you in. Now go on if you really are interested in tending your gut."

"You're ordering me around like you were Colonel Stubby himself," Garrett grinned.

"That's not funny. Now go on."

Garrett obliged, bringing his meager belongings in and then going outside to his horse. He led the chestnut over the parade ground toward the stables, passing several colored soldiers along the way. As he approached the stables, two laughing black troopers marched out. One stopped and stared with stony eyes at Garrett and his horse.

"What's a matter, Jonah? You looks like you just seen a ghost," said Skully.

"It's no ghost, Skully, 'less my eyes is playing tricks on me. That's Master Morgan Garrett."

Garrett, equally dumbfounded at finding one of his former slaves in a cavalry uniform at a New Mexico outpost, stood speechless and staring, as if his feet had taken root. He finally broke the unnatural silence.

"How are you, Jonah?" he said, extending his good right hand.

Jonah paused, uncertain whether or not to grasp Garrett's hand. Then Skully jerked him away before he could decide.

# CHAPTER 3

Jonah toyed with the slumgullion on his tin plate, spooning the stew from side to side without taking a bite. His portion had been scraped from the bottom of the pot and the one spoonful he had swallowed, charred and bitter, had ruined his meager appetite. As the other soldiers cleared their plates and mugs from the roughhewn table, Jonah stared sullenly at supper, his eyes downcast, his broad shoulders slumped over the table, his forearms resting on either side of his plate.

As the noise of the others moved outside, Jonah glanced around the unlit mess hall. Toward the back a couple soldiers cleaned the dishes, grumbling over their chore. Jonah picked up his tin mug and swished the black liquid around before gulping it down. He winced at its acrid taste. He had forgotten to add the brown sugar, but he swallowed the cupful anyway.

"You comin' or sittin' here 'til breakfast?"

Jonah squinted into the shaft of sunlight angling through the door and recognized Skully's lanky silhouette leaning against the door frame. Dropping his tin cup into the scorched stew, Jonah pushed away from the table and walked around the bench, carrying his eating utensils to the dishwashers. He ambled back toward Skully and finally to the door. Skully twisted around, rubbing his back against one side of the door frame. As Jonah neared, Skully lifted his leg and straightened it against the opposite side of the door, blocking Jonah's exit.

"Ain't you forgettin' somethin', Jonah?"

Jonah shrugged and moved to push Skully's leg from his path. He nudged at Skully's leg. It was wedged in place, tight as a lock. Jonah eased back. Though they were friends, Jonah knew not to trifle with Skully's headstrong disposition.

"Your sugar, Jonah. It's been six nights now that you've forgotten Grant. That horse been missin' his sugar."

Jonah nodded and retreated to the nearest table. Into the palm of his hand he dumped clumps of the hardened brown sugar from a battered can. Walking back to the door, he spit in his palm and clenched his hand into a fist three times until he had a single ball of sugar. Skully dropped his leg from the door and Jonah strode past him toward the stable.

"You been quiet lately, forgettin' your horse, not eatin', not sleepin' well, Jonah."

"This army food's not been settlin' in my innards lately."

"It just been the grub, you'd been a bawlin' like a piglet on hind tit. You been too quiet for that."

"A freed man gots a right to ponder when he wants."

Skully grabbed Jonah's arm and halted the corporal's march toward the stables. For the first time, Jonah turned to face Skully. "It's that man Garrett."

Jonah nodded, his left hand squeezing the ball of sugar more tightly. He gritted his teeth, a heavy breath escaping noisily between them. "I fears he may take me back. Maybe harm me for what happened to his wife and sons."

"You kill 'em?"

"I buried 'em. Cholera killed 'em, but with no white folks around then I wasn't sure nobody'd believe that. I runned away."

Skully released his grip of Jonah's arm. Pulling his slouch hat from his head and swatting at a pesky fly, he leaned closer to

Jonah. "I'll help you kill him," Skully whispered.

Jonah twisted away from Skully and stalked toward the stables, squeezing the ball of sugar tighter between both hands. When he heard Skully's heavy footsteps behind him, he spun around. "I been a slave, but I never been caged or chained like some animal." Jonah's words simmered in anger. "Killin' a white man'll get me in jail or hung like a side of beef."

"I's chained more times that I can remember." Skully spit out the words. Unbuttoning his dusty blouse, then pulling apart the wool undergarment, he continued. "I's been beaten like I was nothin' but a mean dog. Looks at these scars." Skully bared a triangle of his chest and with his fingers traced the jagged wounds like trails on a map.

"I've seen 'em before, Skully." Jonah closed his eyes and shook his head. He preferred not to see them again.

"And the ones on my back. I can't scratch and itch without remembering every beatin' I got from masters like that Garrett."

Jonah blinked his eyes at the pink ridge of naked flesh snaking across Skully's chest. "Button up your shirt, Skully. I've seen your scars before. Master Garrett weren't no bad owner."

"We could knife him. Make it look like an Injun done it. If the army thinks we did it, we desert." Skully rebuttoned his blouse. "Just think about it."

Jonah resumed his march toward the stable, kicking at the hardpacked parade ground with each step. Skully matched each stride. "He's got me worried muchly, but he treat me mostly fairly as a slave. I don't have no scars."

"Your scars just don't show."

"My mamma teach me it's not right to kill a man."

"Did she teach you to read, Jonah? You always sayin' how you'd like to read a book. Did Garrett teach you to read?"

"I asks him once, but he never did nothin' but laugh."

"Then you gots scars."

Jonah pushed open the stable door, the smell of old straw and fresh manure enveloping him as he topped to face Skully. "Maybe I carry a few scars, buts it's no cause to kill a man."

"Lot of troopers at this fort be glad to help you if you ever changes your mind, Jonah."

Jonah spun around and stormed away between twin rows of horses until he reached Grant's stall. Stepping up to the tethered animal, Jonah patted Grant's neck and scratched behind his ears. "Sorry, old boy, I ain't been meanin' to neglect you — just had other things on my mind. I brought some nibblin's for you tonight." He slipped his balled hand in front of the gelding and opened his fingers. The horse lapped at the sugar and then nuzzled at Jonah's empty hand when the sweet was gone. "Grant, ole boy, I'm not forgettin' you again. Promise you that, I do."

Skully walked up and slapped Grant on the rump. "You be a lucky animal, Grant. Best tended horse in the cavalry!"

Jonah kicked at the floor beneath the horse. "More hay, you need more hay." Jonah backed out of the stall, running his hand along the animal's spine, then stepped around Skully. Jonah moved to the center of the stable, grabbed a pitchfork and jabbed it into a hive of hay. Returning to Grant's stall, Jonah ignored Skully, tossed the hay at Grant's feet and returned for another load.

Skully leaned against the wooden stall and dropped his hands on the opposite side. "You gots scars, Jonah. Maybe you thinks you be better than the rest of us, but you got scars, too. You gots a chance to get even with the man that gave 'em to you. Rest of us wish we had that chance."

Jonah stepped by Skully and flung the hay

at Grant's legs, the horse nickering and kicking the wooden stall near Skully. "You put that from your mind, Skully, or it's gonna get us in trouble or get us killed."

Jumping from the stall just ahead of Grant's next kick, Skully tripped over a coil of rope and fell. Jonah laughed, then patted Grant's rump and spoke gently to the animal, as if he were talking to a child. With Grant soothed, Jonah looked down at Skully. "Grant agrees with me, Skully, so you best forget about botherin' Garrett."

Skully grunted as he picked himself up and dusted off his britches, but in the dimness of the stable, Jonah could not read Skully's face. "You promise me, you won't hurt him?"

For a moment, Skully stared at Jonah, then he mumbled. "I's supposed to be workin' in the gardens this evenin'. When I became a freed man I said I wasn't doin' no more of farmin'. And now the cavalry's got me doin' slave work."

"We want anything but damn army food, we gotta garden, Skully."

"I'd soon try to do with a little less food if it meant a little less work. What you say we hit the swimmin' hole and forget any more chores, Jonah?"

"It'd be trouble if we's caught, Skully. Go

on and get your work done, we'll talk later in the barracks." Jonah handed him the pitchfork and told him to leave it by the hay stack when he left.

Skully stood for a moment, watching as Jonah picked up a curry comb and stroked Grant's back. Then he slipped sullenly away. Jonah welcomed the solitude.

"How about giving your jaw and my ears a rest, Ben?" Garrett pushed his broom past the clerk.

"Don't be complaining none, Morgan Garrett. It's not the army way to be criticizing your superiors." Benjamin Franklin Tilman laughed as he wiped fingerprints, mostly his own, from the glass panes of a counter display. He snapped his soiled rag toward Garrett. "I only talk when it's necessary."

"And that's all the time," Garrett said. "I heard more quiet at Gettysburg."

"A man that can't sweep any better than that," Tilman said, pointing to a pile of debris in front of the counter, "could learn something if he paid more attention to what his boss was saying."

Garrett retreated to the floor debris and eased it toward a larger pile, his bad arm swinging like a pendulum as his good hand steered the broom. "You knew you was getting a cripple when you took me on. You hired me for my ears. What's it been, six days that I've been here? Already I know more about you than I know about myself."

"But you only know a fraction about me, Morgan Garrett." Tilman laughed.

"I feared so. You keep talking as much and I'll be taking more of a liking to your boss William Fitzgerald, even if he is a crook. At least he don't batter me with his tongue all the time."

"And I do? But you don't understand the depth of Fitzgerald's wickedness. You just met him once."

Garrett paused from his chore, rested his chin on the broom handle and pursed his lips. "And he didn't say a single word to me. My ears needed the rest." Garrett grinned as he resumed sweeping.

"Okay," Tilman said, staring toward a window opaque with New Mexico dust. "It's getting late, about quitting time anyway. I'll finish the sweeping if you'll run an errand for me."

"Anything to save my ears."

Tilman unhooked his wire-rimmed glasses from behind each ear and wiped the lenses with his dust rag. Holding the glasses up against the murky light from the window, he attacked a stubborn smudge and spoke. "Not too many days until the paymaster comes. I want a good supply of blankets — the troopers wear them out in the field — when the paymaster arrives." Tilman lifted his glasses to the light again and studied his work.

"You expect me to weave them?"

Tilman snickered as he hooked the wire temples over his ears, then blinked his corrected sight back into focus. "Bad as you handle a broom, I wouldn't want to see you on a loom." Tilman lifted his hands to his hips. "Fitzgerald cheats the Indians out of their blankets. He gets them cheap on government contracts, then sells them to the troopers and gets their worn blankets in the exchange. Then he issues the Indians the old, worn blankets. Walk on over to the issue house and tell them I sent you for a half dozen.

"Think a one-armed man can handle that many blankets? It's either that or stay here and listen to me a while longer."

"I'll do it, even if it takes six trips."

"You make that many and you just may run into your friend Fitzgerald again. Maybe he'll say something to you this time, like 'Go to hell'. He's quite like a snake."

Tilman motioned for Garrett to follow

and they walked outside to the back of the store. The clerk pointed to a squat building beyond the gardens. "That's the issue house. It's where Fitzgerald rations out spoiled grain and rotten meat to the Navajos and Apaches. He ruins everything he touches. Don't say I never warned you. Now go on and bring back my blankets."

The fort was calm at that hour, the soldiers had finished their evening meal and all but a few of the chores. Garrett walked briskly into the slight breeze that carried a faint but familiar noise to his ears. For a moment it was as if he were walking the grounds of his father's plantation before the war. It was singing, the unmistakable noise of darkies in the field, commiserating about their woes. Maybe a hundred yards ahead, he observed soldiers in the garden. As he drew nearer, he could make out the words to their song and could hear the field music of metal hoes hitting dry ground. Garrett followed the path between the soldier's vegetable patches and the music died away, just as it had in the days of his youth. But now the silent stares had turned malevolent. A voice called out from among the troopers.

"There goes master. Looks like he forgots his whip today."

Laughter, but not Garrett's, answered the comment.

"Look ats that bad arm," another trooper joined in. "Maybe somebody beat him with a whip."

"Probably some Yankee soldier." The troopers guffawed.

Garrett's gray eyes narrowed and he gritted his teeth. The war had changed much, too much, and he didn't like it. He spit on the hard-packed path and glared back at the black soldiers.

"If you is gonna water our garden," one said softly, ". . . then spit on a plant." The others chuckled.

Anger flared within Garrett like a handful of gunpowder thrown in a fire. He clenched his fist until the knuckles of his good hand turned ashen, but he kept walking. Soon he was beyond the garden. Gradually the sound of the hoeing resumed, but not the singing.

Ahead, the issue house, a long squat adobe structure with a wooden porch and awning running its length, stood dark and hostile, an outcast from the other buildings of Fort Bansom. As he approached the building, he observed shadowy figures reclining in chairs and benches against the mud walls. Garrett stepped up on the porch and stopped before a grayed wagon tailgate resting on two empty barrels as a makeshift table. He stated his orders, eliciting only glances from the four seated men. "Blankets," Garrett repeated twice as he stepped to the side of the table. Two pulled their hats over their faces. A Mexican with hawkish eyes stared over a bent nose and gaunt cheeks at Garrett. With a gleaming Bowie knife the Mexican sliced away at a block of wood, as if he would rather be carving something softer — like flesh. Beside the Mexican a squat man in dirty overalls leaned forward, spurting a stream of tobacco juice on the porch near Garrett's feet, then looking up with a toothless grin. Garrett slapped his good hand on the table. The tobacco chewer's lips contorted into a sneer. The Mexican betrayed no emotion.

"Blankets? Six? I heard you, but you don't give me my orders. No lame-armed man's gonna tell me what to do." The squat man leaned back in his chair and wiped a dribble of tobacco juice from the corner of his mouth. He glanced at the whittler beside him, his gaze lingering for a moment.

Garrett jerked his head to the side, looking toward the end of the long porch. There stood William Fitzgerald, nodding, but not at Garrett. "Do what he says," Fitzgerald ordered.

The tobacco chewer dropped the front legs of his chair back on the porch and jumped up. Then he gave a hurried command in Spanish, the Mexican easing his chair forward and standing. "Pronto, Diablo," the tobacco chewer said.

The Mexican dropped the wooden block to the porch, stood and faced Garrett. Their eyes locked together for an instant, then the Mexican slammed the knife into the table, no more than two inches from Garrett's hand. Diablo left his knife impaled in the wood and retreated into the bowels of the issue house. Garrett glanced back toward Fitzgerald, but he had disappeared. The Mexican returned three wordless minutes later and tossed the blankets against the knife. Two tumbled to the ground like wounded birds.

"Blankets, six," said the tobacco chewer.

Diablo jerked his knife from the table top and slid back into his chair. Garrett picked up and refolded the two downed blankets and fought to arrange them with the other four in a manageable stack on the table. He squatted by the table, slipped his arm under the stack, dropped his chin atop the pile and lifted the blankets. As he turned away, the gravelly voice of the tobacco chewer called after him. "How you gonna scratch an itch?"

Garrett stepped off the porch. He had no answer. The cumbersome blankets shifted with each tentative step, an avalanche possible with each stride. He stumbled over a rock, almost dropping his load, and heard laughter behind him. Then more laughter ahead. As he neared the garden, Garrett twisted his neck and shifted his arm for a better grip beneath the bundle. Still the load slipped. He hopped awkwardly and squeezed tighter at the blankets as he reached the gardens.

When he passed the first garden plot, he saw two soldiers throw down their hoes and fall in behind him. Then others from across the garden stalked in around him, a noose slowly tightening around the path. Just ahead two troopers with folded arms blocked his way. Garrett paused, shifting the load wedged between arm and chin and studying the hard faces of the pair, then stepped forward.

"You're blocking my way," he said, easing toward them.

Both soldiers stepped in unison at Garrett and shoved him into the middle of the circle of soldiers closing in around him. Garrett tumbled to the ground, the blankets scattering about him among the bean plants. The troopers laughed. Garrett eased himself up on his knees and gathered the blankets, working quickly to fold and restack them. "Crawl, you bastard," shouted a trooper, shaking a fist at Garrett. "See what's it's like to get treated like an animal."

"Yeah," a chorus of troopers agreed.

Garrett slapped the final blanket atop the new stack. Carefully gathering the pile under his arm and against his ribs, he drew a deep breath, then stood. As he did a soldier jumped in front of him. A lank slice of a man with a broad nose, beady eyes and larcenous lips, the soldier unbuttoned his army blouse, stripped it from his shoulders and tossed it to another trooper. Garrett remembered the soldier. He had been at the encounter with Jonah.

"You teach him a lesson, Skully. One he'll 'member," called a trooper.

Garrett stepped off the path to move around Skully, but another soldier shoved him back toward the middle of the circle, scattering the blankets again. "You're going nowhere," the soldier said. "Skully gonna give you a teaching." Making no effort to retrieve the blankets this time, Garrett stared at Skully as the soldier pulled apart the top of his wool long johns and bared his torso. Sinister scars traversed his chest.

"My papa was a slave and his papa a slave too," Skully said, then turned around.

Garrett winced at the pinkish trails a whip had left on Skully's back. Discolored skin angled in all directions like a savage spider web across his flesh.

"Like me, they had scars on their backs — bad ones." Skully twisted around, doubled one fist and pounded it into his other palm. "I's waited a long time to catch one of you slave owners where I could beat you senseless. When I's through, both your arms will match."

"Then come ahead," Garrett challenged. "You must've deserved every beating you got."

Skully bent over, reached for his boot and pulled an ivory-handled barber's razor from inside. He straightened and slowly opened the glistening blade. A smile spread like a stain across his face as he waved the knife toward Garrett. "You gonna have more cuts than your blood can find when I's through."

As Skully eased toward him, Garrett bent, grabbed the corner of a blanket and twirled it around his arm. Skully lunged and sliced at Garrett's face. Garrett jumped back, holding up his arm as a shield. He felt the blade graze against the blanket. Skully's grin widened. He waved the razor in wide, high arcs, then swung it low for Garrett's belly. Misjudging Skully's aim, Garrett dropped his arm to his midsection then cried out as the razor angled across his thumb.

Skully backed away and looked at the blood-spotted blade. "First scar, but not the last." He spit at the blade, then at Garrett. "Next scar." He lunged for his bleeding opponent, but Garrett jumped adroitly away from Skully's razor hand. Skully turned and charged back. Garrett feinted away from the razor hand, then toward it. Skully swung at the feint. Garrett kicked at Skully's boot. The trooper fell forward, the razor flying from his hand beneath a bean bush. Garrett rushed Skully. As the trooper was scrambling up, Garrett booted him in the face. Skully screamed like a wounded cougar, his mouth bloodied, then dove for the razor. Garrett moved for him, but tripped over a blanket on the ground. Skully plucked the razor from beneath a bean plant.

"Now it's time to give you a close shave," yelled Skully.

Garrett grabbed at the blanket unraveling from his arm and snapped it at Skully's face. As Garrett jerked the blanket back, Skully followed on its tail, the course of his razor clipping a button from Garrett's shirt.

Skully charged Garrett like an enraged bull and Garrett threw the blanket at his face.

"Get him, get him," the impatient soldiers shouted.

Skully flung the blanket from his eyes and rushed forward, butting into Garrett with his shoulder. Garrett crashed to the ground, pain shooting like molten lead up his spine until he could almost feel it in his paralyzed arm. Skully stomped at Garrett's good arm, smashing it once. Garrett screamed. He flailed for the trooper's leg. Garrett felt the boot crash into his numbing hand. He tried to raise up but Skully fell atop him, straddling Garrett, finally pinning the cripple's good arm. Skully raked the razor in front of Garrett's eyes and laughed. Then he held the razor against Garrett's throat as the spectators cheered for more blood. Garrett bucked his legs, then flailed wildly with them. Skully lost his balance. His razor slipped free as Garrett slid out from under him. Skully pitched wildly, madly with his fists at Garrett's face. Amid the dozen glancing blows, one struck Garrett solidly and felt like a cannon exploding inside his brain, the pain shooting in all directions like a bomb burst. Skully climbed back on Garrett and pounded his face.

"Somebody, hand me my razor," Skully

called. "I'll carve enough scars on his face he'll never forget this slave."

A commotion arose among the troopers. "Stop it, Skully!"

"My razor!" Skully roared.

"Don't, Skully," Jonah hollered, but Skully kept pummeling Garrett's face.

Breaking through the crowd, Jonah dove into Skully and knocked him off Garrett. "I tolds you I wanted none of this, Skully. Why don't you listen? He's never did you no harm. So why try to kill him? Damn, he's already maimed for life. Don't make it no worse on him."

Skully jumped up, and Jonah wrapped his arms around him. Skully shook free and shoved back at Jonah. "It don't matter who he owned, Jonah," Skully gasped. "He still owned one of us. That was enough."

Garrett stood up, his legs wobbly, his thumb bleeding. His brain pounded with pulses of pain. While he steadied himself for another charge, Skully turned away and walked toward the fort. Bending to pick up the blankets, Garrett fell to his knees. Through the haze of his mind, he saw a uniformed figure standing in front of him. Garrett looked up at Jonah.

"Thank you, Jonah," he said, lifting his bloody right hand toward his former slave.

Jonah grabbed and shook it. "You go back to the store and get that hand tended, Master Garrett. These your blankets?"

Garrett nodded.

"I follow you with them, Master Garrett."

"Just call me Morgan, Jonah. Morgan, and nothing else."

Jonah smiled and nodded.

# CHAPTER 4

The door swung rudely open on creaking hinges and a blue-capped lieutenant popped inside before the door bounced back and hit him in the face. With his hands on his hips, the lieutenant glowered for a moment over the tables and chairs as his eyes adjusted to the dimness of the room.

Ben nudged Garrett beside him at the far end of the counter. "You're in trouble, I'll betcha," he whispered. "Colonel Stubby must be rampaging again." Ben stood the full length of his short frame and ran his fingers through his stringy hair. "You running from Pachise, Lieutenant, or trying to knock my door through the wall?"

Twisting his body around to face the direction of the voice, the lieutenant growled. "Morgan Garrett, the colonel demands to see you in his office immediately."

"A social call," Benjamin Franklin Tilman sniped.

"I'm just following orders, Ben."

"Of a lunatic," Tilman added.

Garrett eased away from the counter and stretched his arm, then rubbed his shoulders. He was still sore from the fight with Skully. Garrett dropped his hand to the counter and patted his fingers against the surface worn slick from use. "What business has the colonel with me?"

"The colonel does not make me privy to his reasons," the lieutenant paused, his gaze flitting back and forth between Tilman and Garrett. "It's no secret your fight has gotten the troopers all riled up."

Garrett lifted his hand and coughed into a balled fist, his face shooting with pains from the fight. "What if I don't come?"

The lieutenant stepped toward Garrett. "You won't find many friends at this fort. If you decline, the colonel will only order you arrested. It's easier on everyone if you just come along."

Tilman lifted his hand and pointed a finger at the lieutenant. "You mean easier for you," he said, stepping toward the officer and shaking his finger with each stride. "Colonel will tear you apart if you don't bring back Morgan."

Stepping around Tilman, the officer moved toward Garrett. "It's up to you. Though, as one white man to another, I'd encourage you to go peacefully. The troops would like to get another chance at you. It true you once owned one of them?"

"That's all past now." Garrett walked behind the bar and jerked his hat from a peg. "Let's go." He went out the door ahead of the lieutenant.

"Don't slam it," Tilman yelled at the lieutenant, but too late to be heeded.

Garrett marched quickly to the headquarters building, the closest structure to the sutler's store, though it was still fifty yards away. Only with exaggerated strides did the lieutenant catch Garrett without running. The lieutenant pulled in front of Garrett in time to step first into the dry shade of the veranda and then inside the adobe building.

The lieutenant ushered Garrett into a sparse office with a paper-littered table desk, a pair of chairs, a U.S. flag standing in one corner and a rack of guns in another. He motioned for Garrett to take a seat in a worn cane-bottom chair, then straightened his shoulders, thrust out his chest and stretched his frame to its full height. He rapped on the door and without pausing opened the door. "Colonel . . . ," the lieutenant spoke, his voice instantly trailing off into silence.

Rising from his chair, Garrett moved behind the lieutenant to see inside. The colonel had his feet propped between two lonely bottles on his desk and was leaned back in his chair — asleep.

Pulling the door quietly closed the lieutenant jerked it shut when he realized Garrett was standing behind his shoulder. "You should keep your seat until otherwise instructed, sir." The lieutenant's thin face reddened, and his deep voice dripped with apology when he spoke again. "I'm just following orders."

Garrett turned away from the officer toward his seat. "It helps when the source of the orders can be respected." The lieutenant grunted and plopped down into his seat, saying nothing more but busying himself with the papers scattered across the desk. Garrett settled into his own uncomfortable chair, staring across the room at the colonel's closed door and at a long wait. Time, overburdened by boredom, dragged by until Garrett stood up to stretch his aching legs. He paced from side to side of the room, taking hard steps on the wooden floor and watching the lieutenant squirm at the unnecessary noise. When Colonel Fulton's door cracked open, Garrett stepped swiftly into the office before the lieutenant could rise.

"Send Garrett in now," Fulton ordered as he ambled back to his desk. When he turned around to ease into his padded chair, he flinched at Garrett standing erect on the other side of the desk.

"You need to see me?" Garrett asked, reaching to remove his hat, then opting to wear it instead. As the colonel settled into his chair like a hen on a nest, Garrett studied the colonel's whiskey-ravaged face, peppered with prickly whiskers and bloated with distrust.

Surveying Garrett with red, watery eyes, the colonel rubbed his hands together and leaned forward, drumming his fingers across the edge of the desk. "Now, Garrett, you don't seem to understand how busy a man I am, now do you?" he intoned.

"I've had a good indication, Colonel."

Fulton glanced from Garrett to his desk, then shook his head as if trying to wring his thoughts into words. He reached for the two empty bottles and sat them on the floor. "I've got a fort here to run with three companies of cavalry and one of infantry, all darkies." The colonel fumbled among the papers on his desk until he found a cigar butt that he jammed between his teeth. The cigar and a scowl warped his face. "I'm sure you realize only the best among the officers were picked to command these black boys." Fulton paused, awaiting an affirmation that was not spoken, then bit into the cigar butt and continued. "Despite my abilities, I am often hard pressed to keep things under control, particularly with Pachise on the loose. On top of that, I've got to see that this reservation is run according to the book and those savages are taken care of and taught how to be a civilized people. It keeps me very busy, you realize?"

"A lot of responsibility," Garrett answered without emotion. "Even for you, I am sure."

"Glad you see it that way, Garrett," Fulton continued, leaning back in his chair. "That's why it annoys me that you've been agitating my troops."

Garrett leaned over Fulton's desk and slapped it with his good hand. "When is defending myself agitating? The one they call Skully started it."

Fulton clenched the cigar in his teeth, chewed on it momentarily, then spit a bullet of tobacco toward the open window. "I delayed calling you here so my officers could compile a report on the whole incident."

"No one talked to me, Colonel," Garrett shot back.

"The investigation, Garrett, has followed the proper channels, following proper Army procedures. You stand accused of inciting a fight between yourself and a soldier of the United States Army on government property. That's a serious charge to be brought against a Confederate traitor."

"The charge is unfounded," Garrett answered.

Fulton shifted the cigar butt to the opposite side of his mouth and offered a jaundiced grin. "Your statement directly contradicts several statements from soldiers of the United States Army." He leaned forward until his face was opposite Garrett's. "These statements are from men serving their country, not fighting against it like you did."

The words that came at Garrett were as revolting as the alcohol on Fulton's breath. "I will defend myself against lies, Colonel, just as I defended myself against attack in the gardens."

Fulton snickered. "You didn't put up much of a defense, from the look of you. But then what could be expected from a one-armed man? Look, Garrett, you don't have to worry about this at all. You be

68

thankful I'm an honorable man, as I intend to give you another chance. You realize I have the power to have you removed from this fort and the grounds of the Bosque Bonito Reservation." Fulton took a gigantic breath and thrust his chest forward. "That could mean your death, since a one-armed man is unlikely to survive a meeting with Pachise. Instead of that, you can stay in your present position. But take my warning: there'd best be no future trouble."

Garrett stood erect. He clenched his fist, then wriggled his fingers open, a spot of blood seeping from the razor wound on his hand. He spun around and stalked out the office, past the smiling lieutenant and into the stifling heat of an unsympathetic New Mexico sun. Quickly he was at the sutler's store. He spit on its adobe wall and flung the door open.

Benjamin Franklin Tilman, wiping the counter, winced at the sound, then relaxed as he saw Garrett striding in. "You look like you had a good time," the clerk laughed. "Ol' Stubby has a way of doing that to folks."

Marching past the counter, Garrett struck it with his fist, leaving a smudge of blood from his cut hand. Without speaking to Tilman he headed down the darkened hall to his room.

"You were gone so long, Morgan," Tilman said, following him down the hall, "I thought you and the colonel might have gone fishing or got in a friendly card game."

Garrett wheeled around, his arm upraised like he planned to strike Tilman. "Shut up, Ben. You can get on a man's nerves as fast as the colonel." Shaking his hand, he turned and stepped into his room. A bed, a chair and a washstand made up its humble furnishings. From beneath his bed Garrett pulled his bedroll and saddlebags, then began gathering his meager belongings.

"Now just what are you doing, Morgan?"

"I'm getting my things and getting out of this place." Garrett glanced up at Tilman and saw in his eyes fear magnified behind the thick lenses of his glasses.

"Hold on, Morgan, don't get too hasty." Tilman pulled a filthy handkerchief from his pocket and wiped his nose, then his brow.

"The damn fight," Garrett started, "Stubby's investigated it and's accusing me of starting it. As long as I'm here, I'll be the target of the troops and Stubby. I can do without that."

"Just hold on, Morgan." Tilman balled the rag in his hand and dropped it. "Sure, you've been falsely accused. Everybody at the fort knows it, including Stubby. Don't you see? You worry Colonel Stubby. That's why he made you wait a good while. Didn't think I knew that, did you? Yes, sir, he does it to anger people. Stubby makes them mad because he's smart enough to know they don't think straight when they're angry. Hell, the only person he doesn't make wait is your boss and mine, William Fitzgerald. Stubby's too anxious to split the graft. Yes, sir, the Napoleon of the West may be dumb when it comes to soldiering, but he's shrewd when it comes to working people. Otherwise he wouldn't have survived as long as he has in this Army." Tilman squatted down to pick up the rag from the floor.

"I don't need Colonel Fulton and if I stay I'm only asking for trouble — you know that, Ben." As Tilman straightened up, Garrett glimpsed cowering eyes.

"Fact is, Morgan, I need you."

Garrett laughed and turned away. "You're doing okay by yourself gouging the soldiers and cheating the Indians."

Tilman's eyes narrowed and his brow darkened. "You think it sets well with me? I don't like it either," he answered. "And one day I may go to jail for my part in it. That's why I need you to help get me out of here."

"Nothing's keeping you from leaving now. You can come with me to Santa Fe and find honest work."

Tilman shook his head. "It's not that simple, Morgan." He wiped his brow with the rag again. "I'm a wanted man and William Fitzgerald knows it. If I leave him, he'll tell all and I'll wind up going to jail for sure, and maybe worse."

Garrett cocked his head in skepticism. "You? A wanted man?" he laughed. "Wanted for murder, I'm sure." A grin split his face.

For a moment, Tilman stood silent, motionless, then his head drooped forward. "For murder? In a way, yes."

The smile faded from Garrett's lips and he sat on the bed.

"I was wanted for murder," Tilman whispered, "and it was something I just couldn't do. You see, I deserted the Army during the War of the Rebellion. I just couldn't shoot somebody and live with myself, and the thought of getting killed tormented me even more. So I deserted. Never was cut out to be a soldier, anyway. Can't hardly see well enough to know friend from foe, but I was conscripted and had no choice."

Garrett nodded. "Sure, Ben, you've outdone yourself with your talking this time."

Raising his head, Tilman stared at Garrett.

"You don't believe me, do you?"

"Now, Ben, it strikes me rather peculiar that a man who deserted the Army would choose to work in a sutler's at a military outpost."

"Divine punishment, I reckon, because it's a daily reminder of my past," Tilman explained. "I was broke when I got to New Mexico and I fell in with William Fitzgerald. He offered me a meal and a drink. I was so hungry I ate and drank everything he put in front of me. One thing led to another and before long I was drunk. I never could hold my liquor well. In my drunkenness I must've told him my story because the next day he told me he knew of my past. Being a man of honor," Tilman let the word linger on his lips, "he told me either to work for him as he wanted or he would report me to the authorities. I either went along or risked a firing squad. I saw things his way."

"War's past — there shouldn't be fear in leaving."

Tilman wiped his brow with the rag, then jammed it in his back pocket. "No, dammit, shouldn't be, but I'm afraid of the firing squad. That's how they took care of deserters on the Union side. I know this, though — I haven't sipped whiskey since that night."

"So Fitzgerald's scaring you into operating his crooked business."

Slowly, he nodded. "He reminds me I'm a deserter with the same breath he instructs me what to charge our clientele."

"Then you cheat him to get even?"

"To settle our score. He probably knows, but he's making too much to worry about the little I cheat him out of." Tilman jerked the rag from his pocket and wiped the beads of sweat from his forehead. "I need you, Morgan," the clerk said, hiding his eyes behind the rag as he spoke. He ran his nervous fingers through his stringy hair.

"How can I help, Ben?" Garrett stood up from the bed.

Tilman wiped his hand on the rag. "I've got the records to prove my accusations and I need someone to take them to the territorial governor. I can bargain that evidence for a pardon for deserting. But I need someone to help me, because I could never leave the fort with the evidence without Fitzgerald seeing I was killed. I got nowhere else to turn, Morgan." Tilman's head drooped forward. "If I were braver, I might do it myself, but I can't."

Picking up his saddle bag and bedroll from the bed, Garrett dropped them on the floor. "I'll sleep on staying and helping you out — but no promises, Ben."

Tilman sighed, then tossed his head like a frisky colt. "Yes, sir, I knew you'd stay, Morgan, 'cause you're a decent man."

"Now, Ben, I didn't say I was staying. Just that I was going to sleep on it."

"I know what you said and I know what you meant, Morgan." The clerk stepped beside Garrett and with his boot nudged the bedroll and saddle bag under the bed. "And, yes sir, I know you'll be staying."

Tilman stuck his head out the front door, then jerked it back in side. "Okay, Morgan, mind your manners. The officers are coming."

Garrett stepped behind the counter. "I'll let you do all the talking."

The clerk laughed. "You can talk — just don't call Fulton Colonel Stubby again. His temper gets worse each time a patrol returns without Pachise. With Company A returning today with nothing but blisters, he'll be touchier than a wounded grizzly." Tilman scurried around behind the counter as the door swung open and Fulton led in seven officers. Tilman deposited a fresh bottle of whiskey on the counter and slapped eight glasses beside it.

Fulton grabbed the bottle and stomped to

his usual seat. "Damn that Pachise," Fulton shouted. "He can't be everywhere at once, now can he?"

His junior officers mutely picked a glass apiece, the final officer taking the two leftovers and carrying one to Fulton who glared at each officer's face as he uncorked the bottle. Filling to the brim the glass placed before him, Fulton spoke. "First, Company A returns today from the south, reporting Apache raids 50 miles from here during the past week. Then the soldiers on the mail run from the north report his marauding up north at the same time. Now dammit, Pachise can't be both places at the same time." Fulton jerked the disintegrating cigar from his mouth, rubbed the whiskered stubble on his cheeks and gulped the drink down. "Well, somebody answer me."

"Sir," spoke a straight-jawed captain, "we might think better after you've filled our glasses."

Fulton jammed the cigar in his mouth and pointed at the officer. "Captain, none of you deserve a drink and you know it."

The colonel filled his own glass to the brim, then tilted the bottle toward the men, ready to serve. He rationed out half a glass apiece to his officers.

Each man sipped slowly at the meager allowance of whiskey.

"Gentlemen, I am growing impatient with your failure to catch this Apache outlaw," Fulton bellowed. "It's not acceptable for this savage to outsmart us for this long. Unless you do better, I may be forced to leave my administrative duties here and lead you into the field until we find him."

One lieutenant swallowed his remaining liquor hard and braced himself to speak. "Sir," he braved, "the Apaches most likely have broken up into two or three smaller bands so they seem everywhere."

Fulton's teeth ground into the remnants of the cigar butt, now as unsightly as his disposition. Fulton scowled, then spit the cigar across the room. "Brilliant, Lieutenant, absolutely brilliant."

The lieutenant shrank back from the table.

"Everyone in this room can figure that out, even that damned Confederate boy," Fulton said, motioning in Garrett's direction. "I'm not worried about all Pachise's bands. I want him. Once we get Pachise, the Apaches will have no leader and are bound to return to the reservation."

Fulton poured himself another ample glass. "You men think about it and come up with some reasonable suggestions for catching Pachise. I'm tired and I'm retiring for the evening. Report to me with your ideas in the morning." The commander stood up from his chair and a path toward the door parted between the standing junior officers. "Don't fail me this time, gentlemen," Fulton said, "because none of you will ever get a promotion with what I'll enter in your record if you don't catch him, and soon."

No one answered as Fulton marched out the door, though as soon as it was shut the captain called him a bastard. The men grinned, but their smiles evaporated the instant the door opened up and Fulton poked his head inside.

"Benjamin Franklin Tilman," yelled Fulton.

Tilman stepped in front of the counter. "Yes, sir."

"The mail brings news that the paymaster will be arriving day after tomorrow. You'll need to be ready the following day to assist him. Do you understand?"

"Certainly, sir."

"Then good day."

Fulton closed the door and the officers resumed their complaints against him.

"Paymaster's coming. We ought to be celebrating that," a lieutenant said. "Instead we've got to put up with that overbearing son of a bitch."

Tilman sidled up to Garrett. "Bet our esteemed colonel could find Pachise if he thought that Apache was going to expose his crookedness to the governor."

The officers lingered for more than two hours, repeating their troubles to themselves and their bottles.

# CHAPTER 5

The bugle wailed like a mourning woman. The strains of reveille carried sharply through the crisp early morning air, rousing the men from slumber. Perhaps the men on guard duty welcomed the noise, but as Jonah rolled out of his bunk, he cursed the army life of too little sleep and too many chores. About him others were crawling out of bed, damning the darkness, fumbling around for their clothes. It was a damn poor life for thirteen dollars a month, he thought. He wrestled his britches on and stumbled into the adjacent bunk, eliciting a mumbled lament from its occupant.

"Skully," Jonah advised, "you'll be late again for roll call. That happens today, the lieutenant may leave you here to handle chores." Skully grunted in response.

Jonah grappled with his ill-fitting boots, certain the Army could never find an instrument of greater torture. Then he pulled on his blue woolen blouse and hitched his suspenders, ready to relieve himself in the latrine trench behind the barrack. He kicked Skully's bunk and marched to the back door, Skully's curses following in his wake.

An enlistment of five years had seemed so short a time when he made his mark on the Army papers three years ago. Now, though, his enlistment seemed a prison sentence, particularly since Colonel Fulton had forbidden reading lessons for the soldiers. Most days oppressed the troopers with the rote monotony of cavalry life, redoing the same chores that had been completed yesterday and would be done again tomorrow. Little was available to break the boredom around the fort. Jonah valued those days when the routine was altered. Stepping out of the barrack, he smiled to the east as a pink crack of light on the horizon slowly shoved up the night's curtain of darkness. Today, he and nine other men from Company C would ride out to meet the paymaster and escort him to Fort Bansom. Jonah would be rid of the fort, Colonel Stubby and Morgan Garrett, and when he returned, he would be due four months pay. The monotony would recede, at least for a few days.

After roll call, Jonah walked to the stable,

Skully trailing sullenly behind him like a scolded child. Skully awoke each day with venom in his veins, the bile only gradually dissipating, and Jonah had learned to be wary, particularly before breakfast. While Grant crunched an extra ration of corn with his fodder, Jonah fanned the gelding with the saddle blanket. "Gonna be a day's ride, old boy," Jonah said, stretching the blanket over Grant's back, then easing the McClellan saddle atop and cinching it. As Grant finished eating, Jonah picked up a pail and fetched water from the trough in the center of the stable. Grant lapped at the water as Jonah fingered the animal's halter. After the horse quenched his thirst, Jonah fitted the bridle to him. "Be good to get away from this place for a while, won't it, old boy? I'll bring you some sugar after I eat."

Standing by the stable door as Jonah emerged, Skully growled as he fell in beside the corporal. "Damn Army." Jonah grunted and they reported to the mess hall, forcing down a breakfast of hard bread, salted bacon and the mud someone called coffee. Army coffee was a bastard offspring of rodent droppings and grit, made worse at Fort Bansom by the Loco River's brackish liquid, more salt than water. Their taste hardened to the bitter coffee and grub; they tolerated the meal. As he gulped down his coffee, Jonah grabbed a handful of brown sugar and wadded it into a ball for Grant.

After breakfast Jonah, Skully and the other eight men going with them for the paymaster reported to the quartermaster for rations. Then, as the other troops of company C began their daily routine following breakfast, Jonah and those with him returned to their barracks, checking their Spencer carbines and .44 caliber Colt revolvers. Loaded down with weapons, ammunition, haversacks, slickers, rations and bedrolls, the ten black troopers marched to the stables, strapped their gear onto their mounts, then led them outside.

The black sergeant in charge of the patrol ordered the men to mount. "Forward," he yelled, and the horses tramped ahead, single file across the parade ground, past the adobe barracks, beyond the headquarters building and around the gardens and Indian agency. Riding in the strict and hushed formality preferred by their cavalry superiors, the soldiers advanced north toward their rendezvous with the paymaster in precise parade form until they were beyond the prying eyes of their commanders. Then they relaxed their stiff riding poses to chatter and jest.

"Pay day's a comin' day after tomorrow, boys," Skully shouted. "I's gonna have me a good time."

"You sure about that, Skully?" Jonah shook his head like he knew better. "How much you owes the sutler?"

"Not four months' pay, Jonah." Skully spit on the buffalo grass.

Jonah scratched his chin. "I wouldn't be so sure of that Skully, the way my bill grows."

"If they'd pay us when they was supposed to, it wouldn't be this way. Why don't they pay on time?"

"Don't ask me, Skully. I don't understand the Army none too easily." Jonah raised his voice. "Maybe the sarge up there understands, his being in command and all that, but not me. I'm just a corporal. I just wish they wouldn't take what we's owe the store away from us at the pay table before we ever get to feel the money. Not a time since I been in the Army have I held at one time all thirteen dollars from a month's pay."

"I's with you on that, Jonah," said Skully, rubbing his fingers together like he was doling out cash. "Just once I'd like to have my full pay in my hands to know what it's like to be a rich man. Just once."

The patrol followed the serpentine path of

the Loco River as it crawled across the unending flat land. The soldiers rode clear of the canes and tall grasses and occasional cottonwoods that neighbored the water course and offered potential cover for Indian ambushers. And while the soldiers no longer rode as orderly as they had leaving the fort, they were just as alert, because Pachise could be anywhere.

As the scorching sun neared its high, the sergeant pointed to the north. "Cottonwood Crossing," he called. The troopers hollered and their horses, infected with their enthusiasm, picked up their gait. At Cottonwood Crossing, named for the twelve towering cottonwoods which marked the intersection of the north-south and east-west Army trails, the patrol would stand halfway to their destination. The sun wrung sweat from the soldiers' bodies, soaking their uniforms and glistening their faces, making them grateful for each breath of a breeze. Gradually the trees grew larger until the cottonwoods loomed over the troopers, offering them shade, the scarcest of all New Mexico commodities.

As they reached the river, the sergeant ordered half the men to tend their horses while the other half stood guard. Skully jumped off his mount into the water. "It's wet," he laughed. Holding the bridle while his horse drank, Skully cupped his hand in the water and sipped from his palm. "And it's good!" Somewhere between Fort Bansom and Cottonwood Crossing, the river picked up its brackishness, but here the water was as sweet and appealing as a naked woman. One by one each trooper emptied his canteen of its brackish contents and refilled it with the clear water from beneath the tall cottonwoods. The men on watch nibbled at hard bread until the others had remounted, then took their turns watering their animals, quenching their own thirsts and refilling the water in their canteens.

When everyone had remounted, the sergeant suggested they let their horses graze a few minutes on the lush grass which grew in green blankets along the river. "Stay away from the canes and tall bushes," he suggested. "Just in case ol' Pachise's taking a nap in 'em." As the animals nudged at the ground, the soldiers told lies about what they would do when they finished with the Army, and when their stories were done and their horses rested, they continued north toward their rendezvous. An hour before sundown, the troopers reached their destination, a dry lakebed. There they would await the paymaster and his escort from

Fort Hodges. "We beat the white soldiers here," the sergeant said, jutting his chin forward, "because of the good leadership from your commander." The sergeant grinned as the patrol laughed at his jibe.

"Yeah," said Jonah, "you handled us black boys almost as good as Colonel Stubby himself."

"Next man to compare me to Stubby," the sergeant said, dismounting and shaking the aches out of each leg, "will be collecting horse apples out of the stable for a month, even if he is a corporal." The sergeant's eyes smiled as he spoke. "Now we'll pitch camp and wait for the slow boys from Fort Hodges."

The horses had been grazed and staked out, the bedrolls had been spread across the hard ground, the watches had been appointed, and the sun had dropped from sight, leaving only a souvenir ribbon of pink bordering the western horizon when Skully spotted the other party approaching. "Here come the white bastards," he called out.

"Mind your tongue and your Army manners, Skully, or I'll whip your butt," commanded the sergeant, reclining on his blanket. "Time you boys broke out some hardtack and ate. I want your mouths full when the Hodges men get here so no words slip out that can get us in trouble back at the fort."

"Hell, sarge," Skully replied, "they won't set up camp close enough to us to hear a cannon go off."

"Just watch it, Skully — you're the one that worries me the most." The sergeant watched the white troopers come within fifty yards of his camp, then dismount.

"What'd I tell you Sarge."

"Shut up, Skully," the sergeant said, arising from his bedroll. He bent over his haversack and pulled out a corncob pipe, tobacco and a match from a watertight tin. He fiddled with the pipe, stuffing tobacco in, tamping it down, lighting it and drawing heavy on it. He sighed like a man taking a last smoke, then sauntered toward the other patrol. When he came within easy hearing distance, he spoke greetings. The sharp epithet which answered convinced him he was welcome no closer than the fringes of the camp. A white sergeant issued orders to his men, then dispatched a white corporal in the black sergeant's direction.

"What took you fellas so long?" asked Jonah's sergeant.

"Took time to bag some game for a decent meal. You boys eaten yet?"

"My men just settled down to their rations."

The corporal stared toward the shadowy figures of men and horses at ease in the black troopers' camp. He sniffed at the air. "You boys must be eating a cold meal," he laughed. "I don't see no fire. We got us two antelope and a dozen jack-rabbits." He laughed again. "I doubt there's enough to go around for our men, the paymaster and your boys."

The black sergeant knew it was a lie. "We brought decent rations enough that we don't need any of your antelope or rabbits," he answered.

"Well, boy, if you got decent rations from the Army, you must be in a different Army than I'm in," the corporal sniffed, turning and walking away. He halted for a moment, looking back over his shoulder at the sergeant. "The paymaster and his two men will join your outfit in the morning. After breakfast."

Through the dimness of a dying day, the sergeant could see the troops dressing an antelope and rabbits. Two troopers were building a fire. His stomach knotted in jealousy as he turned back toward his own men and cursed their luck in camping downwind from the others. He drew hard on his pipe and the tobacco glowed red like the anger within him. "Men," he said as he plopped down on his blanket. "Get your sleep, we'll have a hard day tomorrow. Won't be no fooling around on the return trip, not with the white officers watching us."

Skully stared past the sergeant toward the white camp. "What are they cooking, Sarge?"

"It's no matter, Skully. They didn't offer us any."

"You'd think we was Pachise and his Apaches much as they shared with us," Jonah offered.

"It's no matter, any of you."

"But it smells good, whatever it is," Skully answered.

Two sentries got up from their beds and moved to their watch posts as the others settled into their bedrolls. The aroma of the cooking meat made it hard for anyone with a half empty stomach to think about sleep.

At dawn the sergeant roused his men from bed. They quickly consumed their hard bread, saltpork and coffee, broke their camp and saddled their mounts. When the light was full, they were ready to travel, but the paymaster ate a leisurely breakfast with the white troopers.

Skully's vindictive eyes fixed on the Fort

Hodges men. "Jonah," he said, pointing to one side of the camp, "I've been studying that splotch of brown to the side of the horses. You know what that is? It's what they left of that a damn antelope last night. The bastards! Us over here starving and them wasting meat."

The sergeant slipped up beside Skully. "Shut up, Skully. Don't be causing no trouble for me."

Skully turned away and pulled another slab of hardtack from his haversack. "Just watching, Sarge. That's all."

The black troops were mounted and anxious to leave when the paymaster and his two clerks joined them. Without a word, the paymaster and his two men, each leading a pack animal, fell in ahead of the sergeant. The paymaster, a captain, motioned with his arm and the patrol lurched toward Fort Bansom.

Travel was slow and the paymaster showed no concern about being behind schedule. It was midafternoon before Cottonwood Crossing came into sight and at that rate it would be three hours after dark before the patrol reached the fort.

As the patrol neared the crossing, the paymaster called for the sergeant. "We're not making good time. Have your men attend to their horses and their own needs here quickly."

"Yes, sir, half'll keep watch while the other water and then the —"

"No, Sergeant, we'll spend five minutes at most here. Everybody at once."

"Few extra minutes, sir, won't matter no way. Even at good time we'll be in fort hours after dark."

The paymaster sneered. "You boys afraid of the dark?"

"No, sir."

"Then do what I say, Sergeant, or I'll have a talk with your commander."

"Yes, sir," the sergeant answered, reclaiming his spot in the formation.

Under the shade of the trees, the sweet aroma of the breeze blowing across the water and over the tall canes and grasses invigorated Jonah, but seemed to confuse Grant. The horse tossed his head and shied out of formation as if he feared the water.

"Okay, men," yelled the sergeant, "everybody down and tend to your needs and water your mounts."

Grant's ears flicked forward and the gelding lifted his head, then threw it forward, as if trying to shake loose from the bridle. "What about the guard, Sarge?" Jonah called. Grant pawed at the ground then reared back.

"Paymaster says we haven't got time for that!" The sergeant was on the ground walking his horse to the river. "Dammit, Jonah, get that horse under control. We don't have time for that."

The horse fretted and stamped the ground with his feet. Something was wrong, Jonah thought. "Calm down now, old boy," Jonah said, patting the horse on the neck. The trooper lifted his leg to dismount. "What's a matter that's got you . . ."

A horrible shriek screamed out from the tall grass, then the retort of a gun. Grant reared back and spun around. Jonah lunged back into the saddle, fighting to steady himself atop his terrified animal. Then more shots exploded from the bushes.

Apaches!

Jonah jerked his carbine from its boot and quickly looked around. He alone was mounted among the troopers. Several horses had bolted for safety while a few of the soldiers struggled to climb aboard their animals. An Apache ran from the tall grass toward Jonah. The soldier leveled his Spencer carbine. Grant spun around as Jonah squeezed off his first round. The gun stock kicked his shoulder and the horizon circled his eyes as he yanked the reins for control.

He shook the blur from his vision, trying to regain his bearings and eject the shell casing from his weapon.

From the corner of his eye, Jonah glimpsed a form racing at him. He flung his arm around. The gun extended his reach and hit the oncoming Apache in the face. The Indian fell at Grant's feet. The animal danced and kicked to get away and the Apache struggled to regain his feet. Jonah brought the muzzle of the gun within a foot of his chest and pulled the trigger. The gun exploded and the dying scream of the Apache echoed in Jonah's ear. He steadied Grant enough to shoot at the clouds of gunsmoke and flashes of weapons. Quickly, he glanced around at the other soldiers. Those without horses were returning fire with their revolvers. Jonah's impulses screamed for escape but he held his ground. Another Apache raced from cover toward the sergeant. Astride his horse, the sergeant held the mount while another soldier clambered on behind him.

"Sarge!" Jonah screamed. "Other side!" Jonah leveled his carbine at the Indian and jerked the trigger. The gun went limp against his shoulder. It had either jammed or he was out of ammunition. He dropped the carbine and grabbed his revolver, then cocked the hammer. The Indian, his out-stretched hand holding a pistol, came within pointblank range of the sergeant. Jonah aimed. The Apache fired. So did Jonah. The sergeant tumbled from his saddle as the Apache assassin clutched his chest, then dropped to his knees, then fell on his face. Jonah slapped Grant and forced him toward the sergeant. From the blank look on the sergeant's face, Jonah knew nothing could be done. Grant smelled the blood and fought against Jonah. The Indians yelled and more rushed from the cover; behind him Jonah heard more gunshots. The Apaches were encircling them. One of the paymaster's clerks had drawn his saber. The fool, Jonah thought, as an Apache bullet ripped into him. A saber can't swat buzzing lead, but the clerk could never use that lesson now.

"Run for it!" the paymaster shouted. "Make sure we get everybody!"

Jonah emptied his pistol at the advancing Indians, then reloaded it as he glanced about him. The soldiers were doubling up on mounts, their return fire slackening. A lone rider in blue raced by and Jonah recognized Skully. Damn if Skully wasn't too mean to die, and Jonah was glad of that. A couple of black soldiers had picked up unmounted men and bolted for freedom. Jonah caught a glimpse of the paymaster clinging to a black trooper as the cavalryman's mount struggled under the officer's extra load. A bitter thought raced through Jonah's mind. The paymaster wouldn't share antelope or breakfast with the blacks, but damn if he wouldn't share a ride with one when his butt was in a crack. A bullet whizzed by Jonah's head and he forgot about the paymaster. Twisting around in his saddle, he fired at an oncoming Indian. He glanced toward the river for troopers still standing, but there were none. "Let's get out of here," he yelled at Grant. Jonah dug into Grant's flanks with his boots and the horse, finally given the freedom he had wanted, shot forward toward the others.

Just as Grant gained his stride, he stumbled. Jonah slapped the horse's neck with his gun. The animal snorted and tossed his head, flinging blood and mucus from his nose and mouth into Jonah's face. "Run, dammit! Run, Grant!" Jonah screamed and beat the animal. Pushed by momentum, the horse stayed upright, one, two, three strides, then his front legs buckled beneath him before the rear legs stopped. The horse flipped, flinging Jonah through the air.

Jonah crashed into the hardpacked ground

and cried at the pain bursting through his shoulder and ribs and exploding in his head. He lay dazed and motionless until a bullet struck near him and showered him with stinging bits of dirt and rock. He remembered where he was and he clambered to his hands and knees. His pistol? Where was it? He groped at the ground, his hand closing around a rock. He stood up and threw the rock at the dozen warriors running at him. He spotted his pistol and lunged for it. He cocked the hammer and fired as one Apache grabbed his arm. Again he fired, and again, until several successive dull clicks told him his gun was empty. From behind him he heard galloping hoofbeats. As the warriors came closer, he drew back and threw his revolver at them. Stupid, he thought, as he let go of the gun. Now he was done for.

Behind him, Jonah heard a frightful whoop. He was surrounded. He turned to face his attacker, but it was Skully swooping toward him. Hunkered low over his mount's neck, Skully had extended his arm. "Grabs on, Jonah!" he yelled.

When the animal galloped by, Jonah clutched Skully's arm and leaped for the animal. Skully moaned under Jonah's load and flailed his feet for a hold on the animal.

Jonah managed to get his leg over the horse's rump just as Skully turned the animal hard around and away from the oncoming warriors. Jonah's leg slipped back off the animal, and the jolt as his legs hit the ground almost broke his hold on Skully. Skully reined up on the horse long enough for Jonah to lift his leg back over the mount. Bullets buzzed around them as he crawled behind Skully and let go of his arm. Leaning forward, Jonah wrapped his arms around Skully's waist to hold on.

Skully screamed, then swatted at his arm. "Dammit!" he yelled. "They hit me."

"Ride, Skully, I'll take care of you now," Jonah called. "We got a jump on them. Even if they get their horses and follow, we'll catch up with our men."

"You sure, with two men on a horse?" Skully groaned.

"Some of them are two to a horse. If the paymaster knows anything about Indian fighting, he'll find a place we can defend and hole up there. Hush up now — I'll take care of you."

They rode two miles. Jonah, looking over Skully's drooping shoulders, spied a soldier waving his hat at them. "We're almost to safety, Skully." As he neared the signaling soldier, he saw the others hiding in a ravine leading to the river. Some were reloading their weapons, others tending their wounds."

Jonah eased the horse into the ravine as a couple soldiers gathered at Skully's side to help him down.

"Corporal."

Jonah turned and stared at the paymaster, he could feel the hate boiling inside of him. If the paymaster had listened to the sergeant and let the men water their mounts half at a time, the sergeant might still be alive. "Yes, sir," he answered.

"The Apaches following you?"

"I reckon not, sir."

"But you don't know, is that right?"

"Nobody knows Apaches but Apaches, sir." Jonah let go of Skully as the other soldiers eased him off the saddle.

The paymaster coughed into his fist. "I tried to tell that damned sergeant of yours to let the men take their drinks and leaks in shifts."

Jonah slammed his fist into his palm. He glared at the paymaster. "Damn . . . ," he let the word hang heavy in the air, ". . . Apaches." He spit on the ground insubordinately close to the paymaster's boots and turned away.

The paymaster followed him. "You're in

charge of your men now, corporal. How many are you missing?"

Jonah took a quick count. "The sarge's dead, one more of our boys's missing and one of your men's dead. And they got Grant."

"Who's Grant?"

"My mount, sir — my horse."

"Hell, boy," the paymaster laughed, "don't worry about your horse. The Army'll get you another one."

"They'll never get me another Grant."

Jonah took off his hat and slipped in the back door, his eyes slowly adjusting to the dimness and his nose wrinkling at the odor. The room had the bastard smell of medicines and maladies, numbing his nose. The sheet-draped beds stood in precise rows along both long walls and as Jonah's eyes came into focus, he stared at the sagging forms, half asleep, half awake, half dead, half alive. He stepped tentatively forward, nervous the doctor or an orderly might discover him. His tension slackened when he recognized Skully rolling over in his bed. He slipped by Skully's side and squatted, tapping the patient on the shoulder.

"Don't bother me," Skully said, peering out of the narrow slits of his eyes, which widened in recognition. Skully sat up, looked to the opposite end of the room, then back at Jonah, grinning. "Didn't knows it was you, Jonah. Good to see you." He thrust his bandaged arm at Jonah.

The corporal grabbed his hand and shook it.

Skully grimaced, let out a low moan, then yelped when Jonah dropped his hand.

"Sorry, Skully," he said, "I didn't know it —"

"Just funning you, Jonah," Skully snickered, then hit the bed with his wounded arm. He laughed. "It weren't much of a wound, but I keeps tellin' the doctor it's sore and he keeps me in here in bed, like I's some rich fellow. They care for me almost as good as we tend the damned horses." He paused, then added an afterthought, "Sorry about Grant — he was a good horse."

Jonah nodded. "You ought to get a medal for savin' me. If the Army don't give you one, I'll do it."

"I wants a solid gold medal, one that's worth a fortune and can buy my way out of this white man's army."

"Can't afford one of those until payday. With A and B companies out looking for Pachise, it may be a while 'fore we gets our pay."

"I'll be ready for my money," Skully grinned. "I plans to stay here as long as I can, but not past pay day. I want to spend my money on some liquor — maybe a little poker." Skully slapped his bandaged arm and laughed at Jonah's grimace. "It don't hurt none. I just don't want to go out on another patrol for a spell."

Jonah nodded. "Me neither. I went back with the party that brought the sergeant back from Cottonwood Crossin'. The Apaches cut him up a terrible sight and the other two the same way. And," Jonah swallowed hard, "you know what they did to Grant? They butchered him and ate him, his bones scattered around a fire."

"Sorry to hear that, Jonah, but you're lucky to be alive. I don't think I'd turned around for anybody else." Skully saw Jonah's eyes misting and turned away from him.

"Next time I run into any damn Apaches, I'm gonna kill a few for Grant and the sergeant."

Skully scratched through the bandage on his arm. "I'd be might glad to help you out on that, Jonah, when I get out of this bed but I plans to roost here until the doctor throws me out. Then we'll kill every Apache in New Mexico Territory."

# CHAPTER 6

"Yes, sir, Morgan, you take my word for it," Benjamin Franklin Tilman said between bites of an apple, "they'll never catch those Apaches until they understand them."

Garrett yawned like a man traveling again down the same road.

"Stubby don't think like Pachise," Tilman continued. "He thinks every Apache move is a military maneuver. Instead it's a matter of survival, not from the soldiers, but from this damned desolate land. To live, you keep moving." Tilman bit into his apple and licked the juice from his lips.

"Ben," Garrett said, leaning back in his chair, "how come you know so much more about the Apaches than Colonel Stubby?"

Tilman swallowed, then rubbed his lips with the back of the hand holding the apple. "He's a fool, Morgan. It's hard for a man to learn if he thinks he has all the answers. That's Stubby's problem, that and all the mash that's pickled everything between his ears."

Garrett laughed. "You've got an answer for everything, Ben."

"I know to outsmart an Indian, you've got to have somebody that thinks like one. Get him a good scout or two and turn them loose on Pachise's trail." Ben slipped from behind the counter to the door and tossed his apple core outside. "You remember Diablo, the Mexican with the knife at the agency?"

Garrett's face contorted as he nodded.

"Well, Diablo lived among the Apaches some, and he could trail sunshine out of a norther. By reputation, he's as good a tracker as in all of New Mexico Territory. Fitzgerald pays Diablo good money and hangs onto him, I suspect, in case Stubby gets in trouble for not bringing the Apaches back in line. It'd sure disturb Fitzgerald's setup here if Stubby was replaced."

Garrett sat forward in his chair, lifted his lame arm onto the table before him, then propped his good elbow on the table and his chin in his palm. "Ben, if you know so much, why don't you just tell your esteemed Colonel Stubby what to do instead of giving me the same lecture day after day."

"I like you better, Morgan." Tilman pulled

another apple from the tow sack before him. As he opened his jaws wide as a steel trap and bit into a hunk of the red fruit, the door swung open.

William Fitzgerald waddled in and Tilman choked, coughing bits of apple across the counter. "Mr. Fitzgerald," he stammered, gulping down the fruit in his mouth and hiding the defiled apple behind his back. "Surprised to see you here this time of day."

"You should be surprised," Fitzgerald grumbled, "when I catch you eating apples you've no intention of paying for."

Tilman sputtered, showing the apple. "I had every intention of —"

Fitzgerald waved his pulpy hand toward Tilman. "A trifle, Ben, a mere trifle."

Tilman coughed, then stomped his foot on the floor. He held up his hand to signal he was okay. "Sorry," he managed.

"Don't get choked up about it," Fitzgerald said. He looked toward Garrett, his lips quivering slightly beneath a walrus moustache that dropped under the weight of his heavy cheeks. It was as close to a smile as Fitzgerald ever offered. "Good to see you've been staying out of fights, Garrett," Fitzgerald said without emotion. "Hate for a man taking my money to get killed, or even worse, kill a trooper here at Fort Bansom. Might cause an investigation."

"And waste taxpayers' money," Garrett said, the flame of disgust burning hotter within him.

"Precisely," Fitzgerald replied, pulling back his coat and hanging his thumbs in his suspenders. "My sentiments exactly, but a hand should owe some loyalty to the man that pays him."

Garrett slowly pushed back his chair and rose. "Tainted though the money may be?"

Fitzgerald rocked on his heels, his massive belly lumbering like a beached whale with each breath. "No man that ever took Confederate pay should complain to me of tainted money." Looking at Tilman, Fitzgerald jerked his thumbs from his suspenders and motioned toward the back. "Let's head to your room, for a little business talk, Ben." When Tilman lingered for a moment, ill at ease, the apple still in his hand, Fitzgerald clapped his hands. "Now," he snapped.

Tilman jumped, dropped the apple, paused to consider picking it up, then shot down the narrow hallway to his room. Fitzgerald dug with his finger into the flesh of his neck and scratched at the sticky edge of his sweat-soaked collar. He clasped his hands on his belly, which spilled over his pants top, and followed leisurely behind Tilman, squeezing down the pinched passageway.

Garrett stared until Fitzgerald turned into Tilman's room and slammed the door. Garrett grimaced at the thought of Fitzgerald — his bloated, toadlike face, his beady, reptilian eyes, and his grotesquely overweight body. Garrett despised his twenty-dollar suits and five-dollar shirts, bought with his larcenous take from cheating the Indians and the soldiers. Fitzgerald was a scavenger, a greater danger than Colonel Fulton because he was shrewder. A man with money can have all the friends he desires, but Garrett was glad to count himself among Fitzgerald's enemies.

At length, Fitzgerald emerged from Tilman's room, huffed through the hallway and exited the building without a word to Garrett. Tilman lingered a moment, then strode out, a broad grin upon his face.

"Have I got good news for you," he said, but then his grin evaporated, as if he were reconsidering. He paused.

"Well, Ben, what is it? Fitzgerald turning honest?"

"Ah . . . ah," he stammered. "Tomorrow is ration day at the issue house. On top of that, Companies A and B will be back in the fort day after tomorrow."

"Nothing special to me."

"Sure it is." Tilman smiled again as if he were more comfortable. "You keep complaining about my chattering like a bird. Well, you'll have your peace tomorrow." Tilman chuckled. "Fitzgerald wants to use you at the issue house tomorrow to help keep books. Then, if A and B Companies get back on time, he'll want to use you at the pay table when the paymaster hands out greenbacks."

Garrett shrugged and stepped toward the bar.

"You don't seem too happy."

"I prefer your company to your boss's."

Tilman ran his hand through his stringy black hair. "I'll be damned. And, we'll get our pay after the soldiers."

"Now that is good news, Ben."

Walking over to face Garrett, Tilman rubbed his chin. "I'm not so sure about that, Morgan."

"What do you mean?"

"Fitzgerald don't seem to be taking to you, and your remarks about tainted money didn't help. He's no fool. No, sir, he may be a lot of things, but fool isn't one of them, Morgan."

"He can't be worried about a lame-armed man like me, now can he?"

"Hell, Morgan, you're smart. He's shrewd enough to know you can see what's going on. He'll do anything to protect this crooked nest of his."

"Come pay day, Ben, I may be gone."

Tilman shook his head. "It won't be that easy anymore, Morgan. Something's come up that'll make him suspicious of anyone leaving Fort Bansom without his okay."

"Well, Ben, what is it?"

Shrugging, Ben took off his spectacles and pinched the bridge of his nose. "I'm not feeling too well, Morgan. A darn headache. Look after the store for me while I sack out for a bit."

"What's your secret, Ben?"

Tilman shrugged and retreated to the back room.

Well past dark, Tilman stayed in his room, quiet but not sleeping. Garrett locked up the store himself and retired to his own room. He had blown out his lamp and was crawling into his bed when there came a tapping on his door.

"Morgan," whispered a voice. "It's me, Ben."

Garrett cursed under his breath. "Why

now, Ben, just when I'm getting into bed?"

"Just get out of bed and don't show any light. Slip into my room."

"This better not be a trick of yours, Ben."

"A trick?" Ben laughed. "This may be my salvation."

Garrett slipped across the hallway toward the wisp of a shadow on the opposite side. In the darkness he could hear Ben's rapid breathing and he followed him into the room. Tilman shut the door as soon as Garrett crossed the threshold. The room was covered in additional layers of darkness; not a hint of moonlight filtered through the window. "Have you lost your mind or have I, Ben? You're acting like a fool."

Scraping a match against the rough adobe wall, Tilman shielded the flame with his cupped hand, then lit a candle.

As Tilman watched the anemic flame take life, Garrett glanced at the window, now covered by a heavy blanket. "What you hiding from, Ben?" Garrett took quick bearings of the room. Like his own, it was sparsely furnished with a bed, a chair and washstand, plus a trunk and an overloaded bookshelf.

Finishing with the candle, Tilman straightened to his full height and stared up at Garrett. His lips parted into a grin. "You mean what am I hiding? My ticket from blackmail, thanks to you."

Garrett grabbed the straightback chair and straddled it, resting his good arm on the backrest, his chin on his arm. "Quit the games, Ben, cause I'm not following you."

"Fitzgerald wouldn't talk about business in front of you today." Tilman clapped, then rubbed his hands together. "When he came back here to give me instructions, he dropped this." Tilman reached under the pillow on his bed and triumphantly withdrew a small black object. He held the rectangle by the light and fanned its pages for Garrett to see. "It's the proof, Morgan — the proof I've been seeking to trade for my pardon."

Garrett stuck out his hand. "You sure about that?"

"As sure as Fitzgerald is crooked."

Garrett snatched the book as it dangled from Tilman's fingers and scooted his chair close to the candle. Holding the book by the light, he turned from page to page, then whistled. "You may be right, Ben."

"No maybe, Morgan. It's Fitzgerald's pocket ledger, every crooked deal he's made — when he bought stolen cattle and who from, when he supplied tainted beef, the inferior grade flour and sugar he's been sell-ing the commissary. Everything. Even Colonel Stubby's payoffs, a pretty healthy cut." Tilman broke into a spontaneous jig in front of Garrett, then folded his arms across his chest. "Before long, I could be making an honest living as soon as I — I mean you — get this to the governor."

"Not so fast, Ben." Garrett closed up the book and tossed it to Ben. He stood slowly up from his chair and paced around the bed and back. "You think Fitzgerald knows it's missing yet?"

Tilman shrugged. "He didn't come back looking for it."

"If the man records everything in the ledger, he'll miss it before long." Garrett thought for a moment. "He could remember this was the last place he had it."

Stepping to his bed, Tilman slipped it under his pillow. "Could be. He dropped a pencil by the bed and when he bent over, the book slipped out of his coat pocket onto the bed. I started to say something, bit my tongue and sat down on top of it. Good instinct, huh? Now, you just ride to Santa Fe and see if you can work out a pardon for me with the governor."

Rubbing his jaw between his thumb and forefinger. "Not so hasty, Ben. Seems odd, this falling into your hands the day before he wants me to work for him at the issue house."

"Damn." Ben pounded his pillow with his clinched fist. "Maybe he suspects something."

Garrett nodded. "A possibility, or maybe just a coincidence. But if I rush away from here, that may show our hand. If he comes back, asking questions, you've got to be able to stare him straight in the eye and tell him a convincing lie. If he detects an ounce of nervousness, you'll give your secret away as sure as if you handed him the book."

"I can lie to Fitzgerald, the bastard," Tilman said. "He has made my life a hell these last few years."

"Let's not make a move, Ben, 'til we get an idea if he's up to anything."

"Okay by me, Morgan. Just knowing I got proof that'll send him to prison will make my days tolerable." Tilman stood up and stretched his arms. "Just knowing he has something to worry about now is a measure of revenge."

"Maybe instead of gloating, you should be thinking about a good place to hide it."

Tilman ran his fingers through his black hair, glistening with sweat in the dim light. With a sweeping gesture, he pointed to the bookcase behind Garrett. "There."

113

"Not very imaginative."

Tilman stepped to the bookcase and from the bottom shelf extracted a book. He pitched it at Garrett, who snapped it out of the air with his good hand.

"Not a bad catch for a one-armed man," Tilman grinned.

Garrett held the book up to the lamp and read the gold-lettered title on its spine. "Uncle Tom's Cabin. This wasn't a popular book back in Alabama before the war. More lies in it than all the abolitionist broadsides ever printed."

"Well, Morgan, we Pennsylvanians liked it, but that's not important anymore. Open it up."

He dropped the book on the bed as near the candle as he could and opened the book to the center. "It's easier for me to catch it than to open it with one hand," he explained.

"You ought to like this copy of Uncle Tom's Cabin."

Garrett grinned at what he found. A rectangular hiding place had been cut out of the book's middle pages.

Tilman explained. "I needed a hiding place for some of my money — a lot of people around this fort you can't trust. I don't worry about protecting my money now as much as hiding this ledger, because it'll buy my freedom."

"Just curious, Ben," Morgan started. "Why Uncle Tom's cabin?"

"Only book I had a duplicate of. I'd a been in a tight spot if some officer or even Fitzgerald had wanted to borrow my book and its innards were missing."

Garrett laughed. "I always heard you had to listen to learn, Ben, but for a guy that talks all the time, you come out darn smart."

"Morgan, I learn by listening to myself — and you'd learn a few things yourself, if you'd pay me more mind." Tilman stepped beside Garrett and inserted the pocket ledger into the hollowed center of the larger book. He picked the volume up and slapped it shut. "Morgan, you just remember where this book is. When the time is right, if I'm not available, you deliver this to Santa Fe to the governor."

Garrett nodded.

"Even if something happens to me, Morgan, I'd like a pardon — if they give pardons to dead men. I'd rest better in my grave."

Garrett reached out with his arm and laid it upon Tilman's shoulder. "Ben, mind your tongue and you'll get your pardon. Now let's get some shuteye. I've got to work at the issue house tomorrow, remember?"

"That's what's bothering me now, Morgan. You watch out for Fitzgerald. He's treacherous."

Face after sullen face, the line stretched from the edge of the issue house porch toward the river, maybe a thousand or more Navajos, waiting between troopers with fixed bayonets, dull in the early morning light. Their despairing eyes stared toward the porch. From where Garrett stood, the Navajos all seemed to be focused on him until the building's double doors swung open. The Navajos surged forward, a single-file human river flooded with hunger. As the Navajos moved forward, the black soldiers stepped before them to dam the surge with crossed bayonets.

"So there you are," Fitzgerald said as he stepped out onto the porch, followed by Diablo and the three other issue house men. Fitzgerald tugged at the waist of his pants, then with a sweeping motion pointed toward the silent Indians. "Impressive sight, wouldn't you say Garrett? The benevolence of these great United States in taking these . . . ," he paused to emphasize his feelings, ". . . *savages* and feeding and caring for them." He turned for acknowledgement, but Garrett stared beyond Fitzgerald to the

116

drained faces and empty eyes. His voice dripping with disgust instead of sincerity, Fitzgerald continued. "Christian charity at its best to save this lowly sample of mankind. And, at its greatest profit."

Garrett looked into the reptilian eyes of Fitzgerald's toadlike face. "For some." As he spoke, he watched Fitzgerald's puffy cheeks flush with the anger he had kindled.

Folding his ponderous arms across his heaving chest, Fitzgerald pursed his lips, then sneered. "Garrett, you're an astute man, but you're not my match."

"In many things," Garrett nodded, "I'm not your match."

Fitzgerald flung back his arm, as if to strike Garrett, but he dropped his hand to his side. "I'll not strike half a man, but consider this, Garrett. I run things on the reservation and have a great say in how the fort is run. If I give the word, you'll be kicked off government property. A lame-armed man wouldn't be too hard for Pachise to murder — like catching a hen with cropped wings."

Diablo stepped between Fitzgerald and Garrett, pointing toward an officer moving in precise military strides toward them. "Good morning, Lieutenant, are your troopers ready to proceed?" Fitzgerald continued, as the officer removed his hat and nodded. "We intend to try a new way of passing out the rations today, one that should expedite things."

Fitzgerald issued orders in Spanish to Diablo, then commanded his other three helpers to take their positions on the porch. "Garrett," he said, pointing toward a make-shift table of planks resting on two empty barrels, "take a seat behind the table. The boys wanted you to tote the hundred-pound flour sacks for their amusement, but I told them you were too smart for that. And I was right."

Garrett slipped wordlessly into his place. After giving final instructions to his men, Fitzgerald landed in the chair beside the lame-armed man. "Ben tells me you're okay handling numbers. All you must do is count the dated ration tickets I pass to you. Every twenty-fifth coupon, you stop the line until that twenty-five receive their rations. It's not a hard job, now is it? I could do it easy, except I've got to inspect these ration tickets. Sometimes they try to slip in bogus ration tickets. Damn Indians."

Clearing his throat, Garrett lifted his bad arm onto the table and spat at the plank. "And we wouldn't want them cheating the issue house," he replied.

Fitzgerald huffed a command at the lieutenant and the line started moving forward, one person at a time passing between two troopers. Another soldier took his place in front of the table.

As Garrett stared at the soldier before him, he could feel Fitzgerald's hard eyes gauging him and despising him. The first Navajo, clutching a clay bowl to his chest, reached the table and with contempt dropped a ticket before Fitzgerald, who examined the stub, then passed it to Garrett. Men, women and children, each clasping a bowl or a tin can they had salvaged from the fort trash heap, passed before Garrett.

"Twenty-five," he called when the requisite number had passed. The soldier before the table stepped ahead of the next Indian.

Fitzgerald snapped his finger. "Diablo," he called and the Mexican appeared from the end of the porch, carrying a hundred-pound sack of flour as easily as if it were a baby. In front of the table, no more than ten feet from the porch, Diablo dumped the sack on the hard-packed ground. Pulling his Bowie knife from the scabbard at his side, he bared his yellow teeth in a wide grin and slit the end of the towsack. Jerking the bottom of the sack by its ears, Diablo laughed as the sack's powdery contents piled up between his feet.

As Garrett watched, he could see disturbed weevils and worms burrowing their way back into the powder. He clinched his teeth.

Diablo backed away from the white pile and three soldiers stepped forward, herding the first twenty-five Indians into a circle by the motions of their bayonets.

The soldiers backed away and the lieutenant nodded to Fitzgerald. "Now?" he called and Fitzgerald nodded back. "Go," shouted the lieutenant and the Navajos rushed the white mound like ants attacking an insect carcass.

Using their bowls and tin cans as scoops, they clawed at the flour and climbed on one another's backs, elbowing each other to get at the pile. And those in the second circle around the ration, shoved their containers between those ahead. Desperate children scrambled between the legs of the adults, tripping the feeble old men and women whose frailties offered them little chance at a fair ration or a full stomach in the days ahead. So placid and emotionless in line earlier, they now screamed their success and failure. The wad of people tightened in a final frenzied flurry like a wild animal in its death throes and then person by person peeled away from the spot where not a smudge of white remained.

For his part in this, Garrett could feel a knot of shame tightening in his stomach, the disgust made worse by the troopers laughing and slapping their knees at the ration spectacle. Diablo laughed loudest and taunted the disappointed Navajos by mimicking their desperation. Garrett turned to Fitzgerald. "Before the war, I owned slaves, Fitzgerald."

"So, I've heard," Fitzgerald replied, snapping shut the cover on his gold watch, then inserting it in his vest pocket.

"And never once did I see slaves treated as poorly as this — not anywhere."

Fitzgerald ignored Garrett. "Lieutenant," he called, "this works well. Let the Indians divvy up their four pounds apiece without us having to weigh each ration and we'll get through in half the time. Your boys can attend to their other chores by noon today." Fitzgerald accepted another ration ticket and the line started moving again, twenty-five Navajos at a time, time after time until Garrett was numbed with disgust.

"Ben was right, Garrett — you can count, but I gather you don't take to this work," Fitzgerald said, as another group grappled for their ration.

Garrett nodded. "I'm no merchant."

Fitzgerald stroked his walrus moustache. "It's more than that, but maybe a little extra money would make this settle more easily on your mind, shall we say. What I'm offering, Garrett, is to double your wages. You make twenty dollars a month with Ben. I'll make that forty dollars and put you over here at the issue house. I know Ben with all his talk and chatter can get on a good man's nerves."

"Your offer is generous," Garrett started, looking down the porch at Diablo and Fitzgerald's other hired hands laughing at the rationing procedure, "but I don't plan to be staying here long enough to make a merchant of myself."

Fitzgerald laughed. "A one-armed man can't be too picky, now can he, when it comes to getting a job for himself. I'll not give you a second chance."

"I just want to make enough money to move on."

"You'll make it faster at the issue house, Garrett."

"I prefer the company where I am."

Fitzgerald sneered. "Like cheating the troopers better than the Navajos, is that it, Garrett? I should have figured that from a former rebel." Fitzgerald doubled his fleshy fist and pounded it into his palm. "You're a smart man, Garrett. I just hope not too smart for your own good."

Standing up, Fitzgerald called to the lieutenant. "Send a message to Colonel Fulton that I need to see him."

The lieutenant nodded and sent a sergeant toward the fort headquarters.

Fitzgerald pointed at one of his henchmen and instructed him to take the ration coupons and to watch carefully for fake ones. Then Fitzgerald disappeared through the doors of the agency.

"You in, Fitzgerald?"

It was Fulton, knocking on the door. Fitzgerald shoved the fresh bottle of bourbon to the opposite side of his desk. Then he propped his feet up on the desk and leaned back in his chair, like a pig settling into mud. He locked the fingers of his hands and rested them atop his head. "Come on in, Colonel."

Fulton slinked toward the chair closest to the whiskey bottle. At the odor of whiskey on Fulton's breath, Fitzgerald smiled.

"What did you learn?"

"We can get the Navajos through in about half the time under our new rationing method, Colonel."

"No, no — what did you learn about Garrett?"

"You should come over next ration day to watch the Navajos fight over their sugar and flour. My men and yours certainly enjoyed the free-for-all."

"But, what about Garrett?"

Fitzgerald motioned to the bottle and Fulton grabbed it. "I believe I will," he said, twisting at the cork.

"Of course," Fitzgerald continued, "not everyone thought the Indian scramble was all that amusing. Your man Garrett was as somber as the Navajos the entire time. I could see it in his eyes he didn't like what was going on. We've got a problem. I regret now that I didn't have Ben let him go to begin with."

Fulton swallowed his liquor hard, then wiped his lips with the wrinkled sleeve of his uniform. "Why don't I kick him off the fort now?" He sucked on his bottle again.

"Won't do, not for a while anyway, Colonel. I've lost a pocket ledger that details all my dealings. I may have lost it at the sutler's. I don't want Garrett leaving the fort until we find that ledger. Some people might misinterpret it, if it fell into the wrong hands."

Fulton choked on his next swig and sputtered. "Am I mentioned in your ledger?"

Fitzgerald nodded. "We've got to find that ledger or take care of Garrett. He could be a threat to you and me. He's smart and dangerous. Tell your men in the stable not to let him take his horse out without first letting you know. Then, the next patrol that goes out, you might do best to lead it. I'll send Diablo along. He can scout for you, and," Fitzgerald growled, "take care of Garrett for us away from the fort and reservation."

Fulton chuckled, then laughed heartily, lifting the bottle by its neck toward Fitzgerald. "I'll give it to you, Fitz, you always know how to take care of a problem."

# CHAPTER 7

Before Garrett even closed the door, Tilman was gabbing. "Well, lookahere, if it isn't Morgan, back all ready." Tilman jerked his watch from his pocket, glanced at the face, then back at Garrett, a wide grin puddling across his face. "It went quicker than normal."

Garrett shut the door, then surveyed the room for customers. Seeing none, he shook his head as he walked around behind the counter to join Tilman. "It went faster because they don't weigh out individual rations any more. They just dump the flour and sugar on the ground like they were feeding hogs and let the Navajos fight over it. I've never seen slaves treated as poorly."

Clearing his throat, Tilman threw out his anemic chest and a worrisome question. "Did Fitzgerald ask about the book?"

"Not a word."

Tilman sighed.

"Don't relax any, Ben." Garrett eased down on a stool. "I just said he didn't ask about the book. Your boss suspects something, no doubt. He offered to double my wages to join the others at the issue house."

Rubbing his hands together, Tilman stared with wide eyes at Garrett. "I knew from the beginning you'd make him nervous. That's one reason I hired you."

Garrett shrugged. "He's not nervous, Ben, just adjusting his plans — don't you see? He offered me the move, he didn't order me to work the issue house. He was testing me, seeing if I'd throw in with him. Now he knows I'm against him and it won't strain his brain to figure out you influenced my choice."

Stepping toward Garrett, Tilman jammed his hands into his pockets and thrust his chest forward. "He can't turn me in to the authorities, now can he, without me telling all about his dealings?"

"That's right, Ben, he can't turn you in," Garrett nodded, giving Tilman plenty of time to recognize the alternative.

Tilman shrugged that he wasn't following Garrett's reasoning.

"Ben, it's too late for him to turn you in. You've been bluffing in a poker game with him having the higher hand. Your stake in this is your life, not from a firing squad but from one of Fitzgerald's henchmen."

The grin melted from Tilman's face like ice under the sun. His eyes grew wider behind the thick lenses of his glasses and he heaved a deep breath from his sagging chest. "Don't guess I'm as smart as I thought." He edged over to the counter and slumped down on the bar, his back to Garrett. "My life's been a chain of mistakes and deceptions since I deserted. It'd have been better if I'd done my duty and been killed and buried in some nameless grave back East." He ran his hands through his shaggy black hair, then slapped them down on the counter. "Why can I never escape my mistakes, dammit?"

"Nothing can save us from this life, Ben. Death'll catch up with all of us. Some sooner and some later, but all of us nonetheless." Garrett walked to the counter, reaching beneath it. He extracted a bottle and two glasses. "Sometimes a drink'll help things." After uncorking the bottle, Garrett filled the glasses with the whiskey and pushed one toward Tilman. "Drink up, Ben."

Garrett downed his quickly, enjoying the rivulet of fire rolling down his gullet. "As long as you've got the pocket ledger and keep it hidden from Fitzgerald, you're buying yourself time."

His hand trembling as he reached for the glass, Tilman stood soldier straight at the bar. "If I take a drink, I may slip and tell Fitzgerald where I hid the book."

"I'll watch for you, Ben."

Tilman brought the glass to his lips, paused for an instant and then spilled the whiskey into his mouth. He swallowed hard, then coughed.

"Any time you expect to see Fitzgerald, have a glass of whiskey. Maybe you won't be so nervous. But no more than a single glass."

"I'll probably give myself away, Morgan, no matter what happens."

"You can't, Ben — your life depends on it," Morgan said. "It's too early for us to make a move without tipping our hand. When the time is right, we'll leave for Santa Fe together. I won't leave without you."

Tilman's face clouded with despondency. "What chance do we have, Morgan, with me a proven coward and you a lame man, against Fitzgerald and the whole U.S. Army?"

"A better chance than if we do nothing."

The bugle at reveille sounded livelier, the

responses at roll call louder, the noises of an Army post coming to life for a new day crisper. This was not just any day, but payday, and the anticipation of money to be spent filled the air like clouds before a storm.

The soldiers were lining up in formation on the parade ground as Garrett stepped out of the store three paces ahead of Tilman. Garrett eyed Tilman for a moment and knew the clerk had slept little during the night. Tilman's bloodshot eyes were empty of life behind his heavy glasses and his slender lips quivered. He carried the store's cumbersome ledger under his arm and after he shut the door, he jerked a handkerchief from his pants and blew his twitching nose. Together Garrett and Tilman marched toward headquarters.

Glancing at Garrett as he put away his handkerchief, Tilman forced a smile. "So hot last night, I had trouble sleeping. Payday won't make my lot any better."

"Payday? Why?"

"A lot of the troopers will be angered when they find out they owe the store more than they've got coming in pay. Those that get paid'll buy out our whiskey and probably my entire stock of razors."

"Razors?" Garrett started walking toward

headquarters.

"That's right," Tilman answered. "These black fellows use them for weapons. Seems they'd rather slice up a fellow than stab him."

Garrett remembered the fight in the garden with Skully, then studied the scar on his right hand. "They do cut nicely," he said.

"Some of the troopers will accuse us of inflating their debts, but I've never had a single one accuse us of having prices too high."

"Comes out the same, seems to me, Ben. They accuse you of one injustice, but you're guilty of another."

"Oh, hell, Morgan — I'm not defending the store. It makes for interesting paydays, though."

As they stepped up on the porch at head-quarters, both spotted Fitzgerald with the paymaster and Ben fell nervously silent.

"Keep talking some, Ben, or Fitzgerald will know you're hiding the book," Garrett whispered to the frightened clerk.

Reaching the paymaster's table, they heard Fitzgerald speaking to the officer. "Awfully considerate of you, Sir, to let my store deduct the troopers debts before they receive their pay."

"Colonel Fulton has suggested that's the

best way to handle his troopers," the pay-master said, ". . . and I'm always obliged to follow the instincts of the post commander, though this is a bit unusual, even for black troops."

Tilman placed the store's account book beside the paymaster's records on the table.

"Ah, good morning, Ben," Fitzgerald said. "Garrett, you'll find this more orderly than dispensing rations to the Navajos. You two know the paymaster?"

Tilman nodded and then introduced Garrett to the officer. Garrett extended his good hand, but the officer ignored it, instead organizing his records and restacking his paperwork. Fitzgerald excused himself and the paymaster acknowledged his departure with a nod. Tilman took the first of three seats behind the table and told Garrett to stand behind him.

"Now, gentlemen," the paymaster said as Tilman scooted under the table, "I expect you to have your books in order. I want to proceed without difficulty and without interruption. Attend to your needs now because I am anxious to be done with this chore and to join Colonel Fulton and Mr. Fitzgerald for a drink."

"We're ready, Sir," Tilman responded.

"We're as anxious as you to get on to other things."

"Very well," replied the paymaster, turning to his clerk. "Sergeant, please bring the cash pouches from the colonel's office and inform his officers we are ready to proceed."

The clerk saluted and about-faced, walking briskly down the porch and inside headquarters. The paymaster pulled the chair out beside Tilman and silently seated himself, holding his shoulders pompously erect.

"Now, Morgan," Ben instructed, "the paymaster will call each soldier by name. As he does, look each soldier up in the ledger and tell the officer how much he owes." Ben pointed to the paymaster. "The paymaster credits our account. You make the entry in the ledger and the trooper gets what's left. It's easy enough until one of them thinks he's been cheated."

"Sounds simple." Garrett nodded.

"Then," Ben continued, "the paymaster credits us and settles with Mr. Fitzgerald at the end of the day."

Garrett looked out toward the troops, assembled in the crisp rank and file of their formations. The smell of pay was in the air and the soldiers seemed tense, like animals before a storm, ready to bolt for the table as if the money might not last for the latecomers. In their uniforms, kipi hats and scuffed boots they looked prepared for their daily chores. But each man wore the white gloves of his dress uniform, his palms sweating as much from the anxiety over the money they would hold shortly as from the gloves themselves. They stood in four groups, two on each side of the center flag pole, facing the headquarters building. As orders were shouted from the porch and echoed down through the chain of command, the first company stepped away from the others and marched smartly toward the headquarters.

"Take your posts," the paymaster ordered. "They're coming." His sergeant jumped into a chair beside the paymaster and two junior officers positioned themselves at each end of the pay table. The paymaster glanced from one to the other, scowling as his eyes glimpsed Garrett behind Tilman. He spoke to Ben. "Pay day is not the time for training your men."

Ben sniffed. "Fulton's request," he lied. "If you'd like, take it up with him."

"No time for that now," the paymaster answered as the first company of troops came to within a dozen feet of the porch, dissolved into single file and stepped forward.

For an instant the troops of Company A tried to maintain their military manners, but as the first soldier stepped to the pay table, their faces melted into puddles of anticipation. The paymaster called each name loudly, shouting with the confidence of a man who believes he is liked for who he is instead of what he is. One by one the soldiers reached the table, each signing the payroll as Tilman called out the debt to the store. After the paymaster calculated the difference and the sergeant noted the payment, each soldier received his pay.

Garrett watched the payroll sheet as soldier after soldier made his mark. So few could write. He thought about Jonah, wondering if his former slave had ever learned. Ben kept repeating instructions and Garrett acknowledged them, even though they were obvious. The procedure was simple, and when Company A was paid in full and its men had disappeared, Tilman arose and offered his chair to Garrett. Company B advanced toward the pay table and the process renewed itself. As the black soldiers stepped forward, Garrett could feel the heat from their burning eyes. Kindled by either his position with the store or his past with Jonah, their hate flared like a pine knot in a fire as he called out their debts.

They grumbled, then resumed their military manners, removing their gloves and saluting as the paymaster dropped greenbacks into their hands.

Behind Garrett, Tilman said "uh-huh" as each man stepped down the line with the sutler's share deducted. At thirteen dollars a month, each private was due fifty-two dollars from the Army, but the sutler's outstanding debts easily made up more than half of that for most and, in a few cases, more than they were due. Those groused the loudest, though their impulses were tempered by the solemn-faced officers standing at each end of the table.

When the last member of Company B had passed, Ben slapped Garrett on the back. "Well done, Morgan — not a single mistake. Not that I didn't trust you, Morgan, no sir, but wasn't sure you could read my hen-scratching in the ledger book." Ben hooked his thumbs in his pocket and whistled softly until the paymaster glanced over his shoulder at him. Ben caught his breath. "Don't believe my man slowed your pay line down a bit, now did he? You'll be able to have that drink with our esteemed Colonel Fulton sooner than you thought." Ben rocked slightly on the balls of his feet.

The paymaster mumbled and turned to

his papers.

The men of Company C advanced to the table as called by the paymaster. At the announcement of each man's name, Garrett read out his debt.

"Morgan," Tilman said between soldiers, "I'm going back to ready the store for business." He strode off the porch without looking back. "Bring the ledger when you finish. We can't open without it and Mr. Fitzgerald'll be angered if all the soldiers gamble away their money before we're open."

When Jonah's name was called, Garrett glanced up from his ledger and smiled. "Well, Jonah, you got much money coming or does the store get it?" Garrett watched Jonah scribble his mark on the government paperwork, then found his name in the ledger. "Eleven dollars and thirty-eight cents owed to the sutler," he called. "You spent less than a month's pay so you've got a fair amount of pay coming, Jonah. Don't go and lose it in a poker game."

Jonah shook his head slightly as he received his pay, then saluted the paymaster.

"No, sir, Mr. Garrett," Jonah said as his fingers closed tightly around the paper. "I'm savin' the money to pay somebody to learn me to read." Jonah's voice dropped. "Something you and your pa would never let me learn."

Before Garrett could speak, Jonah slipped away from the table and the paymaster called another name, but Garrett kept thinking about Jonah and the stinging truth in his comment.

Garrett performed his job by rote and two dozen soldiers, maybe more passed him by, before he looked up into the face of the one who called himself Skully, the one who had tried to kill him. Skully's name was called out and Garrett found it quickly in the ledger book. Garrett announced the debt.

Skully saluted and extended his ungloved hand toward the paymaster.

"No pay this time, Private," the paymaster said. "You owe three dollars and eighty-nine cents more than you're due."

"What?" cried Skully, his gloved hand releasing its salute.

"Watch your buying at the sutler's and you'll have money to spend on next pay day in two months."

"It's a lie," screamed Skully. "I ain't spent money that much at the store. He's cheating me, charging me for things I don't buy." Skully flung his glove at Garrett, then lunged across the table.

The glove glanced off Garrett's cheek. The

two lieutenants at each end of the table jumped for Skully as he grabbed Garrett's good arm and twisted it. Pain jolted Garrett from wrist to shoulder. Skully climbed onto the table with his knees, knocking over the paymaster's inkwell. The paymaster cursed as the two lieutenants jerked Skully off Garrett. The two officers pinned Skully to the table and forced his arms behind him.

Skully's teeth clenched as the officers shoved his arms toward his shoulder blades, but he did not scream out, his hate for Garrett greater than the pain. "You'll pay, dammit," he managed through his labored breath.

Garrett shook the numbness out of his arm, then drew back and slapped Skully with the back of his hand before his two captors could jerk him away from the table. "You son of a bitch, I'll add another scar to your chest if you try."

As the two lieutenants stood him straight, Skully spit toward Garrett, the spittle landing on the ledger. Garrett bent over in his chair and retrieved Skully's free glove from the wooden slats of the porch. He wiped the ledger of the wetness, wadded the glove and tossed it at Skully's head, the glove glancing off Skully's cheek.

"Men, men, settle down! That's an order!"

yelled the paymaster. "Things have gotten out of hand. You officers return this soldier to his barracks."

The lieutenants tugged at his arms, but for a moment Skully's feet seemed rooted to the ground. His sunken eyes seemed to bulge from their hiding place deep beneath his brow. "One of us is to die for this," he said.

Skully's feet gave way as the two officers turned him around and marched him back toward the barracks.

"You heard the threat, sir," Garrett turned to the paymaster.

"It's best we just forget this unfortunate incident," the paymaster answered, then gave orders for his clerk to clean up the mess.

"Gentlemen, you've just been paid." Colonel Fulton chewed on the gnawed remnant of a cigar. "Now what have you done to earn the money the United States government has seen fit to pay you?" Fulton eased back in his chair, staring at the blank faces of each officer across his desk. He propped his feet on a naked corner of his cluttered desk. "I'll tell you what you've done since your last payday. You let Pachise and his band escape from the reservation. You've gone on a dozen unsuccessful patrols. You've lost three Army men when the paymaster was ambushed. Is there a reason for your incompetence?"

Fulton spit a splinter of tobacco toward the floor while he awaited an answer. The room was hot and uncomfortable and had the slight intoxicating hint of an open bottle of whiskey, hidden somewhere. A blow fly buzzed in through the open window and circled Fulton's head even as he swatted at the air to drive it away. A lieutenant's shoulder dropped slightly from his stiff pose and Fulton scowled. "Attention, I've ordered, and I expect to be obeyed." The lieutenant threw back his shoulders and resumed his starched stance.

"I'm awaiting a reply," Fulton repeated. "Can't any of you catch Pachise?" As he waited, the colonel tugged at a tear in the sweat-stained undershirt exposed between the unbuttoned front of his army blouse. The fly landed on his leg and he swatted at it, scaring it out the window. Fulton pointed his accusing finger after the fly. "Somewhere out there you'll find Pachise — if you're worth your pay, dammit." He pulled his feet off the desk and jumped from his chair, striding toward the window. "Out there, dammit!" He twisted around to face them, chewing briskly on his cigar, then stomped back to his desk.

His voice turned soft, like a man talking to children. "Your duties have been performed admirably in all instances," he said, then he yelled, "on the reservation and at the fort, but I want results *out there*! Can anyone among you catch Pachise?"

Once more, he awaited an answer, pacing back and forth in front of his desk. "You won't answer because to do so would be to admit failure, and we all know you've failed. And admitting a failure could ruin one of your carefully planned promotions. Did you ever think that if you succeeded in capturing that damned Apache it might make your career? Now that the War of the Rebellion is over, not many officers are gonna get promotions as soon as they'd like, and I'm sure none of you would like a bad report from me to go on your record. Now would you?"

"No, sir," the officers answered in unison.

"Then I guess to save the reputation of this fort, not to mention your careers, I have no alternative but to go out into the field myself. If my inferiors can't accomplish the task I've set before them, I should show them how to conduct war. Don't you gentlemen agree?"

"Yes, sir," they said together again.

142

Fulton rubbed the stubble on his chin and nodded. "I thought you'd agree, knowing it might save your careers in the United States Army. We'll ride out in three days. One company will accompany me, and . . ." Fulton halted.

The door behind the officers was swinging slowly open.

"Sergeant," Fulton yelled, "I told you I didn't care to be disturbed."

The bloated face of William Fitzgerald appeared through the crack of the door. He pursed his lips and tugged at his moustache. "Sorry, Colonel, I took this upon myself. Excuse the intrusion."

Fulton hurried around the desk before Fitzgerald's head disappeared. "That's all right, Fitz, I was just finishing up. Come on in." He turned back to face his officers. "You men think about whether you deserve Army pay based on your poor performance in finding Pachise, and report to me first thing in the morning. Dismissed."

The officers filed silently out of the office, the last one closing the door sharply behind him. "Damn him," Fulton spat, striding to the door. He jerked it open, then paused. "Aw, the hell with them. Sergeant, see that I am not bothered under any circumstance until Mr. Fitzgerald departs."

Fitzgerald pushed a padded armchair from its place in the corner to Fulton's desk, then squeezed in between its shoulders. He tugged at his moustache and cocked his head. "I hear we had another unfortunate incident today, Colonel."

Fulton circled his desk. "The altercation at the pay table?"

Fitzgerald nodded.

The colonel settled into his chair, then bent over the pair of riding boots on the floor by his desk. He reached inside and retrieved a nearly empty bottle of whiskey. Uncorking the bottle, he reclined in his seat and spit the remnants of his cigar on the floor. "Uncertain how I'll handle that, Fitz."

"Perhaps," said Fitzgerald, planting his elbows on the chair arms and resting his fleshy chin in the cradle, of his interlocked fingers, "we can use that to our advantage."

Holding a swig of liquor in his mouth as he pondered, Fulton slowly nodded his head. He swallowed. "How so?"

Fitzgerald grinned. "This trooper they call Skully and Garrett haven't struck much of a friendship, with the fight in the garden and the dispute at the pay table."

"True, but what of it?"

"Don't you see, Colonel — if we could get the soldier to kill Garrett, it'd end any threat Garrett might pose to our mutually profitable partnership here at Fort Bansom."

"But risky," Fulton nodded. "I'd take a big chance ordering that darkie to kill Garrett. A lot of inquiries might follow."

"Ah, but, Colonel, there's no need for an order." Fitzgerald cocked his head and folded his arms across his broad chest. "It seems every time the two meet they have a misunderstanding. I would suggest we make sure the two are around each other plenty in the coming days."

"Might be difficult, Fitz." Fulton rubbed the stubble on his chin. "I'm leading a company out in the field in three days. It's up to me to catch that damned Pachise. None of my officers can."

"All the better, Colonel." Fitzgerald leaned back in the chair and clasped his hefty hands around his stomach. "Take Skully's company. I'll send Garrett along on some pretext and even Diablo to scout for you and take care of Garrett, in case Skully fails."

Fulton nodded. "Excellent plan," he wheezed.

Fitzgerald wiggled forward in his chair and Fulton jumped up as quick as a junior officer. He moved quickly around the desk.

"Excellent plan," he said again, his words drowned in his own laughter.

Without smiling, Fitzgerald laughed. Fulton slapped the sutler on the back, instantly killing Fitzgerald's small grin. Fulton's hand fell away as awkwardly as if he had touched a leper. Fitzgerald straightened his coat and his shirt cuffs, then marched silently to the door.

Fulton trailed Fitzgerald into the anteroom and stared at the sutler's back until he was out the door. Fulton laughed. "Sergeant," barked Fulton, and the officer sprang to his feet from behind a report-ladened desk.

"Yes, sir," he answered sharply, grimacing at loudness which seemed to echo off the walls.

"Send out the orders for preparation of a patrol." He snickered. "A single company which I will lead to capture Pachise. "We'll leave in three days. That'll give the troopers time to waste all their money. See that the troops are issued thirty days rations and five hundred rounds of ammunition apiece. We'll not return without Pachise."

"Yes, sir. Anything else?" The sergeant scribbled notes on a sheet of paper.

"Which company is in the rotation for the next patrol?"

146

"Company A, sir."

"Sergeant, make the orders for Company C instead."

Softly and sleepily, the music of the mouth organ floated through the long room like flickering lantern light. The harmonica music was the salve that helped ease the lingering sores of payday — the noise of the dice game at the far end of the room, the snores of drunks sleeping it off, and the overblown conversation. Jonah could feel the sleep tugging at his eyelids and he didn't care to fight it. The harmonica's serene refrain felt as soothing as a gentle rain, and then even it fell away into the darkness of Jonah's sleep.

The rest came and then it was gone in a fit. The bed shook, and as his senses gathered on the sleep side of waking, he felt a hand on his shoulder, pressing softly but insistently against him.

"Jonah. Jonah?"

For an instant, the voice startled him and then he recognized Skully's hollow voice. Damn him. "What is it, Skully, that means you gotta wake me for?" Jonah shook the sleep from his head and inhaled a deep breath. The odor of liquor came strong from Skully and as Jonah's eyes took focus, he saw Skully's face not twelve inches from his own.

"I needs a favor, Jonah."

The corporal sat up, as much to escape Skully's rancid breath as to recollect his bearings. At the end of the room, the dice game was still going but the harmonica was silent. "What's your trouble, Skully?"

"Money's my trouble, Jonah. I thoughts I might get in that dice circle if someone'd just borrow me some money."

Jonah turned away and dropped his legs off the opposite side of the bed from Skully. "I'm savin' my money, Skully, for some learnin' lessons. Can't saves none if I loan it all out, 'specially for someone to gamble with."

Skully struggled to his feet and staggered around the bed to sit beside Jonah. "I'll pay you back, you just waits and see. Mights even pay you back tonight . . ."

"In the mornin', Skully."

"Pay you back in the mornin'."

"Skully," Jonah started, "you're drunk. On top of that you've got about the worstest luck of any man, white or black, ever created by the Almighty hisself. I'd just be throwin' my money away in a dice game without even havin' a chance to toss the bones myself."

"Jus' a dollar, that's all. I don't owes you no money now and I won't when I'm through tonight," Skully said, his voice rising with drunken anger.

"You don't owes me no money 'cause I ain't lent you none," Jonah answered, standing up. "You coulda asked me 'fore I went to sleep, Skully, but you've maddened me."

Skully shrugged and struggled to rise, succeeding with a tug from Jonah's outstretched hand. Skully twisted his head from side to side, then mumbled. "Won't loan me no dollar, nots even after I saved him from the Apaches, nots even after I always brought sugar for Grant when he missed meals." Skully stumbled toward the aisle between the long rows of beds. As he stepped, he shook his arm loose from Jonah's grasp. "Not after I saved his curly scalp. Not a dollar."

"Okay, Skully. A dollar." Jonah stepped to the end of his bunk. Bending over a small wooden trunk, he opened the lid just enough to stick his hand inside, then fished around for money. As soon as his hand reappeared, he dropped the lid and offered Skully two half dollars.

"I knowed you'd understand, Jonah," Skully said, holding a coin in each hand and inspecting them in the dim light. "You'll be seein' these here two boys later." Skully turned toward the dice players in the back. "Fresh money on the way so you'd better be careful now, 'cause Skully's playin'.'"

For awhile, Jonah could hear the dice game and the growing number of snores, but then they faded out, not entirely, but enough for him to sleep. Rest came fitfully now, not a heavy curtain screening him from the surroundings, but a thin veil which only blurred them. And then before reveille, like a recurring bad dream, Jonah heard Skully's voice and by the odor of liquored breath could smell his nearness.

"Wake up, Jonah, wake up."

The voice sounded so distant, yet so close. Damn him again, Jonah thought as he twisted away from Skully's touch, he must want more money.

"I's got somethin' for you, Jonah. Your friends have come back and made new friends for me, they have. My luck's changed like I knowed it would." Skully groped for Jonah's hand. Finding it, he dropped two half dollars in his palm, then closed Jonah's fingers around the money. "I came away with five dollars and six bits, Jonah."

Jonah could feel the cold coins in his hand and he was glad to have them back, but they could never buy the rest that Skully had cost him. "That's good. Now would you lets me get back to sleep?" he mumbled.

Turning away from Skully, Jonah could feel the wreckage of his shattered sleep and before drowsiness could overtake him again, the sound of reveille came like an unwanted guest. He clambered from his slumber trough, rubbing his eyes and scratching his belly. As he pulled the covers over his bed, he found the two half dollars and returned them to his trunk. Around him others were begrudgingly climbing out of bed, many moaning and shaking their heads because of their intemperate ways the night before.

Beside him, Skully's bed overflowed with the form of its occupant, motionless except for the gentle rising of his chest with each breath. Disgusted with Skully's deep trance, Jonah pulled a boot on, then kicked with the enthusiasm of a mule. "Get your butt out of bed, Skully, 'fore I kicks it into the river and drown you at the swimmin' hole."

Jonah dressed quickly and left, ignoring Skully at roll call, stable duty, sick call and breakfast, but Skully was waiting for him as he exited the mess hall.

"You're lookin' a little tired this mornin', Jonah."

Appearing no worse for his night of drunkenness and gambling, Skully's comment angered Jonah, who felt a strand of jealousy unraveling within him. "Some fool — certainly weren't no friend of mine — waked me up twice in the night."

"At least you got your money back, and there weren't no fool jackass kickin' your bed this mornin', neither. But to makes up for everythin', I broughts my money and thought we might slip over to the sutler's and buy us a little tobacco."

Jonah grabbed Skully's arm. "You heard the orders at roll call. We march out in two days. We got work to do," he said, knowing it was just an excuse to prevent another run-in between Skully and Garrett.

"By damn, Jonah, most of you fellows got to spend some at the store yesterday. I had extra stable duty. Now that I got a little money, I intends to use it." Skully broke away from Jonah's grasp and strode toward the store, Jonah following in his wake. Skully barged past the door before Jonah could stop him. Jonah breathed more easily to see three men and not just Garrett behind the counter. Tilman and Fitzgerald were with him.

"No trouble, Skully," Jonah whispered as he grabbed the soldier's arm. Though Garrett stared at them without emotion, Jonah thought he saw a glint of treachery flash through Fitzgerald's eyes.

The sutler spoke up boldly. "Just a minute, boys, and we'll assist you."

"Don't you —," Skully started to speak, until Jonah's tightening grip on his arm shut him off.

"As I was saying," Fitzgerald resumed, "Garrett, I want you to ride with the patrol in two days. I got a contract to supply corn and hay to the Army and some of the settlers may want to sell out cheap since there's so much trouble with the Apaches." Fitzgerald shoved his hand inside the lapel of his coat and pulled out a stack of greenbacks.

Jonah felt Skully's muscles tighten and sensed Skully's instinctive halfstep toward the wad of money. Then Skully relaxed.

Fitzgerald waved the money toward the two troopers. "You boys just look around all you like."

For an instant, Jonah's eyes locked with Garrett's, observing an uneasiness.

"Now, Garrett," Fitzgerald said, thumbing through the money, "I'm advancing you two hundred dollars to pay settlers for their crops. I'll expect a full accounting when you return." He shoved the money toward Garrett.

Jonah turned to Skully, watching his beady

eyes widen with greed. This could mean trouble.

"That's a lot of money," Skully whispered, shaking his arm loose from Jonah. "Let's get our tobacco and get out of here."

Fitzgerald stepped around the counter and flaunted the wad of bills before the black troopers as he offered another apology. "Hope you boys weren't in a big hurry." With a wide flourish of his hand, he passed the wad of money within smelling distance of the two soldiers, then put it into his coat pocket. He laughed without smiling. "You boys are from Company C?"

Jonah nodded.

"Good. My man Garrett'll be accompanying you. He's gonna have a lot of money on him, so you fellows protect him from that damned Pachise. I'd hate to lose two hundred dollars to an Indian that didn't know what to do with it." He marched past Jonah and Skully then stepped outside, a perverse smile on his face.

# CHAPTER 8

A sullen sun hovered above the eastern horizon, suspended in a sky without a hint of moisture. A shroud of dust lay lightly over the stables and through the newly stirred haze Garrett could see the ghostly figures of Company C attending their mounts. In half an hour, the troops would ride out of Fort Bansom and Garrett would accompany them. On the porch of the store, he leaned easily against the wall, enjoying the early morning coolness and dreading the long days in the saddle and especially the hard nights on the ground. Sleeping on a straw-filled mattress in recent weeks had softened him.

Benjamin Franklin Tilman scurried around him. Like a lighted fuse with nothing to detonate, he created more nuisance than harm. "Maybe you better go on, Morgan, and get your mount." He unhooked his glasses from each ear and rubbed away a film of dust from the thick lenses, squinting as he stared toward the stables. "The Army's supposed to provide you a horse but that don't mean they'll saddle it for you. If you're late, Colonel Stubby'll be angered."

Garrett eased away from the wall, stepped to a post supporting the porch overhang and leaned against it. "The earlier I get there, Ben, the sooner trouble can start with one of those black troopers. I'll wait on the colonel to leave headquarters, then join him."

Tilman shrugged as he rigged his glasses over his ears, wriggling his nose until the bridge settled comfortably into its accustomed place. "I'd prefer the company of the troops to that of the esteemed colonel."

Nodding, Garrett turned to Tilman. "Yeah, but you've never owned one of them."

"And you haven't cheated them out of as much money as I have and I'd still rather take my chances with them, Morgan."

"Speaking of chances, Ben," Morgan pointed at a figure coming even with the store.

"Diablo." The word caught and hung in Ben's throat. He stepped behind Morgan as if shielding himself from the Mexican, and peeked at him. "He must be going too."

"From his looks, I'd say you were right," Garrett replied, studying the stocky figure. His gliding stride carried him effortlessly forward, like a powerful bull, his bulk more muscle than fat. A jagged scar snaked from his cheek down his neck, suggesting a physical hardness that matched his flinty eyes and his outthrust jaw. Strapped around his waist he wore a cartridge belt with holster and scabbard for his sinister Bowie knife. Two more cartridge belts crossed his broad chest, and in his hand he carried a carbine. He wore a confident smirk that suggested any of the weapons were deadly in his calloused hands.

Drawing abreast of the store, Diablo lifted the carbine to his sombrero, pushing the hat up his forehead. *"Buenos dias,"* he called, tipping the carbine to acknowledge Garrett and Tilman, but his eyes offered no salutation. Then a grating laugh, as dangerous as the noise of a rockslide belched out of his crooked mouth, and he passed.

The sound carried easily in the early morning air, and Garrett could still hear Diablo laughing as he reached the flagpole in the middle of the parade ground. Neither Garrett nor Tilman spoke until Diablo had passed the flag which hung limp in the morning stillness.

"You always said, Ben," Garrett said, "that Stubby needed to use Diablo for a scout. Looks like Stubby's picked up some of your wisdom."

Running his fingers through his stringy black hair, Tilman opened his lips to speak, but the words failed him. He drew another breath and tried again. "I don't like it — not now, not this trip."

"Me neither," Garrett answered, pointing to the headquarters building where Fulton had just emerged.

"He'll be hunting more than Pachise on this trip, Morgan."

"I was thinking the same thing, Ben," Garrett said, tugging at his holster. He picked up his saddlebags, and slipped them over his good shoulder. He plucked his bedroll from the porch and clinched it under his arm before grabbing his carbine. "Almost too much for a one-armed man to handle," he said, but Ben stood silent.

With his back turned to Garrett, Tilman spoke meekly. "You be careful, Morgan. You're all I've got."

"I'll be back, Ben. You just take care of the store. See if you can keep it swept as good as a one-armed man." Garrett stepped off the plank porch, stopped, then retreated to Ben. "My hat, Ben — pull it down a little snugger for me."

Tilman lowered his head and twisted around before Garrett. Without looking up, he reached for Garrett's hat and tugged it down. "That better?" he asked, looking up then quickly averting his eyes.

In that brief instant, Garrett could see Ben's eyes misting up. "That's fine, Ben. You take care."

Tilman shrugged. "I'm not a brave man, Morgan."

"Nor am I, Ben. Sometimes doing what you have to do may seem brave, but it's just reaction, nothing more. We'll manage. Just don't let Fitzgerald see that you're scared." Garrett turned and angled across the parade ground to intersect with Fulton. He knew as he walked he was being trailed by Tilman's eyes and doubts. Maybe Tilman was right.

His path converged with Colonel Fulton's before the flagpole. On this trip, Garrett knew he'd have worries enough with Diablo and Skully so it made little sense to chafe the colonel. "Morning, Colonel," he offered.

Fulton glanced up from the ground and grumbled. As he tucked his cavalry blouse into his britches, he stared at Garrett and stretched himself to his full height. "Garrett, let me get a few things straight with you.

This is an Army expedition and I will try to accommodate your needs to do business with the settlers, but there's no guarantee. If you start any more trouble with my soldiers, I may just leave you out there alone in the badlands."

"You're in command, Colonel. You provide the horse and tack and I'll be no trouble."

Fulton glanced down at Garrett's lame arm, then over to the carbine in his good hand. "A cripple will be some trouble, Garrett, because I'll have to assign someone to saddle your mount for you, but I will not tolerate your bringing your weapons along. You'll have adequate protection with the troops. How the hell does a one-armed man load and fire a carbine, anyway?"

Garrett halted immediately and spun around toward the sutler's store and Tilman.

Fulton turned to watch. "You keep following my orders like that and we'll have no trouble at all, Garrett," he said.

"I ride nowhere without my weapons. I'm resigning. Going to the issue house right now to tell Fitzgerald." Garrett marched away.

Fulton stammered for a moment, then pounded his fist into his palm. "Dammit,

Garrett, don't be so hasty. Fitzgerald needs you to stay with him."

"Not without my revolver and carbine, Colonel."

Vigorously chewing on the omnipresent cigar stub, Fulton nodded. "Very well then. You keep your weapons, but you'd better not use them against any of my soldiers — your reputation is not too clean in dealing with them — or you'll find yourself in trouble with the United States Army and your Confederate past won't help matters."

Garrett reversed his direction again. "Colonel," he said, "I knew you'd be a reasonable man when things were explained."

His face reddening to the color of his bloodshot eyes, Fulton slapped his hands together. "It may be a long trip for you, Garrett. You won't be getting any favors."

Approaching the stables, Fulton started issuing commands and exerting his authority, the troops reacting instantly to his whims and demands. Fulton pointed out Garrett's assigned mount and Garrett loaded his gear on the animal. While the soldiers readied their horses and the pack mules that would carry thirty days of supplies, Garrett slipped inside the stable and found his chestnut. The animal was putting on some weight and its coat was shiny. Garrett wished he were taking the chestnut now, but it would be better to save the animal's strength in case he had to escape from the fort.

Lingering a moment, Garrett patted the chestnut, then weaved his way back outside among the busy soldiers. Finding his government mount, he patted the coal-black horse with white stockings and a white blaze across its face. Untying the horse from the picket line, Garrett threw the reins over its head and grabbed the saddle. Hoisting his foot into the stirrup, he dropped his hand over the opposite side of the horse, and grabbed the edge of the cavalry saddle. The animal sidled away from him, but Garrett managed to hold on, lifting his other foot up and over the animal until he was astride the horse.

Garrett ignored the snickers of the soldiers at his unorthodox mounting. The horse danced and neighed uneasily until Garrett took the reins, then reassured, the animal calmed as Garrett directed it away from the picket line, pacing him along the parade ground. The horse had an easy gait and would be manageable, even for a one-armed man, Garrett thought. For an Army-broken mount, the animal was well trained.

Out of the confusion, Army order gradually appeared as the varied activities and chores began to mold into a single purpose. The pack mules were loaded and the troopers were mounting. When Colonel Fulton took to his horse, Garrett nudged his mount toward Company C. He fell into line behind Fulton and his officers. Twisting in his saddle, he stared down the line for Skully, but did not see him.

Fulton gave the command to the sergeant. "Move out," he yelled, and the whole line lurched forward. The company guidon and the officers led the way, followed by half the troops, the pack mules, then the rest of the troops. Diablo shadowed the procession as it headed north along the parade ground and past the sutler's store.

Except for the thud of horse hooves and the rattle of a fully equipped cavalry troop marching out, the fort grew silent as soldiers from other troops stopped their chores and watched. If Fort Bansom had been a regimental headquarters, a band would have serenaded them out beyond the fort. A foreboding silence shrouded the troop and from somewhere back down the line, a soldier, sensing the sadness, played "Gerry Owens" on his harmonica.

As the procession passed the sutler's,

Garrett spied Tilman staring forlornly. Garrett lifted his reins and touched the brim of his hat, drawing a slight crease of a grin from the clerk. Then Garrett was beyond the sutler's and the gardens and the issue house where, watching from the side, Fitzgerald stood. Garrett wondered who was running Fort Bansom, the man at the head of the procession or the one now watching them leave.

The procession moved slowly along the Loco River. The sun was heating the land into an oven, sapping man and animal of strength. Making good time in this heat would be difficult. Garrett allowed himself to relax. Moving out with a cavalry outfit brought back many memories of the war. Some were pleasant, others disheartening. The one cavalry escapade that had marred him for life haunted him daily. The sudden raid on the Union supply train had caught the Yankees by surprise, but one enemy trooper had been quick with his rifle. As the Rebel cavalry was breaking for the trees after firing the train, Garrett felt a burning sensation in his left shoulder, and never again would he use his left hand. The lead had entered, severing nerve and muscle tissue, then exited. The doctor had said it was a clean wound, but that didn't restore the arm. It was still there, a useless appendage brushing against his side as it did now. There were other memories, too, of friends now deceased, ambitions also dead and a family now perished. Garrett almost felt a traitor to the cause by riding in this blue-shirted patrol. He still preferred gray, but riding in the same outfit as one of his former slaves seemed the strangest of all the twists in his fate.

Jonah felt a knot in his stomach. He still chafed at leaving the fort on a horse other than Grant. He tolerated the animal he was astride, but it still wasn't Grant. He noticed the difference in his periodic checks up and down the line. This gelding lacked Grant's heart, Grant's desire, and maybe most dangerous of all, his endurance.

Up ahead, Jonah could see Garrett riding without a companion at his side. Behind him, Jonah knew Skully was discussing some foolishness or mischief with the other soldiers. As long as he was between them, Jonah guessed he might prevent trouble. But a corporal had more responsibilities on a campaign than keeping enemies apart.

He took off his kipi hat to wipe the sweat from his glistening black face. As he drew his hand across his mouth, he could taste the salt the sun had sweated out of his body. He jerked his mount out of the line and headed toward the rear.

"Keep those pack mules closer together," he called to two privates. "Let's don't be stringing ourselves out too far, case we runs into them Apaches." Nearing the end of the line, he saw Skully, greatly animated, talking to the men. Jonah nudged his horse toward Skully.

"Yep boys," Jonah heard Skully say, "he's carryin' two hundred dollars or maybe more in his pockets. One of us ought to get . . ." Skully saw Jonah approaching. Their eyes met and locked as Jonah eased his horse in beside Skully's. Skully's lips were drawn tight and his face had turned sullen.

"What's this you been tellin' the boys, Skully?"

Skully's beady eyes grew smaller. "Just about watchin' out for them Apaches and what a fine upstandin' colonel we's got leadin' us on this here patrol. Those Apaches don't haves a chance now, Jonah, not with Stubby in command of Company C. I bets it wouldn'ts surprise me none if that Pachise didn't leave this here territory right now and go to Mexico forever once he finds out about this."

Jonah broke his gaze at Skully and looked

up the line for Garrett. "You're rilin' the boys against him, tellin' them he's carryin' a big money roll, hopin' somebody might help you."

"That ain't true, is it boys?" Skully held up his arms and looked at the others around him. No one answered. "See, they'd tell if it was a lie."

"You just stay away from Morgan Garrett, Skully. He never did you no harm, 'cept defendin' hisself. And I'm a corporal ordering you to obey."

"Yes, sir." Skully mocked Jonah with a precise salute, jerked his hand to his side, then spit between his and Jonah's horses.

Jonah slapped his horse on the flank and the animal bolted forward, carrying the corporal back to his place in the line. For miles the troops followed the river, slowed by the pace of the pack mules, and Jonah stared ahead, disgusted by the dust, his mount and Skully. Often his eyes seemed drawn to Garrett, riding ahead, the officers preceding him and the black soldiers following him, none in either group speaking to him. Garrett's lame arm bobbed with every step of his mount, and Jonah felt a sorrow for him, a social and physical outcast on this patrol. But that was what it had been like to be a slave, and even now to be a black in a white man's world, Jonah thought. Even so, Garrett had been a decent owner.

As Cottonwood Crossing appeared on the horizon, Jonah eased his horse out of line and drew up beside Garrett. A smile, genuine and pleased, lighted Garrett's face. He eased the reins down on the saddle and offered his good hand to Jonah. Without hesitation, Jonah grasped it, shaking it heartily and feeling its unexpected strength.

"Thought you might be lonely, Mister Garrett."

"It's Morgan, Jonah," Garrett said, retrieving the reins.

"I keep forgetting, Mister, I mean, Morgan," Jonah answered.

Garrett laughed and Jonah joined him. "Some things are hard to change, aren't they, Jonah?"

Jonah nodded, feeling at once comfortable with Garrett and at the same time uneasy because of the troopers who followed. He could feel their hardened stares and it made his flesh crawl, unsure whether their hate was aimed at him, at Garrett or at them both. "Some things may never change, sir."

"Like your friend, Skully?"

"He had a hard time as a slave, Mister, huh, Morgan," Jonah spoke his name slowly.

"Still hard for me to calls you 'Morgan'. Skully can't seem to understan' that times have changed."

Garrett nodded. "That doesn't make it any safer for me, does it?"

"No, sir," Jonah said, "that's what I came to tell you about. Skully's spreadin' word you're carryin' a lot of money. I'd be careful, 'cause some of them could come after you in the night."

"I've been watching Skully, but there's no way I can be on guard against everyone of them." Garrett nodded toward Cottonwood Crossing looming over the trail up ahead. "Biggest trees I've seen in New Mexico Territory."

"I almost gots killed there last month when we escorted the paymaster in. Would've died, 'cept Skully charged back for me. He's a hard man, but the bestest friend I haves in Company C."

"Between him and Diablo, I'll have to be careful to keep from getting skinned on this patrol. Diablo must share Skully's opinion of me.

Jonah snickered. "Diablo may have more problems than he knows."

"Looking for Apaches? That's plenty trouble, but I expect he's mean enough to handle it. He's well enough armed."

Jonah laughed. "But he ain't well horsed."

"I'm not following you, Jonah."

"When the orders comes down to saddle extra horses, I was told to gives you the horse Diablo's riding. The markin's near the same, but yours be a good horse. Diablo's horse, the one they wanted you on, is gun shy. When the firin' starts, that animal goes loco." Jonah smiled. "When I passed the orders along, I gots mixed up."

"I appreciate it, Jonah. This is a good horse."

"But he's no Grant," Jonah said to himself.

They drew close to the big cottonwood trees hugging the banks on either side of the sweet water of the Loco River. Jonah watched as Garrett surveyed the animal carcasses and bleaching bones left from the paymaster fight.

Jonah pointed to a pile of bones poking from the dried and cracked hide that had once been a horse. "That's all that's left of Grant, best horse in the Army. I'm gonna repay the Apaches for that."

Garrett hobbled his horse and tossed his bedroll down away from the soldiers, but inside the ring of guards on night watch. His body ached from the day's ride and his senses were dulled from exhaustion, a disconcerting condition with Skully nearby.

As the soldiers grumbled over their squares of weevil-infested hardtack, Garrett opened a tin of tomatoes Tilman had slipped in his saddlebags. With the knife he used to cut the lid, he speared the stewed tomatoes and savored their sweetness. He finished off the can by drinking the juice. After the meal, he checked the hobbles on his mount and stretched out, carefully scanning the camp for Skully. Along with Jonah, Skully was in a circle of troops making their beds in the dwindling light of day.

Diablo had disappeared. The last Garrett had seen of him, Diablo had been riding off toward the mountains. In the summer heat, the Apaches wisely preferred the coolness of the mountains, and Diablo went alone into the high country.

Garrett stared at the mountains, purpling in the dwindling light, and felt relieved that Diablo was somewhere among them. But there were still the black troopers, perhaps all of them holding a grudge against him. He bent down and jerked his carbine from the boot beneath his saddle, making an ostentatious display of checking the load. After leaning the carbine on the saddle by his blanket, he jerked his revolver from its holster, broke it open and checked the load. He would sleep each night on the trail with his holster on. He hoped the blacks thought it was for defense, but Garrett knew better. A one-armed man had to struggle to hold and latch a heavy gunbelt around his waist.

After he had made all his gun checks, Garrett reclined on his blanket and pulled his hat over his head. If he got an earlier start on his sleep, perhaps his senses might return enough to protect himself in the early morning when he feared some trooper might try to ambush him.

Sleep came quick and hard to Garrett. His body seemed to melt into the earth, but his senses divested themselves of his body, alert to the dangers that existed from the troops much more than from the Apaches.

Early in the morning, after the second watch had changed and after the coolness of the desert night had chased him within the fold of his blanket, his senses tingled with anticipation and his hand slipped slowly down his side for his pistol. Garrett came awake. Slowly his eyelids cracked. In the black of a moonless night, his eyes strained to see a form around him. He stared at nothingness, then heard his horse blow. Maybe it had been the animal, he thought, his grip loosening on his hand gun.

Then a twig snapped and Garrett pulled the gun from his holster. As he stared toward the sound, he picked out a form moving stealthily toward him. Easing the gun up his side and over his chest, Garrett snorted, as if he were turning in his sleep, then he breathed heavily, like the snoring of a man fast asleep. As he did, the gun drew a bead on the approaching figure.

Garrett could feel his muscles tightening as the figure crawled steadily nearer. Each instant the figure moved closer, the more difficulty he had maintaining the regular pace of his snoring. The figure crawled closer, then as it came within a dozen feet of Garrett, raised on its knees, inching closer still. When the form was almost within reach of Garrett, its arm raised up in the sky. At that moment, Garrett flung back the blanket and cocked his revolver. The figure froze.

"Come an inch closer," Garrett whispered, "and you're a dead man, whether you're Apache or cavalryman."

The form grunted, but the noise was unintelligible.

"Whatever you've got in your hand, drop it."

By the thump of something against the

ground, Garrett knew the form had complied.

"Now back away. You come back," Garrett whispered, "and I'll kill you without asking questions."

The figure eased back away from Garrett. Getting to its feet, the form hunkered low over the ground and moved back toward the other soldiers.

When the would-be attacker had disappeared in the darkness, Garrett leaned over and groped along the ground until his hand touched something hard and cold. It was a razor. It had been a trooper. He stuck it in his pants pocket and rested the remainder of the night with his gun in his hand.

Come morning, Garrett eased out of bed with the troopers. Stretching as soon as he stood up, Garrett hurried to pack his bedroll and saddle his mount. As he worked, he remembered the razor in his pocket. He pulled it out and stared at it. He shivered at the finely honed blade as he pulled it from the ivory handle. It was good for shaving or carving flesh. He folded it up and inserted it back in his pocket, then unhobbled his horse. As he did, he heard the footsteps of someone approaching. He looked around.

"Mornin', Morgan. Just thoughts I'd see if you needed any help getting your animal ready." Jonah smiled.

"About got it taken care of, Jonah. Thanks for the offer, though. You're the only one I've had to turn down today."

Jonah laughed. "If there's anythin' I can do, ask me — I'll do whats I can for you."

"Maybe there is one thing, Jonah." Garrett stuck his fist in his pocket and pulled out the razor. Handing it to Jonah, he spoke. "Recognize this?"

Taking it, Jonah fondled it in his hand, then stared at it. "Did you have some trouble last night?"

Garrett shrugged. "I found it near my bed this morning. Why?"

"I's just wonderin'. This razor belongs to Skully."

# CHAPTER 9

After a while, the days began to run together
with no difference in the boredom or the
heat. The soldiers got up, rode out to
nowhere, camped for another restless night
and arose again the next day to repeat it all.
Never in that time did Garrett see the cabin
of a farmer, nor did he expect to in the territory they traversed. Perhaps in the foothills
and the mountain valleys they might be
found, but not on the prairie lands. This
patrol was merely the pretext for his own
murder.

Periodically, during their futile forays,
Diablo would rejoin the troop and report to
Colonel Fulton, then disappear again as
though he had been swallowed up by the
earth. He was unpredictable, riding out to
the south in the morning and appearing the
next morning from the north. He rode heavily armed, carrying a canteen and little else,
relying on his years with the Apaches to live

off the land and its provisions, meager though they might be. The scrub and thorny plants the white man passed as nuisances, the Apache used to sustain himself and to circumnavigate the vast prairie sea.

Then, the evening of the eighth day, as the men forced down another meal of hardtack and coffee, Diablo appeared suddenly in the camp, his horse soaked with sweat, his scowl covered with the grime of a hard ride. As he sought out Fulton, he walked with the wild-eyed look of a bear that has drawn enemy blood. Spotting Fulton, Diablo stormed up to him, gesticulating wildly with his arms, pointing toward the mountains and giving directions with broad sweeps of his powerful hands.

Fulton chewed vigorously on his cigar, mulling the report, then turned toward the mountains, planting his hands on his hips and staring. Like brooding fortresses, the mountains seemed impregnable and dangerous, more the equal of Diablo than the man he reported to. Waving Diablo away, Fulton called his officers together and for many minutes they huddled together as the sun dropped behind the mountains, taking its light with it. When the meeting broke, orders were quickly passed among the soldiers to prepare for a short sleep tonight and hard ride tomorrow.

In the dwindling light, Garrett searched the camp for Diablo, but he had disappeared. Garrett grimaced at the sound of an unwelcomed voice.

"Garrett," Colonel Fulton called, "we'll leave early. We intend to be into the foothills by first light. You'll go with the main body. We're leaving a half dozen men to see the pack mules into the foothills. You be ready."

"You found Pachise? Or is it settler for me to buy fodder from?" Garrett asked.

"No time for store business now, Garrett."

"Never has been, Colonel, now has there?"

Fulton jerked his cigar stub from his mouth. "What do you mean by that remark, Garrett?"

Garrett turned from Fulton.

"Where are you going?" Fulton huffed.

"To get ready, Colonel, like you said." Garrett strode away, looking without success for Diablo. When Garrett retired into his bedroll, his nerves were taut as a bowstring. If danger did not sleep with him tonight, it surely would accompany him tomorrow.

By first light the cavalrymen had advanced to the base of the foothills. In the darkness the troopers had trotted their horses toward the black silhouette of the mountains, reaching the gentle hills that might shield them from watchful Apaches eyes high in the mountains. As the sun gradually evaporated the long shadows of the hills, the dark forms accompanying Garrett took on discernible identities. Garrett stretched in his saddle and looked about. Though he didn't expect it, Garrett hoped Skully might have been assigned to the pack train. But reaching the top of a knoll, Garrett pulled his animal out of line to stare at the passing troops, strung out single file. Near the end of the sinew of soldiers rode Skully, who spied Garrett and by the nod of his head seemed to understand Garrett's suspicions. Garrett jerked his horse around, cursing his luck, and trotted to regain his position among the others.

Up ahead the mountains jutted from the land, like earthen molars ready to chew up trespassers. Between the steepening hills and the mountains, the land was changing, the yucca and the prairie aster giving way to juniper and cholla, and distant mule deer replacing the occasional pronghorn. Further ahead the mountains were splotched with the dark green of the piñons and the gnarled brown of dead junipers and even though there was green, it was the thirsty green of a stagnant pond, the sparse, hardy green of winter, though the season was newly summer.

Beyond the trail Garrett spied a stream meandering through the maze of hills, and the water's sweet aroma floated up the gentle slope and tickled the nose of man and animal, the troopers straightening in their sticky saddles and the horses lifting their heavy hooves higher. At the stream Fulton passed the word to rest the horses and to fill canteens. The troops were quick to obey, many breaking out squares of hardtack to calm their stomachs for the breakfast they had missed in favor of an early start.

While the others lounged about, Garrett watched Fulton pacing nervously among his black troops, chewing furiously on his stubby cigar, occasionally slapping his thigh, moving with the short, choppy motions of one who does not wear his nerves well or one who desperately needs a drink. Fulton kept glancing toward the mountains as if they would divulge the secrets of the Apaches. Garrett wondered if Fulton might be awaiting Diablo, who had disappeared after reporting to the colonel yesterday.

After a half hour's rest, Fulton ordered the soldiers mounted and led them along the stream dotted with the willow thickets, hackberry shrubs and cottonwood trees that thrived on the waters trickling from the mountains. The Army procession followed the stream until a broad-hipped mountain sliced it into two lesser rivulets, each taking a different route deeper into the mountains. There in the stream's crotch the troopers were ordered to wait. They rested gladly while Fulton paced among them, a scowl his only emotion.

Then the Mexican appeared, like a haunting vision, weaving in and out of sight along the upper stream. A junior officer pointed Diablo out to Fulton and the colonel clapped his hands as he paced back and forth. But Diablo advanced at his own pace, not at Fulton's, and shortly the colonel had jumped astride his horse and galloped up the valley. Like the soldiers, Garrett watched as Fulton drew beside the Mexican, who neither hurried nor slowed his advance but continued his steady pace forward with the confidence of a man who knows others will go nowhere without him. Fulton accompanied Diablo for a few moments, then slapped his horse forward again, splashing through the stream. As he neared the troops, he began to shout. "Mount up," he called. "He's found them in a high valley, eight, maybe ten miles into the mountains. Come sundown Pachise and his renegades will be ours." As he advanced, he waved his hat in the air and whooped like a kid on a new pony.

Garrett struggled into his saddle while about him the soldiers mounted or nervously fingered their weapons.

Fulton halted his horse in front of his men. "Boys," he yelled triumphantly, "not in the months since Pachise and his tribe escaped from the Bosque Bonito Reservation has the U.S. Army been this close to the Apaches without them knowing it."

"You keeps on yellin'," a disgruntled trooper behind Garrett said softly, "and even the dead Apaches'll know we're near."

Garrett twisted around and realized it was Jonah speaking. "Take care of yourself when we get among the Apaches, Jonah," Garrett smiled.

"I been waitin' for this, Mister —" Jonah laughed. "Morgan, I mean. I been waitin' for this."

"Some others have too," Garrett answered as Fulton motioned the troops forward.

"I done some askin', Morgan," Jonah started, then stopped as he raised up in his stirrups, then slipped back into the saddle for a more comfortable roost. "I asked Skully about his razor. He said he lost it on the trail. He's lyin'. I think he meant you harm, but I don't mean you any."

Garrett nodded. "I know that, Jonah."

"If trouble breaks loose," Jonah's words came out slowly and softly, meant only for Garrett's ears, "he may mean to hurt you, so watch him."

"You're a good man, Jonah."

Jonah breathed heavily. "I wondered if you'd think that so, after what happened to your family."

"My family died of cholera, Jonah."

Jonah seemed to sag in his saddle as if he had loosened a heavy load. "I didn't know if you knowed that. I feared you might think I murdered them. In those last months of the war lots of slaves turned nasty, killin' their owners and such meanness."

"Murderers don't bury their victims, Jonah. I found the three graves. I knew." Garrett paused, his throat tightening in a knot of grief. He coughed and shook his head, as if he could jar loose the regrets. "The neighbors said cholera, and I knew you'd done what you could."

"They was good folks," Jonah said, "like you."

"You don't have an apology to make, Jonah."

"I just feels better tellin' you, 'cause I

183

thoughts you'd searched me down to kill me. Your oldest boy, he died first. Your wife and the younger boy, well they did okay for a few days, and then when I thought they'd live, the little one died. It affected your wife. I don't know if it was the cholera or the madness, but she kept sayin' her boys were cryin' for her in the dark and she had to go find them, like she was crazy. And then she seem to come out of it. She told me, 'Tell Morgan the boys'll be okay, and I loves him'. Then she said, 'Morgan, Morgan', and she never said nothing else after that."

Garrett turned his head from Jonah and stared at the side of the mountain.

"And then I buried her between the boys. I'm sorry," Jonah said gently, then pulled his horse to the side of the procession as Garrett rode forward.

For many minutes Garrett rode silently forward, looking neither forward nor sideways but into the past, seeing three lonely graves.

Riding up the narrow shoulders of the mountain and then along its long rocky spine, the patrol advanced deeper into the fortress peaks. When the ridge joined with a taller mountain, the troops skirted its edge until they came to a narrow chasm alive with water. Single file they weaved among the giant boulders littering the stream and its thin banks, the difficulty of negotiating the narrowness in the deep shadows of the channel distorting their sense of time and distance. Then the chasm widened into an earthen bowl and the stream disappeared into the farthest slope. A dead end to Garrett's eyes, there seemed no escape from the mountain hole, but Diablo was quickly moving up the slope's side along a trail made by animals seeking water.

Whispered down the line came orders for quiet. Troopers moved wordlessly up the trail, each horse kicking loose a shower of dirt and gravel which tumbled toward the talus at the base of the hole. Emerging from the lower ground, Garrett glanced around. The air smelled of the scattered pine trees and the ground angled up toward a broad mountain peak to the east. He watched Fulton shade his eyes, then stare toward the sun. After a moment he nodded to his officers.

From the instinct of a hundred past cavalry forays, Garrett nudged his mount into line behind the officers and followed them into a clump of pines, the aroma sweet as vanilla. Advancing to the edge of the copse, Diablo pointed down into a broad green valley.

"By god, you did it," Fulton said.

Diablo smiled, twisting around in the saddle for acknowledgement from the others. Spotting Garrett, the grin changed into a sinister sneer.

Garrett stared beyond Diablo to the high valley, shaped like a dog leg between three mountains, a broad stream running from the far end of the valley and disappearing into the mountain slope below them. Cradled in the bend of the stream, a camp of thirty brush lodges teemed with the activity of children busy at play and women hard at chores.

"Dammit, I told you fellows I'd find them." Fulton wriggled his cigar from side to side of his mouth as he twisted in his saddle. "That's why I'm colonel, you . . ." His sentence died as he spotted Garrett. Fulton spit a wad of tobacco on the ground near Garrett's horse. "What in the hell are you doing here, Garrett?"

"Looking for settlers to buy grain from, Colonel," Garrett said, his words dripping with disdain.

"You give our position away, Garrett, I'll have you court-martialed."

"I'm not one of your men, Colonel. You keep forgetting."

Fulton scowled, jerked his cigar from his

mouth and wiped his lips with the back of his hand. "You forget that on this expedition I am in charge of everything. You be sure and stay out of my way, out of my men's way, or you'll be in big trouble with the United States Army."

"I plan to stay out of everybody's way, Colonel," Garrett said and stared at Diablo. "The Apaches and your men."

"Just see that you do," Fulton said, giving his attention to the camp below for a moment.

Garrett watched too, seeing the adult figures moving about, safe in their ignorance, the children chasing one another among the big rocks that lined the stream. Nearby a dozen horses grazed in grass which reached to their knees.

"We'll attack in half an hour," Fulton said.

Easing his horse nearer Fulton's, Garrett spoke. "Looks like squaws and children only, Colonel."

"Dammit, Garrett, this is Army business — no concern of yours. They're Apaches and they belong on my reservation. I don't care if they are just squaws and children, I intend to take them back with me and civilize them.

"I count twelve horses. Can't be many braves here with that few horses."

"Garrett, get back with the troopers," Fulton commanded.

Wheeling about, Garrett replied. "You're in charge, Colonel." He rode back through the trees and over the summit to the awaiting troops. Descending slowly, he scanned the troops all in a line and spotted Skully at the far end. He pointed his horse the opposite direction.

As Garrett joined the ranks, the soldiers fingered their weapons and nervously checked their loads. When firing broke out, Garrett knew he must be alert, but maybe a fight could be averted. Planting the idea the camp was only women and children — as it had actually appeared to Garrett — might take seed in Fulton's mind. When he topped the summit ahead of his officers, Fulton carried his pistol in his hand. Garrett knew a fight was coming.

Drawing up in front of the soldiers, Fulton called out "Men, the enemy is before us, but we will be fighting on our terms. We cannot be certain how many braves are in the camp, so ride carefully."

Behind Fulton, Diablo stood in his stirrups, inspecting the line of soldiers until Garrett could feel the scout's gaze on him. Diablo broke away from the officers toward Garrett.

Fulton paused to watch Diablo cover the distance between him and the troops. "Let no man, woman or child escape," Fulton commanded, casting a glance at Garrett. "Hold your fire until fired upon or given the order." Fulton held his hand up to the sun. "Advance slowly into the trees over the summit. Halt before you reach the edge of the tree cover. When the sun is shining over our backs and into their eyes, we'll advance on the camp." He paused, then repeated his primary order. "Let no man, woman or child escape."

At the wave of his hand, the troops advanced forward. Garrett spied Diablo gradually working his way closer. Garrett pulled his revolver, broke it apart and checked the load. Snapping the gun back together, he headed parallel along the advancing rank, passing a surprised Diablo, until he came nearer the middle of the rank. When the troops advanced down the hill, Garrett hoped to stay close to Fulton, whose proximity might discourage shots by Diablo or Skully. He fell into line with the troops, looking over his shoulder to see Diablo coming his way again. Slowly, he and the soldiers urged their mounts through the timber, stopping near the edge.

Then he waited for the command.

■ ■ ■ ■

"Advance," Fulton called and the troops emerged from their hiding place, the command echoing softly between the mountains.

The cavalrymen maintained an even line, sliding like a fog down the slope, deeply shadowed by the trees. Their horses moved slowly at first, then reached a full gallop heightened by the incline, their hooves thundering toward the camp. At first the Apaches seemed oblivious to the sound, as if it were some distant storm. "Charge," Fulton yelled and the command bounced among the mountains.

Then the tranquility of a camp at rest was shattered, with children screaming for their mothers, squaws grabbing their offspring and prized possessions, feeble adults throwing their hands to the sky for help from the gods. Everywhere they ran, some into their brush lodges, others up the stream, a few in circles as they gathered young ones.

Jonah beat his horse forward, faster. The animal lunged down the slope, its eyes and mouth wide. Jonah could feel his heart racing and the nectar of revenge pulsing through his body. Now the Apaches would understand surprise as he had known it at Cottonwood Crossing. He would show revenge. He leveled his pistol at a blanket-shrouded figure running among the rocks away from the camp. His finger itched for the command to pull the trigger. Within a hundred yards of the lodges and still no command. He chafed at the order to fire only on command. The blanketed figure was dashing along the stream, moving farther away from the camp.

*Let no man, woman or child escape.* That had been the command. Jonah had heard Fulton give it. And now, fifty yards from the camp, still no permission to shoot. Revenge so near and yet not within grasp! The blanketed figure stumbled and fell, scrambling to pick up something that fell from beneath the blanket. Let no one escape, Jonah thought, but this one was escaping. The order was clear and the figure was fleeing, escaping. Jonah steadied his pistol at the fleeing target. He remembered Grant, the best horse in the army, and how the Apaches had killed him. His thumb cocked the hammer. The Apaches had strewn Grant's bones around Cottonwood Crossing. *Let no man, woman or child escape.* The orders reverberated through his brain. Damn the orders. Damn the consequences.

Damn the Apaches. Jonah's revolver exploded in a white cloud of smoke. Instantly, all along the line other cavalry guns answered and the valley roared with buzzing lead.

Still the figure scrambled away, and Jonah broke out of formation to run it down. Quickly he was behind the terrified form which broke into the stream, jumping among the rocks. Within twenty feet, Jonah jerked on the reins, his horse halting long enough for him to squeeze off a steady shot. The figure fell between two rocks on the far back of the stream and a rivulet of blood stained the water for a moment.

Jonah shouted his pleasure. His revenge had claimed its first victim. He whirled his horse around toward the camp where there would be others.

Garrett cursed as the first gunshot was joined by a deadly chorus of more. He glanced back over his shoulder. Diablo was aiming his pistol in Garrett's direction, but his horse bucked at the noise of the sustained gunfire. As the horse reared, Diablo almost fell, but hanging onto the horse's neck, he rode the animal down then clubbed it under the ear.

The stunned horse stumbled forward, los-

192

ing ground on Garrett, who urged his mount closer to Fulton. Quickly, Fulton was among the brush lodges emptying his revolver at the terrified figures — women, children and feeble old men — dancing with death.

A bullet whizzed by Garrett's ear, too close for an accident. He twisted to his right, spotting Diablo still struggling with his own mount, then to his left, and riding upon him came Skully, his white teeth shining like a wolf's. Garrett ducked instinctively as another shot whizzed over his head. He circled a lodge, his horse trampling a child and almost tripping. Skully followed in a tight circle. Holding the reins in his mouth and jerking his revolver from his holster, Garrett fired a shot behind him with no hope of accuracy. Grabbing the reins again, the gun still in his hand, he maneuvered his horse among the lodges and terrified figures. Skully tailed his every move like a shadow.

Then, as he rounded a lodge, his horse collided with another. Garrett screamed as he was flung forward in the saddle, his head striking that of his horse. A thousand lights flashed through his brain and his eyes seemed to see a hundred quivering Diablos before him, fighting to calm his own mount. As the images gradually focused into a single Diablo, Garrett saw the scout extending his pistol toward him. Garrett lunged at the barrel as it pulled even with his head, then slapped it with his own pistol. He felt the hot breath of the pistol brush his cheek, but in spoiling Diablo's aim, Garrett had dropped his reins. Garrett's horse kept lunging forward against Diablo's mount instead of running away.

Skully rode by. "You bastard," he cried as he fired and missed.

Garrett could not separate his horse from Diablo's. Instantly the two men were face to face. Diablo spit at Garrett, then swung his pistol around for Garrett's chest. Garrett swiped at his face with a downward blow that missed its target, but struck Diablo's gun hand as he fired the gun.

Out of the side of his eye, Garrett caught a glimpse of Skully charging toward him. Diablo raised his revolver toward Garrett's chest. Garrett dodged low over his horse. Skully fired. His leaden caller split the air, striking a rider in the side. Diablo screamed and fell from his bucking horse.

Garrett gathered the reins and raced around the lodges, Skully charging after him. Riding low over his horse's neck, Garrett zigzagged through the camp until he spotted Fulton. He raced up to the colonel. With Skully on his tail, Garrett knew he had but one chance.

"Cease fire," he yelled. "Cease fire. Hold your fire." Garrett guided his horse beside Fulton so the colonel was between him and Skully. "Cease fire," he screamed. Fulton stared, disbelieving, at Garrett.

The fusillade gradually died away except for an occasional shot. A young Apache girl raced from a lodge toward Garrett. As she reached his horse, she grabbed at Garrett's leg and clung to him, crying and mumbling something Garrett could not understand.

Fulton, rage reddening his face, stammered at Garrett. "Who — who gave you authority to halt the shooting?!" he demanded.

As Fulton spoke, Garrett felt another stronger hand on his leg. The girl, no more than ten, was now in the arms of a beautiful black-haired, black-eyed woman who clung to his leg. Her eyes were filled with more hatred than fear, and she spoke in a tongue incoherent because of language, not panic.

Garrett looked to his side. Skully was drawing closer.

Fulton backed his horse next to Garrett, unknowingly shielding the lame-armed man.

"You were not in command of this skirmish, Garrett."

"Neither were you, Colonel. You weren't stopping this butchery of women and children."

"I never issued the command to fire. These women and children fired upon us first."

"The first shot, Colonel, came from your own troops."

"But you had no authority, dammit." Fulton jerked off his hat and wiped the sweat from his smoke-stained face. "No authority at all."

Garrett pointed to the woman at his leg. "Then you take your authority and give the command to resume firing. Start with this woman and child."

"Men," shouted Fulton, swallowing hard before continuing. "Round up the prisoners and check the dead and wounded."

Garrett twisted around in his saddle until he stared at Skully, who waved his revolver menacingly at him. The Apache woman loosened her grip on Garrett's leg as he spoke. "Colonel, your scout is dead." He nodded at Skully. "One of your sharpshooters missed his aim."

"Dammit, Garrett, shut up!" Fulton cried. "We attacked hostiles and he died in the exchange."

"Not a man that can fight in this camp, Colonel," Garrett pointed out. "Quite a victory!"

His face bloating with anger, Fulton shoved his pistol in its scabbard. "Round up the prisoners, burn the lodges and any belongings they can't carry," he ordered, ". . . and bring me all the weapons you find."

Skully leveled his pistol at Garrett, nudging his horse forward.

Fulton glimpsed Skully. "Dammit, soldier, get busy following my orders."

Grumbling, Skully shoved his gun back in his holster and spun his horse around and rode off. Then, Garrett broke his pistol apart over his saddle, dumped the empties onto the ground and struggled to pull cartridges from his belt. The Apache woman at his side lowered her daughter to the ground. She reached for Garrett's waist and worked bullets from the loops in his gunbelt and handed them to him. As he tried to slip the bullets into the cylinder with his one good hand, a cartridge tumbled to the ground. The woman picked it up and slowly offered it, and then her hand, to him. Garrett lifted the revolver from its unsteady perch on his saddle and handed it to her. As she held the gun up to him, he dropped the bullets in place, and when it was loaded, she snapped it shut, offering Garrett the revolver, butt first.

He nodded his thanks and he saw a glimmer of a smile in return. She averted her eyes when he looked down at her upturned face, slim and graceful, unlike the rounded faces of the other women gathering around them. Her high cheekbones and defiant nose, her dark impenetrable eyes and steady lips gave her a defiant beauty. Around her neck, she wore a bearclaw necklace some brave had risked his life to give her.

A dismounted trooper stepped beside her and grabbed her arm, pulling her away from Garrett. She shook her way loose and spit at him. The soldier thinking it safer to push the girl grabbed at her, but realized his mistake as the woman clawed at his face, her eyes flaring with maternal rage. The soldier backed away as the woman and her daughter reached the growing cluster of Apaches. Though around her the others wallowed in fear, her shell was hard as that of a desert tortoise.

A lieutenant counting the captives moved close to the woman, inspecting her, the necklace she wore and her daughter. "Colonel Fulton," he shouted, waving his arms madly in the air. "Come here quick, sir."

Fulton galloped away from a burning

brush lodge toward the lieutenant, jerking his horse to a halt in front of the lieutenant. "What is it?"

The lieutenant put his hand under the squaw's chin, lifting her face toward the colonel. "This is Pachise's wife and daughter," he said, dropping his hand atop the girl, who flinched from his touch.

"Well, well," Fulton said, removing the cigar stub from his mouth. "We did get us a prize, a little bait to capture Pachise with."

"I dare say he'll come looking for her, sir, fine Indian flesh that she is."

"Me, too, lieutenant, but let's leave a message for Pachise." He looked about the huddled clump of captives, maybe a hundred total, then pointed at an old man. "He looks like his fighting days are over. Leave him here with a message for Pachise. Have him tell the Apache chief that his wife will die if his braves try to rescue her. And let Pachise know his wife and daughter may be sent to a reservation so far away he may never find her — unless he returns to the Bosque Redondo."

The lieutenant strode to the feeble man and spoke in the tongue of the Apache, conveying Fulton's instructions. The old man, weak and shaky, trembled more as the lieutenant passed on the instructions, then looked toward Pachise's woman. She nodded to him and he nodded to the lieutenant.

Pachise's wife lifted a clenched fist and shouted to her people. They nodded slowly at her words.

"What did she say, Lieutenant?" Fulton demanded.

"She says Pachise will rescue them and avenge the deaths of their kin by killing us all," the lieutenant paused. "All of us but the man she calls Bad Arm, the one who saved them." The lieutenant looked up at Garrett.

"Bad Arm!" Fulton laughed as he turned to Garrett. "How's it feel knowing you've saved the lives of a murdering savage's family, Garrett? You've made yourself a hero of the Apaches! A great honor, wouldn't you say?"

"The honor would've been yours, Colonel — if you'd been in command." Garrett turned and rode away, a torrent of Fulton's curses following him.

"Finish counting the dead and burning the lodges," Fulton commanded, ". . . and hurry. We must put some miles between here and our camp before dark."

Grant had been avenged, Jonah thought, as

he moved to recount the dead Apaches, but his stomach had turned as he rode among the bodies, awkward in death's distorted grasp. As small fires crackled into consuming blazes at each lodge, he traversed the ground among the flames, his horse edgy at the silent smell of fresh death. He counted nine bodies before coming upon one he remembered downing. He stared closely and his stomach soured more, a wrinkled woman with but half a face, the rest a purple pulp. In the excitement, Jonah told himself, he had been certain that grandmother had been a warrior. Nearby, sprawled over a smoldering fire pit, lay another victim Jonah remembered. The stench of burning flesh attacked Jonah's nose as he stopped his horse beside the body. This one for certain had been a warrior, because Jonah remembered a drawn bow in his hand. But this one too was wrinkled and pitted, though a man, and beside him lay a bow and an arrow, the bow of a child and the arrow a mere stick without a point. Jonah rode away upstream in search of the first body he had downed.

His killings weighted his ride. Revenge had not been so sweet. The Apaches had cheated him, leaving only old men and women and children, not braves, for his slaughter. He knew he had started the firing, but maybe it was a brave who had been escaping. He had been following orders. Now his throat was dry and tight and he wanted to cough out the tightness and he couldn't. Ahead, between two rocks, he spotted the blanket-shrouded body as he remembered it, face down at the edge of the stream, the waters lapping at the blanket. Jonah dismounted, holding the reins of the horse. Taking a deep breath, he jerked the blanket from the form and dropped it in the water. From the buckskin wrap and long unbraided hair, he knew it was a woman. But he had to turn her over, hoping it would be a warrior anyway. By the feel of her unmuscled arm, he knew it was a woman. As he pulled her to her side, a bundle fell from her arms into the water. Jonah reached for it, then recoiled in horror. The bloodied body of a baby bobbed in the stream for a moment, then sank in the shallows. He looked from the infant to the woman, his eyes drawn to the jagged hole in her chest.

And then he retched until his empty stomach seemed it would turn inside out.

# CHAPTER 10

Herding the Apache women and children, all afoot, slowed the soldiers as they worked their way down the great mountain and its lesser neighbors. And, too, Pachise still roamed the country unfettered. Haste bred carelessness and carelessness fathered death in these mountains. So the soldiers rode alert and cautious and quiet, the strain etched in their black faces, their stomachs grumbling from want of anything but hardtack.

As he rode, Jonah took a swig of the water in his canteen and let it trickle down his throat. The water was sweet and still cool. As he closed his eyes to enjoy its wetness, he saw the image of a dead Apache baby slipping from its lifeless mother's grasp and then sinking in the mountain stream, like bait for a huge fish. The water in his mouth seemed to turn as sour as the thought in his brain and he hurried it down and opened his eyes and stoppered the canteen.

Staring at the mountains around him, Jonah spotted so many places for Apache warriors to hide, but the mountains were shrinking and the tree cover diminishing into clumps of junipers and piñons. He looked to the western sky, the sun already hiding behind the taller peaks from which they had ridden. Soon the patrol would reach the rendezvous point where the pack train would be waiting with all its provisions. Perhaps Colonel Fulton would permit fires for a decent meal of saltpork and hard bread and brown sugar.

On the return trip from the Indian camp, Fulton had followed an easier trail instead of the route Diablo discovered. The trail eventually led to a stream, and that stream to another, and the troops had stalked it for miles. Jonah stared ahead for a moment, then searched the mountainsides for attackers. When the column came to a halt at the base of a mountain, Jonah urged his horse past the Apache captive and the other troopers until his ears could pick up Fulton's sulking voice.

"Dammit," Fulton called, his anger rising. "Where in the hell are the bastards?"

Jonah studied the mountain, then examined the stream which met with another, larger stream. Jonah only then realized the troop was back at the rendezvous point. He had expected to see the men with the pack train long before he reached this point, but they were nowhere around.

"Dammit," Fulton said to his junior officers. "They probably got lost, the incompetents. With decent soldiers, I could whip these damn Apaches. But the bastards I've got under my command couldn't find their asses in the dark."

Jonah felt his stomach knot, and it wasn't from hunger.

Fulton jumped down from his horse and stomped back and forth, cursing the absent pack train and the men responsible for it. Holding his hand over his eyes, Fulton stared eastward, the direction in which the pack train had been abandoned. He cursed again as he dropped his hand to his revolver. "They're probably out there moving in circles. Can't anybody in this outfit except me do anything right?" His junior officers shook their sagging heads without responding. "Well, can they?"

"Sir," responded the captain, "maybe they had trouble."

"Excuses, Captain, that's all I ever get — excuses. I want results. Results like I got on this campaign."

Women and children, Jonah thought — some results. The corporal could hear the soldiers behind him murmuring about the missing pack train and could feel the sudden anxiety that enveloped them and their flaring disgust for Colonel Fulton, who alone among all the soldiers was blind to the pack train's fate.

"Dammit," Fulton exploded in a final fit of fury, "we'll camp here tonight — we don't have much daylight left anyway — and maybe the pack train will straggle in and save us from having to find the black bastards."

Jonah heard a horse pull beside his, but his eyes were blinded by too much hate for Fulton to look.

"Disgusting, isn't he?"

The voice belonged to Garrett.

Jonah nodded slowly. "Some of my friends is out there, maybe dead, and him too dumb to think 'bout much but how stupid they are. Lots of the boys'd like to kill him with their bare hands," Jonah whispered.

"You one of those, Jonah?"

Jonah's answer was slow to come to his tongue. When he finally spoke, he could feel the tension in his words. "I had a reason, I thought. But I learnt a lesson about revenge at the Apache camp. Just don't always turn out like you thinks it ought to."

"I can't figure you holding much against the colonel except his stupidity, Jonah."

Jonah looked at Garrett, gauging if his interest was sincere. "Some posts, the commandin' officer lets his boys learn to read. Colonel Stubby, he ordered none of that at Fort Bansom."

Garrett snickered.

Jonah felt his fist tighten around the reins and a spark of anger flash through his body as if fueled by kerosene. "I don't sees that as much funny."

Shaking his head, Garrett smiled easily at Jonah. "If all you boys knew how to read, there'd be no doubt he was the stupidest man at the fort."

Forcing a thin smile, Jonah nodded as if Garrett's laugh had not drawn blood. Garrett meant no harm, but as an educated man he'd never understand, Jonah thought. There would always be a gap between them too great to close even though they'd grown up together, sipped from the same water dipper, ridden the same horses, done most everything together except go to school together when they were kids. "I guess you're mostly right, Mister Garrett," Jonah said. He turned his horse away and trotted back along the line, passing the word they would camp here tonight and worrying they would bury six of their comrades out on the prairie tomorrow.

After a fitful night where the Apache women chanted into the early hours of morning and every spectral noise beyond the camp seemed to carry the touch of Pachise, the troops broke camp quickly and started riding for the red ball rising on the horizon. As the sun changed from red to orange to yellow, it arced across a deep blue sky, draining the heavens of their color until they turned anemic, lifeless and forlorn. The heat was quick upon them and by high sun, the distance shimmered in dry wave after dry wave, each coming from a distant pool of deepest blue that came no closer despite the miles traveled.

And then there was the movement, not of the elusive mirage nor the rippling veil draped by the sun across the distance. In that colorless sky a lazy circling motion like the skeleton of a dust devil rotating over a distant point. Jonah spotted it first and by his unwavering stare those around him looked and saw, lifting their fingers to point for others. Soon the officers noticed as well, and without command the column swung in that direction, moving as fast as possible with the footsore herd of captives.

"Buzzards — damned buzzards," Jonah said to nobody in particular. "Scavengering bastards. Worse than the damned Apaches."

Impatient with the pace of the prisoners, Jonah trotted past them to the leading officers. He saluted smartly as he drew up beside the captain and Colonel Fulton.

"Back to your position, Corporal," Fulton commanded.

Jonah, stuck between his emotion and the orders of his commander, sat for a moment in the saddle like a mute.

"Corporal, did —"

"Sir, I will leads some men to check that out," Jonah said, boldly pointing to the circling buzzards.

"Back to your place, Corporal, as I ordered," Fulton huffed. "The dead will wait."

Stung by the reproach, Jonah jerked his horse around and galloped back to his position. "Damn him."

Eventually, the squawking of the buzzards could be heard and soon after the troops reached the edge of a slight rise. In the depression beyond were hundreds of buzzards dancing among bloated corpses — men, mules and horses in grotesque contortions. Theirs had been a terrible fate and now the buzzards pecked away at the putrid remains of death's indignity.

As the column spread out in a line to survey the massacre scene, Jonah pulled his Spencer carbine from its boot. He aimed at a clump of buzzards and fired, the exploding gun drawing startled cries from the Apache women. His bullet struck into a feather mass. A hundred birds took to their slow wings and squawked at the inconvenience. Jonah pulled down the trigger guard lever to eject the hull. Around him, other soldiers pulled their carbines.

A lieutenant raced from the side of the line. "Who fired that shot?" he demanded, and as he rode by, other black soldiers pulled their revolvers or carbines. "Hold your fire," the lieutenant ordered. "Who fired without orders?"

Jonah kicked his horse to ride ahead of the others. Before he could move out from the line, he felt a tight grip around his arm. He looked at who held him. Skully shook his head and Jonah understood he should not admit to firing.

"Who was it, dammit?"

All up and down the line, the troops shrugged ignorance. The lieutenant stopped in front of Jonah.

"Corporal, did you see who fired?"

"Nobody around me fired."

"The Colonel is upset about it."

Jonah cast a harsh glance at the lieutenant. "Tell the Colonel the dead may wait, but the buzzards don't."

Shaking his head, the lieutenant rode away, reporting back to Fulton. In a minute, after the order to reform had been passed, the column advanced toward the massacre spot. With each step a new horror appeared among the mutilated bodies. More buzzards flushed as the troops came closer. And then the odor of the decomposing flesh enveloped them like a horrible shroud. Jonah could feel his nose twitching and his stomach twisting in revulsion. His senses recoiled from ignoble death and he wanted to turn back, but he rode forward anyway. It was the least he could do for these corpses which had once been men, all friends of his.

Fulton halted the troop and rode down the line giving orders. "Lieutenant," he cried as he drew up alongside Jonah and Skully, "have the damn Apache women dig the graves and bury the bodies."

Before the lieutenant could salute, Jonah rode his horse out of line. "No, sir," he said fighting to keep his voice from reaching an insubordinate pitch. "These men was my friends. I don't wants any more Apaches touchin' them. Me and my men'll bury them."

The colonel stroked his whisker-dotted cheek and nodded. "You do that, Corporal. Lieutenant, assign this corporal to burial detail. We'll see if he has the stomach for it. Have a guard set around the captives and a guard around the burial detail. Get to moving."

As the soldiers divided up into details, Fulton rode alone away from the stench and watched the work from a distance.

Burial detail was a horrible job, but none of the men with Jonah complained. And when the job was done, one of the black troopers produced a tattered Bible and the troops on burial detail stood around the six graves, passing the Good Book among themselves for someone to read. When it came to Jonah, he stepped back from the crowd, looked around the area and motioned for Garrett to join them. When Garrett dismounted, Jonah handed him the Bible.

"Just read somethin' for these men."

Garrett handed the book back to Jonah and Skully stepped from the crowd, drawing his revolver. "Too good to read for a dead black man?"

Jonah looked from Garrett to Skully then

back to Garrett, standing before him with outstretched hand. Then Jonah understood. "Gets back, Skully. Morgan can't holds the Bible and turns the pages with just one hand."

Scowling as he dropped his revolver back in place, Skully stepped back with the others. Jonah cradled the Bible between his outstretched palms and Garrett turned the pages back and forth until, near the middle of the book, he found a passage.

Picking up the Bible with his hand, he stepped away from Jonah toward the graves. "This is from Ecclesiastes," he said, then he started to read as one by one the soldiers removed their hats. "To every thing there is a season, and a time to every purpose under the heaven. A time to be born, and a time to die; A time to plant and a time to pluck up that which is planted . . . ; A time to weep and a time to laugh; A time to mourn, and a time to dance . . . ; A time to love and a time to hate; A time of war and a time of peace. God shall judge the righteous and the wicked: for there is a time there for every purpose and for every work. Amen."

Garrett handed the Bible back to Jonah and turned away as the soldiers began to cover the bodies. When that was done, the burial detail mounted their horses and rode back and forth over the graves to disguise their contents from burrowing varmints that might dig them up.

That done, the column reformed and moved out. For a couple miles Jonah rode trying to forget the Apaches he had killed, especially the young mother and child, and to wipe from his memory the awful bodies he had helped bury piece by piece.

"Jonah, you sure been quiet," Skully said shortly.

"I been thinkin'."

" 'Bout what?"

Jonah glanced over at Skully. "Past and future."

"That just about takes in everythin'."

"Dead men makes you think, Skully."

"All I keeps thinkin' about," Skully said, "is gettin' back to my bunk. That what you been thinkin' about?"

"No, just about bein' able to read, like as good as Morgan Garrett did from the Good Book. Those was pretty words he read over the graves."

"Jonah, you coulda had one of the officers read it."

"They don't care much for us or they'd lets us learn to read."

"You's always got readin' on your mind. Don't you ever think about nothin' else?"

"I gots somethin' to do, Skully," Jonah said, moving away from Skully and up toward the front of the column. He wanted to thank Garrett for his good words. Jonah slipped into the column beside Garrett.

"Sorry about your friends, Jonah," Garrett offered.

Jonah nodded. "I knows that. I just came to tell you we all appreciated your book readin' at the graves."

"Skully didn't care for it."

"He's hard for a lot of fellows to get along with, even black ones. But I just wants to thank you for those words. Those was pretty words you picked out. They gave a decent burial to those men."

Garrett nodded. "Don't any of your men read?"

"A few fellows can reads a little, but not good enough to do it in front of others. I can't even reads a little."

"It'd mean a lot to you, if you could?"

"Most surely."

"I owe you a favor, Jonah, for saving me from Skully. If you want, I'll help you learn, if you promise to keep it quiet. Your colonel and I aren't such good friends and Skully hasn't helped me stay out of trouble."

"I wouldn't tells nobody and I'll pays you

for the teachin'. I been savin' my pay for that."

"No, Jonah, I'll teach you what I can for free. You save your money for when you get out."

"Thank you, Morgan. Thank you, sir."

Half walking, half running, Benjamin Franklin Tilman emerged from the sutler's as the men of Company C herded their prisoners to the center of the parade ground. Wiping his hands on his apron, he hurried toward the flagpole, noting from the somber expressions of the men that not all had returned. When he saw Garrett he whooped and danced on the parade ground, drawing a severe glance from Fulton.

Garrett trotted his mount away from the troops when he heard Tilman and quickly rode up next to him. The clerk stood with both hands on his hips, a broad smile as wide as the eyes behind those thick glasses. "Welcome back, Morgan. I knew you'd make it. Yes, sir, I told myself there was no way you could be stopped if you set your mind to getting back."

"Don't seem that I recall that confidence of yours when I left, Ben, but I'm glad to be back," Garrett said as he dismounted. He tossed Tilman the reins. "I'll let you return this horse to the stables." Garrett pulled his bedroll and his carbine from the horse. He took a step toward the sutler's store, then tossed Tilman his bedroll and held his carbine between his legs. After sticking his hand in his pocket, he pulled out a wad of money. "Return this to your boss, Fitzgerald. It's all there. And tell him Diablo was killed during the raid on the Apache camp."

"Apaches got him, did they?"

"That's what Fulton will say, but the camp was all women and children. Skully's aim was bad — he missed me and nailed Diablo." Garrett pulled the carbine from between his legs and took the bedroll from Tilman. "When you get back, open me a tin of oysters and a can of tomatoes. I want something to eat and to be out of the way before Colonel Stubby comes in to drink with his officers. He and I haven't changed our opinions of one another since this expedition."

"Hell, Morgan, I'd've been awfully disappointed if you had." Tilman started toward the stables. "Napoleon of the West, ha! Now you'll believe me, Morgan."

Fulton rapped sharply on the door several times before it cracked cautiously open, revealing Fitzgerald's eye and the threatening point of a gun.

"Sorry, Colonel," Fitzgerald said, pushing the door open. "Just taking the normal precautions after dark."

Fulton hopped inside and Fitzgerald closed and barred the door behind him. Fitzgerald motioned for Fulton to take a chair in front of the desk. Fitzgerald moved to a cabinet against the wall and pulled a bottle from inside.

"Bet a man whose been on the trail two weeks could use a good drink." He planted the bottle squarely in front of Fulton, then moved the lamp closer to the colonel before taking his worn seat behind the desk.

In the low sallow glow of the lamp, Fulton uncorked the bottle and relished a healthy swig. "I appreciate it, I sure do — It was a long patrol."

"And a successful one, I gather," Fitzgerald answered. He leaned back in his chair, away from the desk and the dim lamp light, propping his feet up beside a roll of greenbacks. "From the prisoners I saw on the parade ground, I believe you proved you could find the Apaches. Now, tell me about Garrett." From out of the shadowy wall, Fitzgerald's pulpy hand appeared in the glow of the lamp, pointing at the wad of bills on the desk. "Ben returned the money I gave Garrett and told me Diablo went belly up in the attack."

Mulling over another swallow and the question, Fulton slammed the bottle back on the desk. "Damn bad luck, I'm afraid. Garrett's back unharmed."

"So I gathered." Fitzgerald's hand reached for the money and took it from the desk.

"Diablo died at the Apache camp. From what I saw, either Garrett shot him or Skully hit him on accident."

"You sure the Apaches didn't get him?"

"Just women and children, no braves. Had the shooting continued, Skully might of plugged that one-armed bastard, but damned if Garrett didn't run upon me and start calling for a halt in firing. The soldiers must of thought it me because they quit."

"Your soldiers — you lose any?"

"One was thrown from his horse and broke an arm in the attack, but the six men we left behind with the pack train were massacred."

"Damn shame, Colonel. Damn shame, but by God you brought back Apaches like you said you would. That should set well with headquarters."

"You never know about these things. Sometimes they notice, sometimes they don't. No way of knowing until it's too late."

"Of course, if your report states your scout was killed advancing upon the camp, then they wouldn't question your attack upon the Apaches. How many did you kill?"

Fulton leaned forward in his chair, looking for Fitzgerald's face, but it was obscured by the darkness. "A dozen or more."

"All braves, I suppose," Fitzgerald suggested.

"No, all . . ." Fulton thought for a moment, then continued, ". . . all but one. We did kill a poor Apache woman by mistake." He grinned widely.

"And," Fitzgerald continued, "your casualties at the camp included your one soldier with a broken arm, one dead scout and three dead cavalrymen."

Fulton nodded. "And in the company's gallant defense of the supply train and Pachise's unsuccessful rescue attempt we lost three more soldiers." He picked up the whiskey bottle by the neck and drowned his low laugh.

"Well there, Colonel, seems like your record won't come off as bad as you feared. And if anyone denies that, they can't deny that you brought back maybe a hundred Apaches."

"One hundred and seventeen, to be exact."

Fitzgerald dropped his feet to the floor and leaned forward into the halo of the lamp. "Now that that's turned out all right, on to other things. Looks like we must figure a way to get Skully to handle Garrett for us. We'll deal with Skully after he takes care of Garrett."

As Fitzgerald spoke, Fulton stood up and paced in front of the desk. "I've been thinking about that. Maybe a strong hint or a little extra incentive from me would help Skully. You know — tell him I'd look the other way."

Fitzgerald tossed the stack of greenbacks beside the bottle. "There's some incentive, but I wouldn't trust one of those ignorant darkies to hold his tongue once the deed was done."

"He'd enjoy killing Garrett and be doing us a favor, but I'd have him arrested, anyway," Fulton laughed. "We'd have to do something to get rid of him then."

"Perhaps you have a point — no doubt there's bad blood between those two fellows."

"Yes, sir, that's what I'll do." Fulton picked up the bottle and nodded to Fitzgerald. "We've settled several important matters here this evening, Fitz."

"Don't forget the money," Fitzgerald pointed to the cash. "Offer Skully the money if he succeeds. If he'll do it for less than two hundred, you pocket the difference."

Fulton laughed as he counted out the money. "Yes, sir, we've settled several important matters here tonight."

# CHAPTER 11

A thousand fears raced through Skully's mind as he was ushered into Colonel Fulton's office by the lieutenant. Up his sleeve he carried a stolen razor, just in case he needed a weapon. He concentrated on standing stiffly erect and unruffled, but his fingers kept twitching. His record was littered with offenses unbecoming to the Army's way of operating, and the shooting of Diablo was only the latest instance. His stomach grumbled and Skully was uncertain if it was from his nerves or his lunch, missed two hours ago while waiting for Fulton to see him.

As the lieutenant was closing the door, Fulton called out to him. "Lieutenant, go grab a bite. I won't be needing you for a while."

Then the colonel arose from his seat and strode to the window, staring out at the parade ground for a couple minutes. Only after Skully saw the lieutenant walk by the window did Fulton turn around. Having never been this close to Fulton before, Skully studied him and was surprised at how much shorter he was than himself. He looked at Stubby's gut and knew the razor would slice it easily — if it came to that. Fulton was only the latest in a long line of white men who had ruled his life, and Skully cared for him no more than he had for the men who had owned him and beaten him over the years.

Fulton returned to his chair, ignoring Skully until he was seated. "At ease, soldier," Fulton said.

Skully could feel the stiffness draining from his muscles, but not the tension. He crossed his hands in front of his belt, the forefinger and thumb of his right hand touching the razor inside his left sleeve.

"Now," said Fulton, leaning forward and propping his elbows on the desk, "tell me what you know about the death of Diablo at the Apache camp."

Skully's jaw tightened and he clenched his left fist. His fears had been confirmed. Maybe Colonel Stubby wasn't as dumb as all the troopers thought. Shifting his weight from foot to foot, Skully struggled for an answer.

Fulton waited a moment, then continued. "Some have said it wasn't Apaches that killed my scout. You have any ideas about that?" Fulton grinned, wiggling the stumpy cigar between his teeth. "Any ideas, soldier?"

"None, sir."

"Suppose it wasn't an Apache that did it. Suppose it was one of my soldiers that shot him. What do you think might happen to him?" Fulton let his arms fall forward and with a clenched fist pounded his impatience on the desk.

"Don't rightly know, sir."

"He could be hung or imprisoned, just like a slave, for years. It would be sad for a fellow like yourself, one that just got out of slavery a few years ago, to spend the rest of his life in a cage like an animal."

"Yes, sir, it would be a shame." Skully's two fingers closed around the razor and he inched it out into his left palm.

"Now then, soldier, did you shoot Diablo?"

"No, sir," Skully answered loudly.

Fulton shot up from his desk. "Don't give me that, soldier," he screamed. "We both know what happened that day, and don't deny it."

"Was an accident, Colonel!" Skully stuttered. "I saw an Apache and shot at him, but the scout rode into my bullet."

Leaning over the desk, Fulton scowled. "Don't lie to me, soldier. You meant to kill one of the men riding with us, now didn't you?"

Skully toyed with pulling the razor and attacking the colonel then, but where would he escape to? Alone he might share the same fate as the pack train escort. Their bloated bodies kept running through his mind as he considered the options. "I don't understands what you's gettin' at, sir."

"Sure you do, soldier. You were aiming for that fellow Garrett."

"I was just shootin' the Apaches. So much was going on, I couldn't'a kept up with him. I thoughts them Apaches was shootin' at me."

Fulton threw his cigar butt to the floor, then picked up a sheaf of papers from his desk. "Let me read you something, soldier. It's my report to headquarters. You listen carefully.

'On the eighth day away from Fort Bansom, our column found an encampment of some thirty Apache lodges. Riding in with drawn weapons, Company C was fired on. Company C returned fire. In the exchange the Apaches lost a dozen braves and one squaw. Cavalry casualties were three men and scout killed, one trooper injured in fall from his horse.' "

Skully scratched his head, then dropped his right hand to his belt, his left hand squeezing the razor. It didn't make sense, the report and what the colonel had figured out. "I'm confused about this," Skully offered.

Fulton dropped the report on his desk. "Let's be honest about this, soldier. You aimed to kill Garrett?" Fulton's voice lacked a sharp edge. The anger Skully was expecting was missing.

Slowly, Skully nodded, wondering if it were wise to confess.

"That's better, soldier."

Having second thoughts, Skully spoke. "But, sir, I was shooting at Apaches."

"Dammit, soldier, don't lie to me again," Fulton shot back, his words sharply honed with anger. "You were aiming for Garrett, weren't you?"

Skully nodded again.

"That's better," Fulton said, the anger in his words had evaporated again. "Now, the report I just read is the report I intend to send headquarters, if you do what I tell you. But if you foul up, I will see you are punished for everything."

Slowly, Skully pushed the razor back up his sleeve.

"This fellow Garrett," Fulton began, "has been a nuisance around here ever since he arrived. I ought to throw him in the stockade and have him tried for interfering with the work of the United States Cavalry. But that takes too long — too much paperwork." He slapped the campaign report for emphasis. "Now, if he were killed, that would sure save a lot of time and work."

Skully scratched at the scar on his cheek, then at the corner of his mouth, his tongue licking his lips as he weighed what the colonel seemed to be suggesting.

"I'm serious, soldier. Here's the proposition. You see that Garrett gets murdered, and we'll take care of you here at the fort. We'll pay off your store debt and treat you better with your purchases and pay you fifty dollars to boot. Interested?"

"He and I has had some differences I'd like to settle, yes sir."

Fulton backed away from the desk, grabbed the arms of his chair and sank back into it. "Now think about what you'll be doing. Don't just go out of there and shoot him yourself. If it comes to that, do it, but you'll still get paid when he's dead no matter who does it. It'll be safer for you if

228

someone else does it, though perhaps not as satisfying."

Skully grinned, nodding with each word.

"Two don'ts, soldier," Fulton cautioned. "Don't feel like you've got to do it today. Take a little time, say a week, to work it out. And don't come to see me or remember this conversation unless I call for you. Can you remember that, soldier?"

Skully nodded.

"Then be gone and be careful."

Sleep was slow in coming as it had been for the past several nights and Skully tossed restlessly in bed. He was no closer to getting Garrett than he had been after the talk with the colonel. Damn if he didn't just want to shoot Garrett or bleed him to death with the razor, but he had grown cautious. No white man had ever done him a favor before. Maybe the colonel was setting him up for something. It would be wise for someone else to do the killing, but how could he spark that?

His thoughts were interrupted by a noise from the adjacent bunk. It was Jonah, sitting up in his bed and looking around the room. Skully feigned sleep, but through the slit in his eyelids he could see Jonah slowly getting up and gathering his clothes, illuminated by the glow of moonlight streaming in through the windows. Jonah was slipping away from his bunk for yet another night. The first few nights, Skully had attributed it to restlessness or the need to take a leak, but now he realized it was more than that.

Jonah pulled on his pants and blouse, then picked up his boots and tiptoed down the center aisle toward the door. As soon as Jonah was out the door, Skully shot up from bed, jerked on his pants and his boots and grabbed his razor and the pistol from the shelf behind his bed. He slipped out the door in time to see Jonah disappearing around the side of the barracks.

The moon was bright and Skully stepped cautiously by the building, clinging to the shadowy recesses as best he could. Up ahead Jonah turned around suddenly and Skully jerked himself as close to the wall as he could, holding his breath. Jonah moved on, from barrack to barrack and then into the clear at the north end of the parade ground. There he ran across the open ground to the front of the sutler's store, then lingered in the shadows, staring back at the barracks. Skully waited until Jonah moved around the side. Then he dashed toward the store. His steps were heavy and when they died beside the building, his heaving breath seemed loud enough to wake up the world. When his breath was under control, he scooted along the side of the adobe wall, ducking under the windows until he reached the back corner of the building. He peeked around the side. He saw Jonah knocking on the back door. After three soft knocks, he heard a voice.

"Is that you, Jonah?" the voice came softly and Skully recognized it as Garrett's.

"Yes," Jonah answered.

Skully heard the door open, then close. When he glanced around the corner, his thumb cocking the hammer on his pistol, Jonah was gone.

What was going on, Skully wondered. He waited several minutes to make sure no one was about to leave the store, then he slipped to the first window. It was dark. On the other side of the back door a soft glow lit another window. Skully squeezed the revolver in his palm. Squatting, he slipped past the first window and the door. The exertion was slight, but his heart pounded little beads of sweat out of his forehead and he fought to hold back his heavy breaths. As he slid his head along the cool adobe wall, his ears detected an unsteady, almost incoherent mumbling coming from a familiar voice — Jonah's. Skully held his breath, then peered quickly through the window, jerking his head back as Garrett walked by inside. Skully's hand shivered for an unsteady moment, then he looked again. Jonah, his back to the window, was standing in the middle of the room as Garrett paced back and forth. Then Garrett stopped, pointing to something in Jonah's hands. Skully smiled. It was a book. Jonah was learning to read.

"Morgan? Morgan!" Tilman called, rapping on the door. "Wake up. You've overslept."

Garrett roused slowly, shaking the sluggishness out of his head and rubbing his eyes with his good hand. The room was awash with light and as soon as his eyes opened to the unexpected brightness, they closed again. The knocking persisted. "Okay, Ben, I hear you," he mumbled.

The door swung open. "We're gonna be late if you don't get to moving." Ben stepped to the chair by the door and tossed Garrett his pants.

Garrett stared at Tilman through narrow slits of eyes. "You've opened the store before without me."

Running his fingers through his disheveled black hair, Tilman grimaced, then smiled sheepishly. "Maybe I forgot to tell you. Today's ration day. We'll help at the issue house."

"Damn. Doing more of Fitzgerald's dirty business."

"If you don't start getting to bed earlier, you're not gonna be doing anybody's business, Morgan. That Jonah is gonna tire you to death. What time did he leave last night?"

Garrett jerked his britches on. "After midnight. He's learning pretty quick."

"Hell, Morgan, don't rush it. What's it been, more than a week of nights like this?"

"About so," Garrett answered, pulling his shirt over his limp arm, then wrestling his good arm down the sleeve.

"You've got time to take it slower. You don't need to wear yourself out."

Garrett shook his head. "Ben, I'm leaving. Plan to tell Jonah tonight, then leave after midnight. Ride hard, in case they come after me."

"But, Morgan, you can't leave me here without —"

"Ben," Garrett said, shoving his feet into his boots, "I plan to deliver your book to Santa Fe and the governor."

"You mean Fitzgerald's book."

"That's a promise I made to you, Ben, and I intend to keep it."

"I knew you would. Yes, sir, I knew you

would, but I'm not sure the time is right."

Garrett laughed. "No good time, Ben. At least this way, we make the first move instead of them surprising us."

Ben rubbed his hands together and stared at the floor. "It makes me uneasy, a churning in my gut, like a coward."

"Even brave men get a feeling like that, though not all are brave enough to admit it."

His shoulders drooping forward, Ben clenched his fist until his knuckles whitened. "I wish you were right."

"We can talk about it later," Morgan suggested, motioning to the door. "We wouldn't want to anger Fitzgerald by not being on time, would we?"

Face after empty face, staring at him with hollow eyes, passed before Garrett at the issue table until he could no longer look back. He tugged his hat over his eyes and stared at the stomachs, taut with a hunger that Fitzgerald's meager rations would never fill. Their faces etched with submission, their shoulders slumped like those of a dog well beaten, the Navajos advanced one by one like a line of interminable ants, all morning and through the noon hour until Garrett thought he could stand no more. Their progress was slowed by Tilman, who Fitzgerald had assigned to Diablo's old duties of carrying the rations from the back and slitting the sacks open. Though weaker and slower than Diablo, Tilman refused to dump the flour and sugar on the naked ground, leaving the rations in their sacks instead. When the Navajos had finished the last sack, Garrett stood up and sighed. At least Fitzgerald had excused himself from the rationing table after the first allotments and had not returned, not even after the last Navajo passed before the table.

After the last sack, Tilman, his eyes heavy with exhaustion, staggered to the table and fell into Fitzgerald's empty chair.

"You're not big enough in the britches to handle all that lifting," Garrett said. "At least it's done. You can fall into bed at the sutler's and I'll watch after the store."

Tilman shrugged, trying to control his heaving breath. "It's not over yet."

Garrett looked down at the ledger book totals. "My figures show we've fed all the Navajos, Ben."

"You're forgetting something, Morgan." Tilman leaned back in the chair and ran his fingers through his sweat-matted hair. "The Apaches."

"Damn," said Garrett, "I've had about all

of this I care to take."

"Let it pass, Morgan," Tilman said, his chair settling forward and nearer Garrett as an officer passed. "Tonight you'll be through with this." Ben ran both hands through his hair, then unhooked his glasses to wipe away a film of grime.

"Ben, you're right. You're talking now like some of my smarts have rubbed off on you."

"Yeah," Tilman spit at his feet, "and some of my distaste for this place has finally caught up with you." He struggled to his feet at the sound of the guards, shouting and cursing, as they brought the Apaches to the issue house. "By the sound of things, damn troopers haven't forgotten about the pack mule massacre." Tilman turned to bring out more ration sacks.

"If I had two good arms, I'd handle the hauling for you, Ben."

"Divine punishment, Morgan, for my spineless part in this fraud." He walked away without looking at Garrett.

Garrett dipped his pen in the inkwell and waited for the first Apache to step forward upon the command of the troops. The black sergeant at the head of the line ordered the first woman to advance and when she hesitated, he shoved her with the butt of his carbine, almost daring her to try an escape.

The squaw stumbled to the ground, picked herself up as quick as a cat and spit at the soldier's boots before he realized what she had done. Then she moved forward, as did the others behind her, until she reached Garrett's post.

As Garrett looked at her, she said something he could not understand, then stepped beyond the table. Though her face was lined with hunger, like that of the Navajos, there still burned in her eyes a flame of defiance. She carried herself erect and proud, and the women, children and old men that followed shared her burning hostility. When the Apaches were turned loose on the open sacks of flour and sugar, they scrambled for the food with a determination equal to the Navajos, but by their scowls they seemed to be telling the soldiers that the ultimate revenge for their treatment would belong to their Apache husbands and sons, brothers and fathers.

Though each Apache spoke to Garrett, he could not understand them and shortly he took to avoiding their gazes, ashamed of his part in their humiliation. Finally one Apache woman stood before him and said more than a few words. He glanced up from the ledger. It was the wife of Pachise. She continued to speak, even as a gruff trooper stepped toward her, motioning with the butt of his gun for her to advance.

"Move on, up there," the soldier yelled as he neared her.

The woman planted her feet in front of the table and extended her hand toward her daughter, who advanced shyly to her mother's side, half hiding behind her.

Garrett smiled and reached across the table, patting the young girl on the cheek.

"Dammit," the soldier yelled, "advance so we can proceed with our business."

Ignoring the soldier, the wife of Pachise lifted her hands to her neck and for a hesitant moment fingered the bear-claw necklace hanging over her doeskin blouse. The black claws were separated on the rawhide thong by scarlet, black and brown stones, highly polished by a mountain stream. Then she bowed her head and pulled the necklace over her raven hair. Cupping the necklace in both her hands, she offered it to Garrett as she lifted her eyes to his.

At first Garrett held his hand back, but as she leaned closer, he opened his palm. She placed the necklace gently in his extended hand, then squeezed the necklace a last loving time.

"No," Garrett said, "you must keep it."

The woman did not comprehend for a moment, but then she smiled broadly, the whiteness of her teeth a sharp contrast to her hair and sun-darkened skin. Taking the necklace from him, the woman stretched even farther across the table and draped the necklace over Garrett's head and around his neck. Garrett nodded his appreciation and Pachise's wife offered a final smile.

But her grin was fleeting as a soldier stepped beside her and shoved her away from the table. Though stumbling off the porch, she kept her balance. Instantly, her daughter kicked the soldier in the shin. The soldier, more embarrassed than pained by the girl's leather moccasins, swung the barrel of his carbine at the girl. She ducked out of danger and under the table.

Garrett shot up from his seat and grabbed the barrel of the carbine. "No need for that, soldier."

"Don't talk to me, Injun lover," the soldier scowled. "My orders say keep this line movin', an' I'm gonna do my job."

The little girl scampered from under the table on Garrett's side and circled the soldier to her mother.

"Now we'll continue, soldier," Garrett said, shoving the carbine barrel away from himself.

The trooper scowled. "You don't give me orders 'cause I ain't your Jonah."

Garrett nodded as he settled back into his seat. "You don't have enough pride to be Jonah." Looking down the line at the remaining Apaches, he called, "Next."

Skully was waiting as Jonah emerged from the stables.

"You's looking a little tired, Jonah, like when Grant was killed. You been gettin' good sleep?"

"I has, Skully," Jonah said, then stared back. "What makes you think different?"

"You just been gettin' up a lot lately to take a leak."

Jonah shrugged and walked away. "We gots work to do in the gardens. Won't be long until we gets some good eats for our meals."

Skully trailed after Jonah. "Tells you what, Jonah — I ain't interested in no garden work, but I could sure use a swim." He caught up with Jonah and stared into eyes reddened from too little sleep.

"Maybe this one time, Skully. I don't much wants to do any field work tonight." Jonah hesitated. "Fact, that sounds good to me, maybe give me a little more liveliness."

They circled behind the barracks to the

cottonwoods lining the Loco River. They advanced from tree to tree until they were beyond the fort compound, the gardens and the issue house. At a narrow river crook about a mile from the fort, they undressed quickly, Skully all the time staring at Jonah and gauging him. When both were naked, Jonah waved his arm at Jonah. "You first."

Though the river where they stood was only five feet deep, it was the deepest spot the soldiers had ever found and they called it their swimming hole. Jonah stood on a rock above the river, poised for a moment like a flawless statue, then jumped into the murky water.

"Whoa, it's cold," he shouted as his head shot out from under the water. "Damn, it feels good. Are you comin' in?"

Skully scratched the pink scars traversing his body from his chest to his back, then jumped for Jonah, who dodged his assault. Skully sprang up from beneath the rippling brown surface. "Weeee, jubilee, you is righter than rain! This water's like ice! Don't it feel good? I could stay here all day and night. Hell with the Indians, hell with the Army, hell with all New Mexico, 'cept for this damned salty river."

"I sure agrees with you, Skully." Jonah splashed water at his partner and Skully fired back. "This a good way to end issue day and all the extra chores we's got to do."

"Ain't it funny on issue day, Jonah, to see them savage Indians scramblin' around on their hands and knees when they pass out the rations?"

Jonah stood up in the water, shaking his head. "I's always wondered if they feel likes we did when we was slaves."

"Don't know about that, Jonah," Skully said, floating on his back, "but I did hear that Garrett man received a necklace from Pachise's squaw and he keep on wearin' it."

"Now you leave Morgan, er, Mister Garrett out of any plans you has got for trouble. He's been good to me."

"But he's been friendly with that squaw, and her buck husband's the one that killed Grant — you haven't forgots your favorite Army horse, have you — and the one that ambushed the pack mule detail."

Jonah didn't answer. For several minutes the two men squatted in silence in the river, watching the last hues of the sun casting colorful coins upon the river. When Skully felt Jonah was totally relaxed, he spoke.

"How's the readin' lessons goin'?"

Jonah stopped, deathly still, except for his widening eyes and gaping mouth.

"What's that?"

"How's the readin' lessons goin'?"

"What you talkin' about, Skully?"

Skully maneuvered closer to Jonah. "Now, Jonah, you knows whats I'm talkin' about. That man Garrett been teachin' you to reads at night. Colonel Stubby probably won't likes it if he find out."

"Ain't nobody supposed to know about that but me and Morgan and the other runty fellow there at the store. How'd you find out?"

Skully's eyes narrowed and his lips tightened. "Jus' keeping my ears open and I picks it up."

Jonah shook his head. "That can't be, 'cause I didn't tell nobody. Must be that runty Ben."

"Not the way I heard it, Jonah."

"No," Jonah said, shaking his fist at Skully. "No, it wasn't Mister Morgan Garrett — he's not that way."

"Believes what you wants, Jonah, but I's been hearin' things from our buddies. Fact is, they been laughin' at you for lettin' Garrett snooker you like this."

Jonah scratched his head, then plowed through the muddy water toward Skully. "He's not snookering me. He's helpin' me out." He turned from Jonah and waded to the bank.

"Helpin' you out?" Skully laughed. "He's gettin' you in trouble. Wait till word gets around to Colonel Stubby what you've been doin'. Then you'll sees who's your friends and who's not. I hates to say it, Jonah, buts you've gots a thick skull when it comes to learnin' to read. The boys won't admits it, but they're snickering behind your back."

Shaking the wetness off his glistening body, Jonah turned to face Skully. "Don't bother me none if they wants to laugh at a man tryin' to learn to read and better hisself. Might do them some good instead of all playing poker."

"It's not jus' the readin' lessons they laughin' at. They . . ." Skully stopped, turned away from Jonah and swam toward the middle of the river.

"What do you means by that, Skully?" Jonah pulled his trousers on and waited for Skully to swim back. Then he repeated his question.

"I don'ts really wants to tell you 'bout that, Jonah."

"Spit it out, Skully," Jonah ordered. "We been friends, no secrets between us."

"I hasn't been wantin' to have to tell you, Jonah." Skully stood up in the water and cut toward the bank. "You see, Garrett's been braggin' to some of the white officers

244

you and he is brothers. He tolds them his pappy slipped down to the shacks and rapes your mammy. You're the result."

Jonah's chin dropped to his chest. "It's not true, Skully," Jonah answered calmly.

Shrugging, Skully spoke lowly. "Now, Jonah, I ain't sayin' it's the truth. I's just telling you whats I've heard."

Reaching down for his Army blouse, Jonah looked up at Skully. "Why would he want to tell lies like that?"

Skully spit in the water. "You got to remember, Jonah, all you are is a one-time nigger slave, and now you're just a nigger to him."

"But he's tryin' to help me learn. I's reading some small words, thanks to him. He wouldn't'a taught me the alphabet, if he was sayin' those things abouts me."

Skully emerged from the water and approached Jonah. Patting him on the back, Skully answered. "He's a hard man to figure out. Sorry I had to bust your gut on it, but somebody did 'fore things went too far and you was in trouble."

Jonah looked up from the ground, his jaw set, his eyes aflame. "I may want to see Garrett tonight, show him we ain't brothers."

# CHAPTER 12

Jonah was late and for half an hour Garrett paced his narrow room, anxious for his student to arrive. The knot of dread in his stomach drew tighter as Garrett wondered how best to tell Jonah that tomorrow he would leave Fort Bansom. Jonah deserved an explanation, maybe for a lot of things, but this desertion most of all.

Garrett fingered the bear claw necklace still around his neck like an amulet. He was anxious to leave this cesspool of corruption. He would take Tilman's purloined book to Santa Fe, but he had his doubts, though he had never expressed them to Tilman, that the governor would do anything. The governor might be profiting from the graft himself. Garrett shrugged as he sat down on the edge of his bed and started to pull off a boot. Jonah must not be coming, Garrett thought, and perhaps just as well. No explanation could ever erase the disappointment that would wash over Jonah. He removed his other boot and dropped it on the floor, then laid back on the bed and unfastened his gunbelt. As he arched his back and pulled the gunbelt from under him, a pounding came at the back door and a pulse of dread tightened in his muscles as he pushed himself up from his mattress. The knocking came again, harder, louder than was Jonah's custom.

Slipping into the hall, Garrett glanced at Tilman propped up on his bed, reading. "Anxious for his lesson, isn't he?" Tilman said, glancing up from his book.

Garrett eased down the narrow hall to the door. Lifting the bar, he called out, "Who is it?" At the sound of an unfamiliar voice, he let the bar fall back in place.

"The stable sergeant," came the reply.

"What do you want?" Garrett asked.

"Need to see Mr. Garrett."

"You're speaking to him." Down the hall, Garrett heard Tilman moving about.

"Sorry to be botherin' you this time of night, sir," the trooper began.

Before the stable sergeant could finish, Tilman was by the door, inserting Garrett's revolver in his good hand.

"Go on soldier," Garrett called.

"It's your hoss, sir. Somethin' seems to be

247

wrong with him. I don't know what to do with him, acting funny an' all. You might want to come see for yourself."

Garrett motioned for Ben to unbar the door and the clerk responded quickly. With the same hand that held his gun, Garrett cracked the door open. In the bright moonlight, he saw a solitary soldier with hat in hand. "I'll be with you in a few minutes," Garrett answered. "You go on back and tend to him until I get there."

The soldier nodded, replacing his hat and moving around the side of the building. Garrett stuck his head outside, quickly glancing both ways for others, then slipped out the door to the corner of the building. He spotted no one but the sergeant walking back toward the stable. Garrett retreated inside.

"Damn bad luck, Ben, if it is luck."

Tilman barred the door behind him. "You're mighty suspicious, Morgan."

"Could be a ruse," Garrett said as Tilman trailed him back to his room. "You ought to be a little suspicious, too. You've got a stake in my well-being." Garrett placed his revolver on his pillow, then slumped onto his bed and gathered his boots. He struggled with them until his feet were inside.

"Anything I can do, Morgan?" Tilman

asked, the thick lenses of his glasses magnifying the worry in his eyes.

Garrett bent over and fished his carbine from under the bed. As he stood, he dropped the carbine on the bed by his pistol. "Help me buckle my holster on, Ben. Unless you change your beliefs enough to carry a gun, that's all you can do." Garrett watched Tilman's eyes tear up with a film of fear, and he regretted his remark.

His face reddened with shame, Tilman edged toward the bed, retrieved the holster and buckled it around Garrett's waist without once looking up. Garrett picked up his revolver and shoved it deep into his holster, then grabbed the carbine, holding it for a moment over the bed, then releasing it onto the covers. "No sense carrying more guns than a lame-armed man can handle," he said, turning to Tilman. "Let me out the front door, in case someone figures me to leave by the back." Garrett led the way down the hall to the front room. Tilman fumbled at the bar across the door, almost dropping it before he cracked the door enough for Garrett to exit.

"Good luck," he whispered as Garrett vanished into the shadows where no moonlight could seep.

For several minutes, Garrett clung to the

dark porch, his eyes searching the surroundings for something out of order, his ears straining to pick up an unnatural sound, his muscles tensing with anticipation. Then he shot off the porch like a surprised coyote looking for cover. His good hand riding on his holstered revolver, he covered the distance from the store to the nearest barrack quickly, staying long enough out of the moonlight to catch his breath, then dashing for the next barrack, carefully avoiding the graveled path between buildings. There, as he attached himself to another reclusive shadow and held his breath, the noise of hesitant boots on the gravelly path behind him pricked his ears. Drawing his revolver, Garrett stared toward the noise. He glimpsed a sudden movement. A narrow figure evaporated into the shadows before Garrett could focus on it. Lifting the revolver to his chest, Garrett felt the cold steel through his shirt as he cocked the hammer. Clinging to the shadows like moss to a tree, Garrett slipped along the barrack's wall to the corner and out of line from his stalker. Garrett waited a moment, then peered with one eye around the corner. As he watched, a rifle barrel emerged from the shadowy side of the adjacent building, the moonlight slowly crawling along its shiny metal. It had been a trick, Garrett thought as he brought his pistol around toward the vague figure lingering uncertainly in the edge of the shadow. His stalker had lost his quarry, Garrett thought, and feared leaving his hiding place.

Then the stalker shot from the shadows. Garrett caught his breath. It was Tilman. Damn if that wasn't a good way to get killed. Garrett eased the hammer down on his pistol and shoved it back in its holster, both pleased and annoyed that Tilman had followed to help after all. Now Tilman was in the shadows of the building that offered Garrett cover and Garrett could hear Tilman's heavy breath and his light footsteps as he approached Garrett's corner. As Tilman walked by, Garrett's good hand struck like a snake for Tilman's mouth, covered it and jerked Tilman hard back against him.

"It's me, Ben," Garrett whispered, gradually letting loose of the trembling Tilman.

"You — you," Tilman stammered, then caught his breath. "You scared me, Morgan."

"I appreciate your help, Ben," Garrett whispered, "but you best let me know next time or I might kill you instead of scare you."

"Sorry, Morgan, it just took me a while to

screw up my courage."

"Now listen, Ben — follow me at a distance. Stay outside the stable unless you hear trouble. Then come in firing. You understand?"

Tilman nodded.

"Let's get it over with," Garrett said. "I still don't like this."

Garrett moved away from the cover of one building to another until he reached the clearing between the final barrack and the stables. He trotted across the open ground to the stable door. He drew his revolver again and cracked the door enough to spy inside. Nothing seemed out of order so he opened the door enough to pass through. Moving slowly, cautious as a thief, he entered.

"Over here," a voice called from toward the end of a row of stalls. Garrett recognized the voice as that of the stable sergeant and turned to his right. The stable sergeant was waving a lantern above his head. "Your horse is down."

Reholstering his pistol, Garrett marched quickly between the twin row of stalls. As he passed, the other horses turned skittish. Though he could see their heads and rumps above the stall slats, he could not see his chestnut. The animal must be down as the stable sergeant said. Garrett trotted forward staring intently at the last stall, too late to react to the sudden movement he saw out of the corner of his eye. A mob of blue-clad soldiers lunged from the cover of the stalls at Garrett, one grabbing his legs, another pinning his good arm, a third pushing him backward. Garrett tumbled to the ground and gasped as the weight of three or more soldiers collapsed on him. He twisted his arm free and grabbed for his holster. His hand brushed against his revolver as it was jerked from its holster by one of his attackers. As he tried to yell, he felt his mouth covered by a sweaty hand smelling of damp hay. He bit it and the soldier screamed but held on. He struggled briefly, but there were too many of them. Now it was up to Tilman.

"Pick him up," ordered a recognizable voice. It was Skully. "We don't want to get these horses too riled up."

A dozen hands jerked Garrett from the ground, as if he were a side of beef, then stood him straight up until Garrett stared into the beady eyes of Skully.

His lips twitching with anticipation across his taut face, Skully lifted Garrett's gun and pointed it between Garrett's eyes. "I ought to kill you now, with your own damn gun."

He cocked the hammer. Garrett spit at him and Skully laughed. "I want to kill you, but only one man here deserves to. Take him out in the corral, boys." Skully eased the hammer down on the pistol and threw it at the stable door. "You won't be needin' that ever again."

With his captors shoving him toward a rear door, Garrett struggled to hold his balance. Where was Tilman? Half shoving and half carrying him, his captors kicked open the back door and pushed him through it into the moonlight. Garrett felt a boot in the small of his back and it propelled him forward onto the ground as the others released their grips. As Garrett stood up, his eyes adjusted to the moonlight and he saw more soldiers, several now lighting lanterns, gathering about him in a broad ring. There was no avenue of escape now. There was only Tilman, his only ally — a weak one at that. Garrett turned slowly around, staring silently at his captors, standing quietly behind the circle of lanterns. Garrett looked for Skully and was surprised when a shirtless black man, tall and muscular, stepped into the circle opposite him. It was Jonah.

"You been tellin' lies about me, Mr. Garrett," Jonah called out for everyone to

hear. "Now I intends to change that forever."

Garrett backed away from Jonah. "What
are you talking about, Jonah?"

"I may be a slave once, but I ain't as dumb
as you may think, spreadin' all those lies."

"What lies, Jonah? Dammit, what lies?"
Even in the dim light, Garrett could see the
anger in Jonah's eyes. It was ready to
explode and Garrett could not understand
why.

"Thoughts you could make an ass out of
me in front of all these boys, now didn't
you?" Jonah circled Garrett step for step. "I
ain't that dumb. May not know how to read,
but I ain't that dumb."

"Somebody's been telling you lies, Jonah."
Garrett could feel his own futile anger rising. "Who? Skully?"

Jonah jerked off his hat and threw it
outside the ring of lanterns. "Thought you'd
give me readin' lessons, then turn me in to
Stubby and get me in big trouble with the
colonel."

"I didn't tell anyone."

Spitting at Garrett, Jonah yelled. "It's a
lie. Skully and the others knew." The watching soldiers grunted agreement. "And then
you spreadin' stories about my momma

havin' me by your father and you laughin' at it."

"What Jonah? Which of your black bastard friends started that? Was it Skully?"

Jonah lunged at Garrett. "Damn you, Garrett, don't you be callin' any of us bastards after whats you said of my momma."

Dodging Jonah, Garrett shouted. "Damn you, Jonah, if you aren't crazier than a loon."

"Been tellin' people around here your pappy was my pappy. It's a lie. You know it's a lie?"

"That's right, Jonah, it is a lie, one somebody else started. I told no one you were learning to read. I was helping you. Thought you wanted that."

Jonah lunged at Garrett again, like a cat pawing at a trapped mouse. "Your folks coulda let me learn to read when I's a slave, but they didn't and you didn't help."

Garrett nodded. "That's right, Jonah, I didn't. They could've beaten you like some masters beat their slaves, but they didn't. Maybe if they had, or if I'd whipped you before now, you'd learned to accept the truth when a man speaks it."

"Take back what you said about your pappy rapin' my momma or I'm gonna kill you."

"I'm not taking back what I never said, Jonah. If you want to kill me, then come ahead. The odds are on your side. But when it's over, you just remember you made a bastard out of yourself by believing this. I didn't do it. So come on — the talking's over."

Jonah half squatted, then lunged forward. In his anger, he swung blindly and missed. Off balance, he stumbled forward, Garrett turning in behind him and kicking him to the ground.

"You need help beating this one-armed man, Jonah?" Garrett sneered as the corporal picked himself back up.

Answering with a big roar, Jonah lowered his head and plowed forward into Garrett, both men crashing to the ground, breathless. Garrett clambered to his feet first, but not soon enough to have any advantage over Jonah.

Garrett charged Jonah and with his fist tried for Jonah's belly, but the corporal dodged and retaliated with a massive blow that grazed Garrett's ear and glanced off his shoulder.

"It's not as easy to whip a cripple as you thought, you bastard," Garrett shouted out, knowing his only hope against Jonah was to enrage him so he could not control himself.

Jonah lunged for Garrett and the crippled man flung himself away, dodging Jonah's swiping hand which brushed the bearclaw necklace. Jonah backed away and flexed his arms, then screamed, wrenching the anger from deep in his lungs. He launched his rush with a second scream and flung his fists wildly at his crippled prey.

Feinting to his left, then sliding to his right, Garrett felt the heat in Jonah's breath as he slipped by him. Before he escaped Jonah's reach, he felt the iron in the corporal's fist as it struck his good shoulder. A searing pain burned its way into his chest and his arm. He wriggled his fingers and they seemed to work, despite a terrible throbbing the length of his arm.

Jonah, sensing Garrett's vulnerability, stopped a moment. "Now you'll die."

Doubling his fist, Garrett charged at Jonah. With all the strength he could muster he slammed his fist into Jonah's jaw. The corporal flinched, but stood as if his feet were anchored to the ground. Garrett screamed at the agony flooding his arm, but drew back and aimed for Jonah's nose.

As Garrett flung his fist at Jonah's face, the corporal laughed, his hand grabbing Garrett's wrist and wrapping around it as tight and unbreakable as iron manacles. As

Jonah pulled him closer, Garrett could see a trickle of blood running down the corner of the corporal's mouth, could smell Jonah's spiteful sweat and could hear the heavy hatred in his labored breath. Jonah opened his mouth to gloat. But before he could speak, Garrett kicked him in the crotch. Jonah shrieked, his hand falling away from Garrett's wrist toward his groin. He stared blankly at Garrett, then doubled forward onto his knees, groaning, his torso swaying at the agonizing spasms pricking his body like a thousand briars.

Garrett stumbled away from Jonah. "No bastard children for you now, Jonah." He shook his arm hard to rid it of its numbness, as he backed to the edge of the ring of lanterns. Reaching the perimeter, he stooped over a lantern and grabbed the handle before anyone could stop him. He twirled the lantern above his head and stepped for Jonah, still gasping for breath on the ground.

"Watch it!" cried Skully as Garrett flung the lantern at Jonah.

The corporal flattened himself on the ground, and the lantern sailed past him, striking the ground and flashing into a puddle of fire. Like the flames beyond him, Jonah rose up and staggered toward Garrett, his arms stretched wide and dangerous like an angered bear's. Garrett kicked savagely for Jonah's groin again, but his boot glanced off his thigh away from the crotch. Jonah grabbed Garrett around the chest, squeezing until he sucked for air, and then with all his muscles, Jonah heaved Garrett to the ground.

As he crashed into the dirt Garrett felt pain exploding so savagely through his body that even his limp arm tingled. He struggled up on his knees, his stomach tumbled in queasiness made worse when his nose drew in deeply a breath of the smoke from the burning lamp. Lifting his head, he could see Jonah towering over him. Garrett backed away from Jonah until the heat from the fire scorched his flesh, then he drained the last of his strength to stand up and stagger away from the fire. Jonah followed. Garrett turned around to face Jonah and saw only the darkness of a huge black fist plowing into his jaw and across his nose. A thousand lights burst through his mind and dimly he could feel the pain receding into some distant corner of his brain as he fought with himself to stay conscious, to stay alive. He could sense Jonah's hard fists striking his face, but in his numbness they seemed to be hitting some other man. Jonah mumbled something as he pummeled Garrett, but the downed man could not understand what he said.

And then the barrage of fists stopped and Garrett felt a tightening around his neck. He heaved and bucked against it, not because of the pain — there was none — but from instinct, but he could not shake the heavy weight upon him. The pressure around his neck grew stronger and Garrett gasped for air, but none came. Then the pinpoints of pain seemed to ring his neck and he remembered the bearclaw necklace. He realized he was being strangled. His strength rapidly draining from no air, he bucked at Jonah, but the corporal was a solid, bullish brute not to be denied. Garrett clawed weakly at Jonah, but with so little strength Jonah's skin seemed as impenetrable as a tortoise shell. He could taste blood in his mouth. He was thirsty and his mind could no longer sort out what was happening. And then as he blacked out, Garrett heard an explosion that seemed to come from outside his body instead of inside his brain. Instantly, his body flattened beneath a heavy load.

When he came to, Garrett first thought he had been buried without a coffin, the weight of dirt heavy upon him. But there were noises, too. From somewhere nearby came the sounds of shots and yelling. Garrett's head seemed to spin around like a wagon wheel as he tried to open his eyelids. He pried them open through the stickiness upon his face and he batted them toward the sky, the moon and stars twirling around the heavens. He shut his eyes and the dizziness lingered, made worse as he tried to sort out for himself what had happened. The dizziness worsened his pain and he wretched, but there was nothing in his stomach to sacrifice to the agony. He pushed against the lump atop him and remembered Jonah and the fight. Jonah's shoulder pressed against Garrett's neck, and as Garrett squirmed from under him, he brushed against the black man's kinky hair. With his good arm, Garrett pushed at Jonah's face. From the cool of Jonah's flesh, Garrett knew the corporal was dead. Dragging himself from under Jonah's weight, Garrett drew a deep breath, and the air, still reeking of burning coal oil, seemed suddenly invigorating. Garrett crawled to his hands and knees, opening his eyes again. The ring of lanterns and the stable to one side seemed to move in a circle like a carousel. Gradually, the circle of a thousand spinning lanterns took focus along with the stable nearby.

Somewhere beyond the corral and down by the river, Garrett could hear gunfire and confusion, but at the stable he was alone, except for Jonah. A pool of Jonah's blood puddled on the ground, almost shining in the light of the lamps. Garrett crawled closer to Jonah and drew his hand across the corporal's forehead. "I'm sorry, Jonah. I wish I knew who'd killed you." Tilman had finally saved him, and though he had pulled the trigger, Garrett knew Ben wasn't the real murderer. Whoever had filled Jonah with lies was responsible, and Garrett figured Skully the culprit.

Garrett struggled to his feet. The earth quivered beneath him and he feared for a moment that he would fall. Though he willed his muscles still, they shook and quivered as he tried to control them. Down beyond the river, the noise of yelling and shooting seemed to be fading into the distance. Ben? The thought suddenly cracked through the mud in his brain. Were the troops tracking Tilman after he shot Jonah? Damn. Garrett wanted to aid Ben, but there was nothing he could do in his condition. He staggered to the rear stable door, with each step watching the ground to make sure it was still there. Inside the stable where the smell of manure and hay was thick, he stumbled on something and realized it was his pistol. He bent slightly forward, then straightened, knowing if he dropped to get his pistol, he might lack the strength to get up. He would leave it. Left foot, right foot, left foot, right foot, one in front of the other, Garrett kept reminding himself as he marched out of the stable and the length of the endless parade ground. When he reached the sutler's store, he lifted his heavy leg upon the wooden walk, but stumbled into the door which flew open as he collapsed onto the rough-hewn wooden floor.

The cool moisture soothed the heat of his bruised face. He squinted through the slits of his eyelids and made out the blurred form of Ben. As his senses fell back into place, Garrett realized he was sprawled across his bed. He tried to lift his head and winced from the pain shooting through his brain like hot lead. He sank back into the bed.

"Easy, fellow," Tilman offered. "You took quite a beating. Don't look none too pretty, neither, but best I can tell you'll make it. You got to, Morgan, for both of us."

Nodding softly so as not to rile the aches in his brain, Garrett swallowed the little moisture his cotton mouth could muster. The effort hurt from the top of his jaw down into his stomach and he reached instinctively for his neck, his hand tugging at the bearclaw necklace.

"I tried to get it off your head," Ben apologized, "but failed at it, just like so many other things. He almost strangled you with it from the look of the bruises about your neck and the cuts where the claws dug in." Tilman drew the damp rag across Garrett's face a final time and dropped it in a basin beside the bed. "Maybe this will help."

Garrett heard Tilman uncork a bottle, then felt Ben's soft hand slipping under his head and lifting him gently up.

"This is easier to do when you're awake and not groaning," Ben apologized again. "This'll help you once you take a swig."

Smelling the liquor's pungency, Garrett parted his lips and let the whiskey fill his gritty mouth. He relished the wetness. Sloshing it around his mouth, he swallowed easily, but the pain trailed the liquid all the way into his stomach. After a second mouthful and tentative swallow, he signaled he had had enough and Tilman eased his head down.

After a few minutes the liquor eased some of the pain and Garrett worked his jaw from side to side as he opened it wide. It felt like hell, but at least it worked. "Thanks, Ben," he struggled for a breath, ". . . for helping me last night."

Tilman sighed deeply. "It was the least I could do, Morgan, cleaning you and putting you back in bed."

"No, Ben," Garrett said as he peered up through the narrow crack of his eyelids, ". . . for shooting Jonah."

Walking away from the bed, Tilman took a swig from the amber bottle. "I wish I had, Morgan, I wish I had — but it wasn't me."

Garrett fought the spinning pains in his head to sit up but he fell back down from the dizziness. "Dammit, Ben, no one else on this fort would've done it."

"Somebody did, but it wasn't me. Honest, Morgan. I shouldn't tell you this, but I just couldn't pull the trigger, even with you being my only friend." Tilman's voice trailed off into fog of embarrassment.

"Bring me the carbine, Ben," Garrett commanded with all the force his aching lungs could muster. "Hold the barrel up to my nose."

Tilman shrugged and returned to the bed, pulling the carbine from beneath. Reluctantly, he lifted the barrel to Garrett's head.

After sniffing at the barrel, Garrett brushed the carbine away with a sweep of his hand. "It smells fresh fired. Too much powder odor, Ben. Quit lying to yourself."

"I tried to squeeze that trigger, Morgan, really did," Tilman's voice was almost breaking. "Then a shot was fired from behind me and I panicked. I ran back to the store as fast as I could." He paused, then added in a lesser voice. "In my panic, I tripped and the gun went off when I fell."

"You killed him or he'd've killed me." Garrett paused to catch his breath. "I know you got beliefs about killing, but no god will hold that one against you. If you took one life, you saved another."

Tilman shoved the carbine back under the bed. His shoulders slumping, he moved to the window. "I wish it were true, Morgan, but I failed you. And then after that first shot, all hell broke loose. Shooting seemed to be coming from everywhere. I was scared and didn't know what happened. And then today, with all the activity at the fort, I find out Pachise raided the reservation and escaped with the Apaches."

Garrett coughed and cried out as the movement seared his tender ribs. "Your secret's good with me, Ben, but don't try to hide the truth from yourself."

"You gotta believe me, Morgan," Tilman said, anger mounting with each syllable. "I was trying to pull the trigger. I could feel my whole body straining to pull it, but I couldn't. My cowardice stopped me. I was scared. I thought you were dead. Then I heard a shot from behind me. I heard the bullet whiz over my shoulder. I got more scared because I figured someone was after me. I glanced in the corral, saw the soldiers scattering like quail and you — dead I thought — beneath Jonah in a heap on the ground. I ran back here faster, scareder than I'd ever been in my life. And when I got here, I was shaking like a flag in a breeze, and all I could do was wait and cry." Ben swallowed hard. "That's right — cry like a child because I'd failed to save my only friend in this world. I'm sorry, Morgan, but you don't owe me thanks. You ought to shoot me yourself for failing you." Tilman shrugged and strode to the door. He stopped for a moment as if he were pondering what to say next, then slipped into the hall shutting the door behind him and his guilt.

"Thanks, Ben," Garrett whispered, settling back into his mattress. "Your secret's safe with me."

Garrett's body demanded sleep and instantly he obliged, falling into a deep, dreamless trance. Not knowing when it started, he could not tell how long it lasted before he felt someone briskly shaking his shoulder.

"Morgan, Morgan, wake up."

It was Tilman and he was careless with Garrett's aches.

"Out front, Morgan — there are two officers that want you to go with them to see Colonel Stubby."

"Tell the bastards I'm not well."

"But, Morgan . . ." Tilman's voice trailed off into a gasp as he looked up at the two officers standing in the open door.

"Tell him," the captain stated, "the bastards are here for him, and here for him now."

Garrett opened his eyes slowly and, thankfully, without pain. He twisted his head toward the door, noting the captain standing with drawn service revolver. "Hunting Apache women today? None are hiding here, so you won't be needing the gun."

"We need you, Garrett, and no foolishness, not after the Apaches escaped last night," the captain said. "Colonel Fulton demands to see you immediately and you'd best accompany us. A lot of the troopers'd like to get their hands on you for killing the corporal."

"Your facts are wrong, captain."

"That'll be for the colonel to decide, Garrett."

Sitting up slowly on the thin husk mattress, Garrett rubbed his eyes with his sore hand and could feel a dull throb of pain in his lame arm. He eased his feet off the edge of his bed and leaned forward, then upward until he stood shakily in front of the captain. Garrett glanced at the bruises on his arm, then caught the shirt and britches Tilman tossed to him. Still slightly dizzy, he tottered a moment after catching his clothes, then his sore chin jutted forward with determination. These soldiers would not see him stagger again. As quick as his good hand would let him, he pulled his clothes over his bruised body and then tugged on his boots and marched wordlessly out of the store ahead of the two officers.

The distance between the sutler's and the headquarters seemed insurmountable as Garrett stepped into the midday sunlight. The glare and the heat, shimmering in waves across the parade ground, uncovered the bursting pains that had been buried in the recesses of his brain. And when Garrett finally reached the headquarters porch, his muscles grew slack with fatigue. He stopped by a window and steadied himself against the wall until the faintness passed. Stepping away from the wall, his gaze lingered on the window. Slowly he realized Colonel Fulton was staring out at him. Anger surged inside him and propelled him forward just as the captain spoke.

"Move, dammit — don't keep the colonel waiting." With exaggerated steps, the captain vaulted ahead of Garrett to the building and straight to the colonel's door, pausing only for Garrett to catch up. "Colonel," the captain stated, "I've brought your man."

Fulton grunted his acknowledgement without turning from the window where he stood like a disheveled emperor surveying his declining kingdom. When the door clicked shut behind the entering lieutenant, Fulton turned around, his lips distorted around the ugly stub of an unlit cigar. His lips quivered with glee as a sliver of a smile squeezed between his unshaven cheeks. "Nothing but trouble from you since you arrived here, Garrett," Fulton started.

Garrett gathered his strength and straightened his aching body to its full height. "Won't be half the trouble that I cause for you after I leave."

"Ha!" Fulton cried with an unstable

laugh. He stepped to the desk and leaned forward on balled fists, his unblinking eyes wide with the anticipation of a wolf over downed game. "You won't be leaving this fort, not after killing one of my boys."

"Didn't kill him, Colonel, and you know it, even if you won't admit it." Garrett jerked his hand to his mouth to cover a cough and Fulton flinched back away from the desk.

"Didn't kill him?" Fulton mumbled. "Didn't kill him? Then how do you explain this?" The colonel grabbed something from his desk and shoved it toward Garrett. "Recognize this? You should — it's your own damn revolver." He dropped it back on the desk. "My officers found it beside Jonah's body. How you explain that?"

"Your men stripped it from me at the stables, not that an explanation matters in your court."

"How do you explain being at the stables, Garrett?"

"A trooper came for me, saying my horse was sick."

Fulton plucked the cigar stub from his mouth and threw it on the floor. "That's not what my witnesses say. You're gonna have a hard time explaining your actions, Garrett."

Garrett stepped forward toward Fulton,

but felt the lieutenant's hand close around his good arm. He grimaced as the captain poked a revolver in his back. "It'll be easier for me to explain Jonah's death than for you to explain your doings at this fort to the governor, colonel."

"You don't seem to remember, Garrett." Fulton leaned over the desk again. "You are going nowhere. You are under arrest and confined to the stockade until further notice."

Garrett felt his muscles tense instinctively, but they lacked the strength to resist, even if there hadn't been a gun shoved into his back. Garrett weighed his options and knew he had none.

Fulton seemed to read his mind. "If you expect any leniency, Garrett, then I suggest you offer no trouble and deal forthrightly with the Army in this matter. Otherwise it's not going to be too pleasant for you. A former Confederate officer killing his one-time slave on federal property won't play too well before a judge in this territory. Further, the trouble you instigated offered the Apaches a diversion to make good their escape. You can expect to remain in the stockade until we return all of them to the reservation. You behave and I'll put in a few words for you. But if you cause any more trouble, try to get out of the stockade or as much as look cross-eyed at a guard, I'll see that you hang."

"Do me no favors, colonel." Garrett's words came out slow and deliberate. "Because I'll offer you none."

Fulton slammed his fist into his desk, Garrett's gun bouncing on the wood surface. "Get him out of here, men."

The two officers jerked Garrett around and shoved him at the door, the lieutenant opening it just ahead of Garrett's stumbling gait.

Fulton picked up Garrett's gun from his desk and followed them out into the adjacent room. He dropped the gun on the orderly's desk. "Put two guards on duty instead of one."

As he was herded outside with a soldier holding each arm, Garrett closed his eyes as the soldiers steered him across the parade ground toward the stockade. When he finally opened his eyes he was within spitting distance of the stockade, a squat adobe building, barely high enough for a man of Garrett's six feet to stand without bumping his head. A black trooper unlocked the padlock on the iron grate door and the officers shoved him inside. In the midday sun, the jail was the first cousin of an oven.

For a moment, as his eyes adjusted to the darkness broken only by the shaft of light from a single barred window, he could see nothing, though he could feel the stifling heat and smell the rankness of stale urine and worse. Finally, he made out a crude bunk. After taking off his boots, shucking his shirt and pants, he collapsed onto the bed, his body sticky with sweat He swatted at a pinpoint of pain pricking his leg and killed a small scorpion. Except for the scorpion's kin, he might now sleep undisturbed, though not without roasting. Rest was all that would cure his aches, rest and maybe some food, the possibility of which he was uncertain. Right now, though, he didn't care about that. He just wanted to sleep off the past twenty-four hours, and he did.

# CHAPTER 13

Tilman was slumped over the counter, his head in his hands, breathing heavily, a river of regrets surging through his body. He had watched three men march to the stockade. Only two had returned and now Tilman was alone, without an ally and without hope. He rubbed his hands through his sweat-matted hair and looked across the room empty of everything but overpriced merchandise. This store was his prison, a cell of his own making, one only he could break out of. But did he have the courage to even try? His cowardice had tangled Garrett, his only friend, in a sinister snare.

Tilman was jolted from his confused thoughts by the slamming of the door. His hands flew to his glasses on the counter and his fingers fumbled with them, almost dropping them once as he held them to his nose and hooked the wire frames over his ears. He hoped he was mistaken about what he had seen and that Garrett would be standing before him, grinning at the joke. But Tilman's breath sank like his heart when his eyes focused on William Fitzgerald. "Mr. Fitzgerald," he stammered. "It's been a slow day, not much business to report."

Fitzgerald waved his comments aside with a sweep of his fleshy hand. He lumbered up to the counter, his breathing as hard as a locomotive with dying steam. When he towered opposite Tilman, he spoke. "Your eyes look red, Ben. You not well?"

Instinctively, Tilman poked his fingers behind the lenses of his glasses and rubbed at his eyes. "Didn't get a good night's sleep, sir, with the excitement and all." His fingers doubled into fists as he eased them away from behind his glasses. He wanted to slam his fists into Fitzgerald, but banged them against the counter instead.

"Nothing to be upset about." Fitzgerald nodded as he talked. "Last night helped us get rid of your friend Morgan Garrett. He's been arrested for killing his former slave."

Tilman shook his head slowly, his only answer to the false accusation.

Fitzgerald licked his bulbous lips. "He's in a lot of trouble now. I hear he told the trooper to meet him at the stables last night, then shot him in the back."

"Morgan — I mean Mr. Garrett — was pretty beat up this morning when the two officers came to get him." Tilman paused, mustering all the courage he could. He struggled to say he had witnessed the shooting, but the words came out cowardly. "Mr. Garrett didn't seem the type to shoot somebody in the back."

"Ben, I should have fired him the first day I saw him because I knew he'd be trouble. Your work damn sure didn't improve any while he was here — I even thought of getting rid of you."

Tilman swallowed hard, opened his fists, then closed them tighter.

"But then again, Ben," Fitzgerald laughed without smiling, "I didn't want to divulge the little secret about your desertion. Trouble the colonel's had capturing Pachise, he might relish taking a deserter into custody."

Turning away from Fitzgerald, Tilman's voice squeaked meekly from his dry throat. "No, sir, we wouldn't want to give Colonel Fulton something he didn't deserve."

"Well then, Ben, you just forget about your friend Garrett and him ever being here. He's got enough legal troubles without complicating our nice setup here."

"What about the pay he's due?" Tilman spun around to face Fitzgerald.

"Damn it, Ben, he's not due anything now. When he murdered that soldier, our responsibility to him ended. You gather up his things and take them to the colonel tomorrow. He'll be taking care of Garrett from now on."

Nodding, Tilman answered. "Yes, sir, whatever you think best."

"And one other thing, Ben," Fitzgerald said, then pursed his lips for a moment. "If you find a small black pocket ledger among his belongings, you see that I get it. You understand?" Fitzgerald's tone mixed menace with his words.

Tilman gritted his teeth and nodded, desperate that his demeanor not give away his secret. Concerned that his voice might crack with fear if he spoke, Tilman nodded again without answering aloud.

Fitzgerald rubbed his chin as he studied Tilman. "You know something you're not telling, Ben?"

"No, sir," Tilman answered, but his simple response was taut with tension.

Then Fitzgerald rubbed his two hands together. "You'd best not be, Ben. Good day."

As soon as Fitzgerald exited, Ben raced down the back hall to his room. He flew to his bookshelf, fumbled for the copy of

Uncle Tom's Cabin on his bottom shelf. Opening the book to the middle, he sighed. Fitzgerald's pocket ledger was still nestled inside its hiding spot. He felt a wave of relief push through his body, until he remembered the book was worthless without Garrett to take it to Santa Fe. A sudden panic overwhelmed him. He spun around. The window! What if Fitzgerald were watching? The sudden motion dislodged the pocket ledger from its secret compartment and it flew to the floor. Tilman fell to his knees to cover it, then cackled nervously at the empty window. Where he had feared Fitzgerald might be watching, he saw only an oppressive New Mexico sky. Unnerved, he hurriedly fumbled the ledger back in place — it was easier to hide than his fear — and returned the book to the shelf.

For a moment he stood rooted in indecision, then collapsed on his bed from the weight of the burden of his deceptions. He thought about his desertion and regretted it. His cowardice had brought him to a living hell in New Mexico and until now he alone had suffered. But Garrett sat caged in the stockade, a victim of Tilman's own deceptions. Since the war, his life had been nothing but deceit and one more would make no difference, Tilman thought as he crawled from his bed. His leaden feet hit the floor and he stood up slowly. What he was about to do was the hardest thing he had ever done. He'd tell one more lie. Though he had not fired the shot, Tilman decided to tell the colonel it was himself, not Garrett, who had ambushed Jonah. Suddenly he was confident and pleased about himself, a feeling he had not known since the war.

He marched from the store. It was later than he thought. The soldiers that remained at the fort were gathering at the mess halls and Tilman feared Colonel Fulton might already have closed up his office for the day. Though his stomach churned with anticipation, he walked erect and direct to headquarters and onto the porch. Drawing a deep breath, he opened the door and marched into the vacant outer office. The orderly must be at mess, Tilman thought as he stepped toward the colonel's door, slightly ajar. At the sound of voices, he paused before knocking. He listened.

". . . figured you were involved in the matter some way. Damn shame, soldier, that your friend got shot. Damn, I'd like to know who did that. You sure it wasn't one of the other troopers that had a score to settle with Jonah?"

"That's one thing I's sure of, colonel."

Tilman recognized the voice. Skully's. The colonel was visiting with the troublemaker Skully.

"Nobody held nothin' against Jonah, an' all the men hates Garrett, for sure," Skully said.

Fulton coughed and Tilman flinched at the noise. "Puzzling, mighty puzzling, isn't it, soldier?"

"Yes, sir buts I still wanna get that man Garrett."

Instinctively, Tilman leaned closer to the door. "You can have him tonight, soldier," Fulton laughed.

"Tells me how," Skully answered.

"I'll see that you replace the guards at midnight. Then it's up to you to see that Garrett tries to escape. Unbar the door and shove him out, if you have to. Once you get him outside, shoot him. Get it done with. Just make sure he doesn't get away. I want him dead by morning."

Tilman swallowed hard at the cold words. He must get out, quick. Backing away from the door, he bumped into the orderly's desk. He averted his eyes from the door to the desk top and the pistol there beside an ink blotter. Recognizing it as Garrett's, he grabbed it and jammed it inside his pants, knocking the blotter onto the floor. He froze, then bent to pick it up. As he stood, he realized he had company.

"What the hell do you want, Benjamin Franklin Tilman?" boomed Fulton.

Tilman slapped the blotter down on the table with his right hand, his left shielding from Fulton the gun in his britches. "I came to tell you," Tilman stammered for a moment, wiping from his forehead the suddenly bothersome beads of perspiration, "that I, I gathered the things of that murderer Garrett and wanted to know what should be done with them."

Fulton folded his arms across his chest and chewed vigorously at the stump of a cigar poking out of the corner of his mouth. "You're nervous, Benjamin Franklin Tilman, and why'd you knock the blotter on the floor?"

Tilman jerked a soiled handkerchief from his back pocket, wiped another wave of sweat from his forehead and held the cloth in front of his waist and the stolen gun. "I heard you had someone with you and was going to write you a note." Tilman pointed at the pen and inkwell beside the blotter. "I knocked it over."

"Just going over the orders of tomorrow with one of my officers, Tilman," Fulton lied. "With so many men out in the field trying to recapture Pachise and his band, those that are left can't keep up with duties on the post without careful planning."

"Certainly, colonel," Tilman nodded, hoping the gesture would cover the disbelief in his eyes.

"I'll send a trooper over tomorrow to get his things, though I doubt he'll be needing them for a while."

"Thank you, colonel," Tilman said, looking behind Fulton into his office, but Skully was hidden from view. He turned from the colonel and reined himself in, controlling the urge to run and hide like he'd always done. In maintaining his poise, he discovered a sudden exhilaration he had never before experienced. As he stepped outside into the dying daylight, he heard Fulton shut and latch the door behind him.

A strange emotion was welling within him as he strode back to the store. Garrett was marked for death tonight and Tilman was confident he could save him.

Smelling of sweat and wracked with hunger, Garrett watched the sky darken through the barred window of his cell. He had endured the heat of the day in this adobe oven, but his throat was parched from want of water.

The evening coolness sent a chill through his flesh but it could not put out the burning dryness in his throat. He arose from the bed, the bearclaw necklace rattling as he shook his head, and put his clothes back on, pulling his pants gingerly over the scorpion sting.

As he buttoned his pants, the sound of a conversation outside penetrated into his thirst-dulled brain. He listened and smiled as much as his parched lips allowed. Never had he been so glad to hear Ben's voice before.

"That's what I was told to do, fellows," Tilman preached to the guards.

Garrett slipped through the growing darkness to the door and stared out through the iron grating.

"I don't likes it none 'cause I don't knows if you is telling the truth," one of the guards said.

In the growing dimness, Garrett could see Tilman hold up a bottle in one hand and what appeared to be a sheet of paper in the other. "You boys don't believe me, you can take it up with Colonel Stubby himself. Here's his orders." Tilman offered the paper to the taller of the guards. "I'm only doing what he told me. He said you was to give this whiskey to the prisoner."

The arguing soldier waved away the paper. "No, sir, I jus' don't believes it — not at all. That don't sounds like what the colonel would do. He never done that for any of the soldiers and there's been a lot of them in here before."

"Hell, soldier, you don't think he'd send good whiskey to you darkies, do you? You know by now he's not too fond of black boys."

"It still don't seems right," the soldier answered, the uncertainty growing in his voice.

"Right's never had too much to do with Stubby's decisions." Tilman shrugged. He extended his hand with the bottle to the suspicious soldier. "Then you just take this bottle and worry about it yourself. I was told to deliver it to the stockade and I've done it. Now do whatever you wish — it's out of my hands."

The soldier hesitated. Tilman grabbed the soldier's hand and fashioned a reluctant grip around the bottle's neck with the uncertain fingers. "There you go, trooper." Tilman backed from the soldier, then turned away. He paused for a moment, looking over his shoulder at the two guards. "Now don't you boys drink that or you might develop a taste for better whiskey than you can afford."

Garrett watched as Tilman disappeared in the twilight. He ached for the wetness in the bottle to quench his thirst, but quickly saw his night would be dry. The two soldiers unstoppered the bottle and alternated swigs of its contents. His throat raged with jealousy. It would be a long night, Garrett thought as he turned toward the bunk.

Tilman moved swiftly from the stockade to the cover of the barracks. He hoped those damn guards didn't offer the whiskey to Garrett or he'd have a hell of a stomachache by midnight. He had mixed half whiskey and half coal oil in that bottle. Slipping cautiously from building to building, he worked his way toward the stables. Tilman moved with his right hand near his waist and near Garrett's gun which, hidden under his shirt, dug into his stomach with each step. He had to secure horses or his plan would never work.

He reached the stable without seeing another person and pushed open the thick, hoof-beaten doors. "Hello, anybody here?"

"Back here," came an uneven voice.

Tilman looked in the direction of the voice, but darkness shrouded the inside of the building which smelled of foul fodder and manure. A flame of light flared in the far corner as a stableman touched a sulphur match to a lantern hanging from a slick stall post. The soldier brushed the hay from his stable frock as Tilman approached. He had been asleep, Tilman thought.

"What's your business?" the stableman stretched his arms.

"Came to get some horses, soldier."

"Don't knows nothin' about that. Hadn't hads no orders."

"I came to get horses," Tilman paused, ". . . if you were awake." He extended his hand with the same piece of paper he had offered the stockade guards. "I've got the orders with me."

"Whose orders?" the stableman asked, thrusting his hand and his chin forward.

"Why, Colonel Fulton's himself, soldier. He wants that chestnut horse of that Garrett man saddled and out of here to cover the lame man's debts at the sutler's."

The stableman grabbed the papers and held it up to the lantern, then handed it back. "Mighty unusual, this time of day."

Tilman nodded. "And so's this." He paused. "The colonel wants his top horse saddled, too."

"Huh," offered the soldier, jamming his

hands on his hips. "How comes the colonel didn't sends one of his officers likes he usually does?"

"May be, soldier, that with three companies out chasing Pachise he don't have enough soldiers left to run all his errands." Tilman's right hand slipped closer to the gun hidden behind his belt and shirt. "Who knows why Colonel Stubby does anything?"

The stableman laughed. "Even Stubby hisself doesn't knows what he's doing most of the time. He's the dumbest white man I ever did see."

"Ain't it the truth. Now you think you can saddle the horses?"

The stableman shrugged, took the lantern off the nail and worked toward the back of the stable. Tilman breathed easier, though it seemed to take the stableman forever to get the two horses saddled. When he finally returned with the two horses, Tilman grabbed the reins. "Good work, soldier," Tilman said. "Must help when you take a nap on duty." He smiled weakly. "Your secret's good with me." He led the horses away from the frowning soldier and out the door into the darkness.

He made a wide swath around the barracks and came upon the sutler's store from behind. His business there would be brief.

He had to get Garrett's belongings, including his carbine, and most importantly Fitzgerald's pocket ledger.

Moving more cautiously as he neared the sutler's store, he paused to stare in case something were amiss, but the building was dark and quiet. He eased the horses up to the back door, tying the reins to a hitching post. Tilman opened the door and slid through toward Garrett's room. Quickly he lit a lamp and grabbed Garrett's coat, carbine, canteen and saddle bags stuffed with provisions, then retraced his steps out to the horses and tied his load onto the chestnut.

Finishing his chore, he looked around him. The fort was still. He scurried back inside to Garrett's room, fetched the lamp and carried it across the hall. He stared straight at the bookshelf and his heart skipped a beat. The duplicate copy of Uncle Tom's Cabin, the one holding Fitzgerald's pocket ledger, had disappeared from its place on the bottom shelf. How could it be? He opened his mouth to curse but his eyes alighted on the top shelf. There it was. He must have forgotten to replace it earlier when he'd checked it after Fitzgerald's visit. As he put the lamp down, he sighed, then grabbed the book and opened it to the middle. Then he gasped.

The ledger had disappeared. The hollowed out space of the book held only emptiness.

Tilman stared from the book to the wall. "Damn," he called softly and turned around.

"Looking for this?"

Startled, Tilman dropped Uncle Tom's Cabin to the floor. In the opposite corner of the room sat Fitzgerald, his fleshy hand cradling the incriminating ledger.

Tilman backed away from Fitzgerald. "What are you doing here now, Mr. Fitzgerald?"

"Just tending my property, Ben," he said, waving the book at Tilman and using his other hand to push himself up from his chair. "What were you looking for, Ben?"

"Something to read, that's all," Tilman said, easing his right hand toward his belt buckle.

Fitzgerald's bushy eyebrows arched with disbelief. "I'm no fool, Ben. This book'd make some interesting reading in the wrong hands."

"I'm not sure I understand what you're talking about."

"From the day I misplaced my tally book until today, Ben, I knew you had it. Too bad I couldn't trust you." Sticking the ledger in his pocket, Fitzgerald doubled his right fist and pounded it menacingly in his open left palm. He stepped toward Tilman. "Too bad I can't trust you any more, Ben."

"You never trusted me. You just manipulated me with my cowardice."

The hulking Fitzgerald took another step toward him.

"You'll not do that any more."

Another methodical stride brought Fitzgerald closer.

"Now, you'll listen to me for a moment," Tilman said, jerking Garrett's revolver from under his shirt.

"Come on, Ben, you don't scare me. I've seen the coward you are. You're too frightened to hurt anybody. You fear you might get hurt yourself."

Fitzgerald advanced with impunity until he was within an arm's length of the revolver aimed at his chest.

Tilman's finger tightened against the trigger, but he could not squeeze that final fraction of an inch that would fire the gun. Fear had overtaken him again, but a fear of a different type. If he shot, the noise would create a commotion and reduce the chance of helping Garrett escape.

Slowly, Fitzgerald lifted his hand and swatted at the pistol, his pulpy fingers snapping at it.

Tilman dodged the blow and slid backward until he was against the bookshelf.

Fitzgerald shook his head. "Hand over the gun and no one will get hurt, Ben." He moved a step closer then grabbed for the pistol, laughing without smiling as he did.

Lifting the gun out of reach, Tilman brought it down hard against Fitzgerald's ponderous hand.

"Damn you." Fitzgerald lunged for Tilman's neck with outstretched hands.

Tilman ducked under his arms. As he jumped up, he sliced a blow down Fitzgerald's cheek, drawing a trickle of blood from the corner of the big man's mouth.

Stunned, the big man turned toward Tilman, then half stepped and half stumbled toward the nimble clerk. Tilman sidestepped a sluggish punch from the big man, then slid toward Fitzgerald. He drew back his arm and slammed the pistol into the side of Fitzgerald's head, a solid blow. Fitzgerald froze a disbelieving instant, then his knees melted and he collapsed. Ben stood over him and spit at him. Bending over Fitzgerald, he grasped the revolver by the barrel and clubbed the sutler one, two, three times for all the wrongs of the past three years. Then he fished the ledger from Fitzgerald's coat pocket. Standing over the corpulent form, Tilman kicked Fitzgerald in the stomach and for a moment he pondered smashing the lamp against the floor and sending Fitzgerald to an early hell. He took a step toward the lamp, but stopped to look at the incriminating ledger in his hand. That would cause Fitzgerald enough hell on earth. He stepped over his unconscious tormentor and walked calmly to the horses.

Garrett lay uneasy on his bed, the groaning noises of the two guards gnawing at his brain almost as much as his thirst. Whatever Tilman had given the two wasn't just whiskey. Sleep would not come and only it or blessed water could lessen his agony. And while his mind languished on a single thought — water — his throat grew tighter and his cracked lips parted from the pressure of his swollen tongue. He wanted to cry out for water, but checked the impulse at the sound of a voice outside.

"Evening, soldiers."

It was Benjamin Franklin Tilman.

"I see that you two fellows have been drinking while on duty." Tilman laughed. "You can get shot for that. Not to mention sick," he added as an afterthought. "And I'm disappointed you uncorked that bottle after I told you it was for the prisoner."

The soldiers groaned.

"Don't say I didn't warn you two. I recall telling you it was better whiskey than you could afford to get accustomed to drinking. Maybe I lied about it being good, boys, but I was telling the truth when I said you couldn't afford to get used to it."

Garrett stood up from his bunk and feebly put his boots on before staggering to the cell door. He peeked outside and could make out Tilman gathering the two soldiers' carbines, revolvers and ammunition belts. Then he took the stockade key. "Water," he called, but the word came out like a whisper. "Water, Ben, water," he repeated without attracting Tilman's attention.

Tilman stepped to the door. "Morgan, you there?"

"Where you think I'd be, Ben," Garrett gasped. "Down at the river swimming?"

"You don't sound so good, Morgan," Tilman said as he unbarred and unlocked the door.

"Water, Ben, I need water," Garrett said. "Haven't had any all day." Leaning against the door, Garrett stumbled outside when Tilman pulled it open.

Tilman, his arms loaded with weapons, awkwardly caught Garrett, providing enough support for him to maintain his balance. Neither trooper could stand up, much less stop the escape. One trooper was retching with great effort against the side of the stockade and the other seemed unconscious.

"Canteen's on your horse behind the stockade, Morgan. Can you make it?"

Garrett nodded. "If there's water." He stumbled away.

As Ben dragged each trooper into the stockade, he could hear Garrett's noisy gulps on the canteen. He barred the stockade door behind him and ran to join Garrett.

"Can you ride, Morgan?"

"Now I can," he said, his voice stronger.

"Then let's go," Tilman said, shoving a carbine in the boot on the colonel's horse and tucking the soldiers' revolvers in his belt. He handed the second carbine to Garrett. "We may need this. Let's ride hard for Santa Fe while we've got good cloud cover."

# CHAPTER 14

Skully fingered his revolver as he walked toward the stockade. A brilliant moon shone through a break in the clouds and cast a column of death's pallor upon the earth. In the pale light, Skully could see ahead the squat adobe stockade with its barred door. He smiled to himself. His moment of revenge was nearing. Once he sent the guards away, he would have Garrett to himself, but Skully had yet to see the guards.

Reaching the stockade, he called out. "Boys, where is you? Your relief's here."

No answer.

"This is no time to be pulling no jokes on Skully. Now shows yourselves, boys," Skully yelled, and in the subsequent quiet, Skully heard a groan.

"Dammit, boys, quits your spoofing and shows yourselves right now or I just might shoot you if you don't."

He heard another groan and realized it

was coming from inside the cell. Skully cursed, hoping the guards hadn't already taken care of Garrett.

"What's going on in there?"

Someone mumbled an answer.

"Names yourself," Skully challenged, his grip tightening on his revolver. Perhaps it was one of Garrett's tricks, he worried. He approached the door cautiously, peering through the iron grating without seeing anyone. As he cocked the hammer on his revolver, he lifted the bar and jerked the door open, crouching to meet whatever emerged. He saw nothing but a rectangle of moonlight illuminating the cell's dirt floor.

At the sound of another groan, Skully inched into the blackness of the cell. He tensed at the sound of a scraping noise. A trap? He squinted to make out what danger hid beyond the rectangle of moonlight on the floor. A dark form slipped forward from the darkness and collapsed into the lighted door. Skully's finger pulled against the trigger, then eased off. This man was black and wore a uniform.

Skully jumped beside him. "What happened?"

A faint voice whispered. "He's escaped."

Skully whirled around and ran toward the parade ground, firing his pistol twice.

"Prisoner's escaped. Prisoner's escaped," he shouted.

Gradually lights began to appear in some of the barracks and in Colonel Fulton's quarters. Skully raced to the commander's porch. Arriving at the door, Skully beat against it until the colonel, revolver in hand, opened up.

"Garrett's escaped, sir."

"Damn you, soldier, I should've known he'd outsmart you."

Skully held his revolver up under Fulton's chin. "It wasn't me, sir. The guards I wents to spell was in the stockade. That's all I knows except that he's gone."

As soldiers gathered around Fulton's porch, Skully lowered his revolver. An officer stepped up beside Skully.

Fulton turned to the lieutenant. "Prisoner's escaped. Check the stables," the colonel ordered, "and see if he got a horse. If he did, have my mount saddled and assign twenty soldiers to accompany me."

"We can't spare that many, Colonel, not with three companies out in the field," the lieutenant answered.

"Fine, dammit, but I want six soldiers whether you can spare them or not." Fulton pointed at Skully. "I want him to go with me. Now get five more."

The lieutenant saluted hurriedly, then scurried across the parade ground.

"You wait here, soldier," he ordered Skully, "until I get dressed." Fulton shut the door, but was back within five minutes, carrying his carbine in the crook of his elbow as he buckled his pistol scabbard on. He stepped beside Skully, ordering the milling soldiers around the porch to make themselves useful or go back to bed.

Fulton paced back and forth on the porch awaiting the return of the lieutenant. "Damn the luck, soldier. How in the hell did he escape?" Fulton shouted. Hearing a noise behind him, Fulton whirled about just in time to see Fitzgerald trip and fall forward onto the porch. In two steps, Fulton was at the big man's side.

"Get a lamp from inside, soldier," he commanded Skully. Fulton twisted Fitzgerald over as Skully returned with the light, illuminating the dried blood on Fitzgerald's left cheek and the swelling knot on his head. Fulton spoke, then shook Fitzgerald without result. In desperation he slapped Fitzgerald's face. "What happened?"

The big man's eyes slowly opened, staring blankly toward the light.

"What happened?" Fulton repeated.

"Ben helped Garrett escape. They've got

my ledger." Fitzgerald coughed and tried to sit up, but fell back into Fulton's hands. "Could be . . . trouble . . . for both of us," he whispered.

Fulton nodded and eased Fitzgerald back down onto the porch. He remembered Garrett's threat to go to Santa Fe, and he cursed.

The breathless lieutenant ran up to the colonel. "Sir," he saluted, "two horses were taken out, the stable orderly reports. The man Garrett's horse and yours, but it wasn't Garrett that did it. The sutler's clerk, Tilman, took them."

"Have another mount saddled for me, lieutenant. We've got to catch them. Then see that Mister Fitzgerald is attended."

The lieutenant scurried away again.

"Soldier," Fulton said to Skully, "we'll not fail this time."

"We've got trouble, Ben," said Garrett, looking back over his shoulder toward Cottonwood Crossing.

Benjamin Franklin Tilman turned in the saddle and spotted a cloud of dust rising on the horizon like a sinister whirlwind. The two men slowed, then stopped their mounts atop a foothill and let them blow. Garrett rubbed his bruised face and stretched in

301

the saddle, his muscles still aching from the fight with Jonah. He and Tilman watched the distant dust.

"I'd been hoping they'd wouldn't come after us," Ben said.

"No chance, not with you stealing Fitzgerald's book, Ben. They'd ride through hell to catch us now." Garrett pointed to the west. "We're in the foothills and once we get in the mountains we'll have places to hide, places to make a stand if we must."

Tilman nodded. "They've made good time, haven't they?"

"Could be, Ben, but it depends whether they've drained their horses. We've kept a good, but not demanding pace. If they've run as hard as I figure, our horses'll have an advantage."

Still nodding, Tilman stuck his hand in his britches pocket and pulled out the little black book. Grinning, he shoved the book in Garrett's direction. "You hang on to this in case we get separated. If something happens to me, promise you'll deliver it to Santa Fe."

"Nothing's gonna trouble you but your conscience, Ben," Garrett said, taking the book and tucking it in his britches pocket. Garrett raised his hand to his neck and fingered the bearclaw necklace. The bearclaws clattered as he lifted the leather thong to his chin, wondering why he hadn't discarded it earlier.

"What are you doing, Morgan?"

"Getting rid of this damned necklace."

"Apaches think some of those trinkets have magical powers. Maybe you should leave it on for powerful Apache medicine. We may need all the help we can get."

Garrett detected a nervousness in Tilman's eyes. He dropped the necklace. "Instead of trusting a dead bear's luck, maybe you better pray."

"I have been," Tilman smiled uncomfortably, "but I'd feel better a riding."

"Then let's move," Garrett said and they sent their horses racing down the hill, toward the next higher hill and toward the mountains. They left behind the yucca and cholla and rode into the scrub junipers and piñons which grew taller as the hills grew higher and then they were in the mountains, and their spirits soared with the hawk that floated leisurely on the air currents flowing from the mountains.

Up the trail in a distant valley, the first pines were visible and the green sheathing of the mountains beyond promised good hiding spots. The nearest cover was off the trail, up in an outcrop of wind-sculpted boulders scattered like toys on the mountainside. Garrett motioned for Tilman to follow him off the trail and they rode up the mountain to spy for a moment on their pursuers and maybe to hide, if the cover seemed defensible. Shortly after abandoning the trail, Garrett realized his mistake. The mountainside was wickedly deceptive, creviced with fissures snaking in all directions, potted with sink holes unthreatening to a man on foot but dangerous to a rider, and studded with a thousand daggered plants among the piñon and juniper and occasional scrub pines. His horse maneuvered through the obstacles and Garrett thought he might make it to the boulders, but Ben was less of a horseman.

"Head back for the trail," Garrett called, but too late.

Tilman swerved his horse to avoid a rock that had suddenly appeared in his path. As he jerked on the reins, his horse turned sharply and its hooves slipped on the flint shavings covering the ground. The horse stumbled, its forelegs brushing the spines of a spidery ocotillo, but regained its stride too late to avoid a wide fissure. A front leg sank into the crevice, the bone snapping and the animal shrilly whistling. As the animal's back legs propelled it over its leading pair, the horse's back arched. Tilman screamed as he flew forward into a scrub piñon which broke his fall and his glasses. The horse thrashed wildly, neighing in wide-eyed terror as it fought the useless leg from the mountainside crack. Struggling free, the horse tried to stand but tumbled forward, then tried again.

Garrett turned his horse around and headed back for Tilman, who was gathering himself from the bush, holding his glasses to the sky.

"You hurt, Ben?"

Ben stared through the shattered left lens of his glasses. "My spectacles," he cried, "they're broken!"

"They'll have to do," Garrett answered, turning his head at the thrashing horse. Garrett tugged at the bearclaw necklace. "This damn sure didn't bring us any luck. Now we got trouble," he said, letting go of the necklace. He pulled his carbine from its boot and aimed at Tilman's horse. The gun exploded, echoing down the valley and giving away their position as sure as a flying flag. "Grab your carbine from the horse and climb aboard, Ben. This is bad, but our trouble hasn't really started yet."

The chestnut was strong of body and heart, but even Ben's small frame was too much extra weight for the animal's stamina. Riding double sapped the animal's strength, but not his heart. He struggled forward, deeper into the valley. His awkward gait and sluggish response to the reins told Garrett the animal could not hold out under the load.

Ahead the valley narrowed like a funnel around the trail and huge boulders stood guard around the narrow passage. Towering over the boulders, ponderosa pines stood watch over the trail like fragrant sentries. Within three hundred yards of the boulders, they heard the first shot. Garrett knew the soldiers had caught them, but he could feel Ben twisting around to look.

"We're dead now, Morgan."

"Forget it, Ben. We'll make those boulders and make our stand there. How many are there?"

From Ben's tightened grip around his waist, Garrett knew Ben was making count. "Six or seven," he yelled as the buzz of a slug died into the ground.

The tiring chestnut made it to the boulder, and Ben and Garrett clambered off the instant the winded animal stopped. Ben stumbled, falling to the ground ahead of the cartridges spilling from his pocket. He scrambled to pick them up as Garrett led the chestnut up from the trail into the boulders and tied the reins to a scrub juniper. Pulling his rifle from its boot, Garrett motioned for Tilman to climb for a position within the stone fortress.

"Steady up, Ben," Garrett called. "It'll be easier than shooting Jonah because you'll have incentive. They'll be firing back."

"Dammit, Morgan, I didn't kill Jonah, whether you believe it or not."

"No matter what I believe now, Ben — we're in a bind. I've got to depend on you now as much as that night." Garrett climbed atop the highest boulder and stood tall against the sky. The troopers rode hard for the rocks, seemingly without noticing Garrett. He lifted his rifle and fired into the ground ahead of Colonel Fulton. The line of troopers broke in two, one side heading for the cover or rocks on one side of the trail, the other for trees on the opposite side.

Garrett jumped down between two boulders. "Shoot for their horses if you can, Ben. It'll be easier to explain than killing a cavalryman," Garrett yelled as he squeezed off another shot. He smiled as he heard Tilman's gun explode. "Good shot," he said without seeing where the bullet hit. A returning bullet whizzed through the rocks, a ricochetting menace that splattered stone chips around them. "Steady up, Ben," said Garrett. "You can do whatever has to be done. If I go down, fire a few rounds and run for the horse. You might make it."

Tilman squeezed off a shot. "I've run all my life, Morgan." He fired again. "I'll not run from this fight."

Garrett saw the profile of a horse in the distant trees and took steady aim, slowly squeezing the trigger, feeling the punch of the rifle against his shoulder and seeing the cavalry mount tumble to the ground. Across the trail, he saw a stocky man advancing between rocks and jump for cover as a bullet struck at his feet. It was Colonel Fulton.

"Nice shooting, Ben," Garrett yelled above the noise. "I knew you had gravel in your craw."

"It helps when you hate your enemy," he answered.

By the rain of bullets falling among them, Garrett knew the soldiers had found their position. He leaned back against a rock and awkwardly reloaded his rifle, a difficult chore for a one-armed man. He glanced over at Ben, who was squinting behind the broken lens of his spectacles. Ben raised slightly and squeezed off a shot. "Damn," Ben said, "missed Fulton again."

A barrage of bullets splattered against the

rocks around them and Garrett heard a thud. Tilman slumped forward like a sack of flour. Garrett shoved his rifle aside and scrambled to Tilman's side. "Ben! Ben!" Garrett cried. "How bad are you hit?" He turned Tilman from his stomach and flinched at the gaping hole in his side. "How bad is it?"

Tilman's eyes cracked open and his lips parted, a gurgling noise coming with each breath. "Don't know, Morgan, I've never been shot before," he gasped.

"I've seen worse, Ben. I'll give up and maybe we can get you back to the fort in time." Garrett started unbuttoning his shirt to wave as a flag of surrender.

"Damn, Morgan, you don't lie too good. I'm dying." He struggled with the next word and coughed up blood. "Do one thing for me." He spit out a bright red liquid that was more than blood.

"Name it."

"Santa Fe," he gasped. "Go to Santa Fe. Deliver the book to the governor. Clear my name so folks won't think too bad of me."

"I will, Ben," he said, helping Tilman to a seated position.

"Then you need to be riding."

"Can't leave you, Ben."

"Suicide to stay," he gasped. "Leave me a

loaded pistol and I'll give you cover."

"Never ran out on someone before, Ben."

"Go, dammit. You leave now, I'll die believing my name was cleared. You stay, I'll not have that satisfaction."

As much as Garrett hated to admit it, neither Tilman's life nor anything else would be saved by his staying. "I'll tell the governor you were an honest man."

Tilman said nothing more, just struggled to keep himself propped up against the rocks where he could see a portion of the trail. Garrett pulled a pistol from Tilman's britches and wrapped the dying man's hand around it, then wiped the mingled sweat and gunsmoke from Tilman's head and ran his fingers through his unruly hair.

"Ben, I've been in a lot of scrapes, but you'd stand with the bravest I ever fought with."

Tilman nodded and Garrett saw in his eyes a brief flare of satisfaction that even the pain could not hide. Tilman had proved himself a man. Tilman lifted his hand feebly to wave Garrett away and then pointed the pistol in the direction of the soldiers and fired.

"Goodbye, Ben, and good luck," he whispered.

Garrett clambered through the narrow

openings between the rocks to reach the chestnut. He mounted and rode out of the rocks and deeper into the valley. Behind he could still hear the occasional report of a gun and finally even that could not be heard over the sound of the pounding hooves. He rode as hard as he had ever ridden, with as precious a cargo as he ever carried — a man's integrity.

# CHAPTER 15

His pistol was still loaded as best he remembered, but Tilman was weak and confused, struggling to keep his eyes open. His brain was muddled, his senses dulled. He felt his finger wrap around the pistol as he leaned his back against the rock. The pistol settled in his hand at his belt buckle. The world seemed to be spinning about him, as if he were the center of the universe. Then he passed out, and all was quiet for several minutes.

Below him the soldiers began to creep toward the rock which screened Tilman. Now that the shooting had stopped from that position, the black troops began to smile at each other and to grow more reckless in exposing themselves to the vantage point which minutes ago had been belching leaden death in their direction. A couple troops managed to crawl right up to the base of that rock. Cautiously the two soldiers circled the rock from opposite directions. There before them on the ground was one of their assailants, his clothes red-stained, his face bloodied.

Moment by moment other troopers gathered around the motionless clerk. Shortly, Colonel Fulton joined the six black soldiers staring at their assailant.

"Damn," said one of them, "the other one gots away."

The evil sound of that voice awakened something deep in Tilman's dwindling reserve of consciousness, though he could sense he was surrounded and knew he was dying. There was little he could do about either. Except for his right hand! His fingers were wrapped around the revolver Garrett had left him. Perhaps he could lessen the odds against Garrett, give him a better chance of making Santa Fe.

"Colonel," called the same sinister voice, "this is the one I got."

With effort, Tilman placed the voice as that of the trooper Skully, the one who had tormented Garrett so. Tilman cracked his eyes just wide enough to see where Skully stood, then saw the black soldier draw back his foot and kick his own.

With all the strength he could muster, Tilman jerked the gun from his waist and fired into Skully's chest. He knew Skully was dead, but before he could know more or before he could fire a second shot, a score of bullets punctured his chest.

The stench of sweating horseflesh overpowered the sweet aroma of white pine mingling with the cool mountain air. Through beautiful country the desperate Garrett raced on his tiring mount. Only once since leaving Tilman behind as a sacrifice for a headstart had the rider allowed his horse to stop. That came as the trail crossed a cool mountain stream. For a moment both man and beast had quenched their thirsts, but it was the only respite since leaving Tilman behind.

Uncertain any more if he was still on the trail to Santa Fe, Garrett had lost track of time as well. High sun was gone, but Garrett could not tell how much daylight he had left. He was too cautious a man to assume he had outdistanced his pursuers, so he pushed his horse mercilessly. That was what worried him now. Unless he pulled back and gave the chestnut a chance to gather some of its strength, the animal might be useless if the troops did draw within rifle range. Still, the horses of the soldiers had been ridden hard during the night and might be in no better shape than his own. Garrett worried when he eased off on the chestnut and the animal stumbled an instant before regaining his stride.

Up ahead the mountains began to close in on the faint trail. It was there that the trail appeared to turn sharply toward the north. The timber was not thick, but it was adequate for cover. Garrett gambled, deciding to stop and rest his horse. The risk seemed no greater than riding on and possibly riding his horse into the ground. From the time Garrett had deserted Tilman, every move and strategy of escape had been a gamble, the outcome depending on factors Garrett knew nothing about — the freshness of the soldiers' horses, and whether he was still being pursued.

Reaching the crook in the trail, Garrett rode up the incline off the south side and into the trees. He tied his horse to a hardened stump in a patch of grass. Not until then had Garrett realized his true exhaustion. His knees seemed to buckle with each step and his body ached with the residue from Jonah's beating. He had been in the saddle at least fourteen hours, possibly longer, stopping only at Cottonwood Crossing, the site of the fight, the mountain stream and this place for rest. He walked around on his mushy knees for several minutes, trying to prevent his muscles from stiffening in case he had to leave fast, but his eyes were heavy and his mind muddled from so much trouble. Walking hurt as much as riding so he sat down on the ground by the stump where he had tethered his chestnut. His horse was by him and he could see down the trail. He would wait a few minutes, rest himself and his gelding, then continue on the long ride to Santa Fe. He stared at the trail intently for a long time, but his exhaustion finally pulled him to sleep.

How long he slept, Garrett did not know. He might have slept until his death had not the chestnut tossed its head and jerked on the reins tied to the stump where Garrett leaned. Garrett opened his eyes, glancing at his nervous gelding dancing beside him, then realized what was happening. Cursing, he cast his view down the trail and cursed himself again. Soldiers and Colonel Fulton were approaching at a canter. Garrett scrambled to his feet and untied the reins, disgusted that he had fallen asleep. The soldiers, a half a mile away, seemed not to see Garrett at first. The gelding, though, was nervous, jerking on the reins and tossing his head. Garrett thought about trying to slip up higher into the woods, but that plan changed the moment he placed his foot in the stirrup and mounted. Colonel Fulton pointed his direction and shouted orders, and the soldiers came at a gallop. Now his only alternative was to make a dash for it. He fell hard into the saddle, slapped the reins against the animal's neck and aimed the gelding deeper into the mountains.

Garrett never looked back. The muffled cracking of a carbine told him all he needed to know. With slaps of the reins and nudges of his heel, he urged the chestnut ahead, seeking every ounce of its stamina and strength for one final escape bid. The animal was still sluggish, but the rest had helped, giving Garrett a slight hope that once again he could escape the troopers. The trail through the trees narrowed even further; a good sign, thought Garrett, because it would force the soldiers to ride single file. That would cut down the number of guns that could fire at him. Still, Garrett could hear the sound of rifle shots behind him and of occasional thumps into nearby trees or whizzing bullets overhead. The shots grew muffled and Garrett was unsure whether the forest was merely absorbing the reverberations or whether he was leaving them behind. When he glanced over his shoulder for a look, the soldiers did, in fact, seem to be falling back. Their horses were tired. He had done the right thing in stopping for rest, although it might have cost him his life. With the cover of the trees, Garrett was certain he could get enough of a lead on them that he could slip into the woods and hide out, letting them pass unaware. His confidence returned.

Then just as quickly it disappeared like the trees crowding in on the trail. Garrett found himself in a clearing, a beautiful meadow about two miles long and a quarter mile wide. Cursing his luck, he glanced around looking for a suitable hiding place. He saw none, though something in what he did see puzzled him. It was as if other men were already hiding in the trees. It was strange, maybe the mental aberration of a desperate man about to face death. Now the real race was on as Garrett tried to make the other side of the clearing. About midway across the meadow, the intensity of the gunfire picked up and Garrett knew the soldiers had emerged from the trees and spread out to fire.

All about him the air was filled with angry lead. For a moment, his chestnut seemed to falter, giving rise to the fear that his horse had been wounded, but Garrett realized the animal had only misstepped. Garrett did not look behind, but felt the soldiers gaining on him because the rifle shots sounded louder. Then suddenly, the number of shots intensified dramatically, thundering throughout the meadow, yet the bullets overhead trickled to nothing. It sounded as though dozens of carbines were firing behind him, but the bullets were magically disappearing. Above the din of exploding gunpowder, Garrett heard a shriek, then another, and finally an avalanche of screams like a giant wounded animal caught in a steel trap. The whole meadow reverberated with awful noises.

Garrett glanced over his shoulder and held his breath. Nearly fifty Apache warriors had appeared in the meadow, most converging on the soldiers, but a handful heading for him. The soldiers were surrounded and fighting a desperate battle of their own. For Garrett the problem now was not the troops, who stood little chance of survival, but the Apaches, whose thirst for blood, particularly the blood of trespassing white men, was well known throughout New Mexico. Garrett was getting all his horse could give, but it seemed so meager compared to what his horse could do when well rested. Behind him, the noise of battle still raged and for the first time in hours he wished well for the soldiers, wanting them to survive as long as they could to buy him additional time, just as Tilman had done earlier in the day. The gunfire lasted no more than three minutes, and Garrett realized the silence meant the end of the patrol and Colonel Fulton. But Garrett also realized his chances had diminished, too, because with no one else to distract them, there could be no hiding from the Apaches. They would easily catch him and make a sport of his death.

Behind him, Garrett heard the same shrieks and yells that had preceded the soldiers' demise. Glancing over his shoulder, he saw a half dozen warriors gaining fast. Though he pushed his chestnut as hard as he could, the animal was losing ground, its heart no longer in the race. Garrett let out a long breath, knowing he could never escape, regretting most that he would not make it to Santa Fe to clear Benjamin Franklin Tilman's name. That had meant more to the clerk than life itself.

Twisting quickly to look, Garrett saw the Apaches drawing even nearer. They planned to make sport of him, maybe torture him, because not one was pointing a gun or an arrow at him. It was just a matter of seconds before they would catch him. Garrett attempted to hold the reins in his mouth, so he could pull his pistol with his good right hand and fire at his pursuers, but he almost lost his balance. He clutched at his saddle then jerked the reins from his mouth slapping them against the chestnut, but the gelding could give no more and actually seemed to slow. His only goal now was to draw out the hopeless chase as long as he could. He just rode, never looking back, his face grimacing against the bullets or arrows he expected.

In no time, two sullen Apaches were riding beside him. They pressed their mounts toward Garrett, sandwiching the chestnut between their paints. One of the Apaches jumped on the tired chestnut behind Garrett, grabbing Garrett's good arm and the reins in one sweep of his muscled arms. Pulling back on the reins, the Apaches brought the chestnut to a halt while the other Indian caught the abandoned pony. When the horses came to a halt, the Apache pulled Garrett's pistol from his holster and tossed it to another of the stern-faced Apaches who had ridden up. Then the Apache holding Garrett pushed him to the ground, holding onto his arm so that he landed on his feet.

Garrett now stood encircled by emotionless Apaches, all staring silently at him. The

Indian on his horse rode the chestnut out of the circle, leaving Garrett alone. Garrett began to turn slowly around, looking at his captors, not a one of which had a weapon drawn against him. Another group of horsemen approached from the meadow. At least twenty more Apaches halted their ponies in the circle surrounding Garrett. The new arrivals were more talkative, joking among themselves. Several were holding up trophies of their battle with the troopers. A couple waved Army weapons they had removed from the dead and one was wearing an Army blouse, splotched with fresh blood.

Finally, one of the Indians spoke and the others nodded in agreement. The Apache who spoke dismounted and approached Garrett slowly. Garrett studied the man, wondering if he would be the one to kill him. Already this Apache had killed one man today — likely Colonel Fulton — because an officer's blouse was draped over his pony.

Cautiously, maybe even reverently, the Apache approached Garrett. The Indian, dressed in a breechcloth, leather leggings, a calico shirt and two gunbelts, was not a tall man. His sharp cheekbones and authoritative nose were the dominating features except for the eyes. They were coal black and afire with pride, eyes Garrett had seen somewhere before. His mind raced for the answer. He had known no Indians except those at the fort. Only the woman who gave him the bearclaw necklace at the ration table had he observed up close. Her eyes were black, but not like these. Then it struck him. The eyes belonged to her daughter, the one who had run to Garrett and grabbed his leg during the ill-fated raid on the Apache camp. She had her father's eyes, eyes that burned with Apache pride. This man was Pachise, the dreaded Apache warrior. Garrett's good hand touched the bearclaw necklace still around his neck.

The Apache warrior with the burning black eyes nodded at Garrett's unplanned gesture, then spoke his words in surprisingly good English. "Many suns ago, Bad Arm, you saved my woman and child. That you still wear the necklace she gave you is good, for it is a good gift, one that I gave her. Without you, my family would be dead. You can travel in peace, Bad Arm, among our people, for even today you did not fire your gun at us."

"You are an honorable warrior," Garrett replied.

"You honorable, too, Bad Arm. You save two lives — my wife's and my child's — and now I have saved you two times."

"Two times?" Garrett shrugged. "I don't understand."

"The night I retook my people from reservation, I pass fight outside horse house. Black soldier beating you. I shoot black soldier, save you first time."

Garrett was silent, stunned for a moment as he realized Tilman had been telling the truth. The clerk had not shot Jonah. Pachise had.

"I owe you thanks," Garrett stammered.

"I do it again to save the man who save my family. All white men not bad, all Apache not bad. White man that steal our land is bad and we fight them. Until we die we fight any man that steals from us and goes back on his word. White man promises food and clothing at reservation but gives us rotten food and little clothing. Now you go. Apaches not bother you."

Pachise spoke in his native language to the others and into the circle a rider led Garrett's horse. Another Apache whistled at Garrett, then tossed him his pistol. After re-holstering his gun and starting to remount, Garrett stopped and opened the flap in his saddle bag. He sought and quickly found the black book that indicted Fitzgerald for his misdeeds at the Rio Bonito Reservation.

Smiling, he closed the flap and mounted his horse. As he did, a path leading down the trail to Santa Fe opened up among the Apaches.

Garrett rode through without looking back. He had a delivery to make in Santa Fe. Now it was a delivery not just to right a wrong for one man, but for two — Tilman and Pachise.

# ABOUT THE AUTHOR

**Preston Lewis** is the Spur Award-winning author of 30 western, juvenile and historical novels. In addition to his two Western Writers of America Spurs, he is recipient of the 2018 Will Rogers Gold Medallion for Western Humor for *Bluster's Last Stand,* the fourth volume in his comic western series The Memoirs of H.H. Lomax. Two other books in that series — *The Redemption of Jesse James* and *Mix-Up at the O.K. Corral* — were Spur finalists. His comic western *The Fleecing of Fort Griffin* received an Elmer Kelton Award from the West Texas Historical Association for best creative work on the region.

Lewis is a past president of both WWA and the WTHA. He resides in San Angelo, Texas, with his wife Harriet. He holds bachelor's and master's degrees in journalism from Baylor and Ohio State universi-

ties, and a master's degree in history from
Angelo State University.

The employees of Thorndike Press hope you have enjoyed this Large Print book. All our Thorndike, Wheeler, and Kennebec Large Print titles are designed for easy reading, and all our books are made to last. Other Thorndike Press Large Print books are available at your library, through selected bookstores, or directly from us.

For information about titles, please call:
  (800) 223-1244

or visit our website at:
  gale.com/thorndike

To share your comments, please write:
  Publisher
  Thorndike Press
  10 Water St., Suite 310
  Waterville, ME 04901